COSEGA STRIKE

BRANDT LEGG

LAUGHING RAIN

Cosega Strike (Book Six of the Cosega Sequence)

Published in the United States of America by Laughing Rain

Cataloging-in-Publication data for this book is available from the Library of Congress.
ISBN-13: 978-1-935070-73-3
ISBN-10: 1-935070-73-8

Cover design by Eleni Karoumpali

PUBLISHER'S NOTE
This book is a work of fiction. Names, characters, places and incidents are products of the author's imagination or are used fictitiously. Any resemblance to actual persons, living or dead, businesses, events or locales is entirely coincidental.

BrandtLegg.com

As always, this book is dedicated to
Teakki and Ro

ONE

Three Eysens illuminated the darkened room, as if a trio of meteors had exploded in soundless slow motion. The eleven million-year-old artifacts, created by a futuristic ancient civilization of humans unimagined by modern day science, and otherwise lost to the eons, could be used as a conduit to connect those in possession of the remarkable orbs with all the knowledge of existence—and to the creators themselves.

"Is the alignment correct?" Rip Gaines asked. The renowned archaeologist, along with his late friend, Larsen Fretwell, had been the first to discover an Eysen. They'd known immediately it was remarkable, but what they'd found that day in the mountains of Virginia could never have prepared them for the onslaught that was to follow.

"Precisely accurate," Savina, a brilliant physicist, said. She'd spent weeks working on the proper placement of the three functioning Eysens in relation to the fourth darkened one. Normally she might have been offended at Rip's redundant question. However, she, better than anyone, knew the stakes of the procedure they had undertaken. *Fate of the world . . .*

Rip's wife, Gale, and their teenage daughter, Cira, were also present, even though none of them considered it a safe environment. "Any gauge on the stability?" Gale asked in a hushed tone. There was considerable risk to unleashing the power of four Eysens in one place, at one time. Eysens were as dangerous as they were miraculous.

Savina scanned the instruments. "Still okay." She had devised a way to quantify the energy content and its exponential output.

Rip checked the door, set to a biosensor lock that only the four of them could access. Even Booker Lipton, the owner of the facility, the small island it was located on, and the wealthiest man alive, could not gain entry without one of them present—or at least that's what he'd told them. Booker was their backer, protector, and savior. He was also a mystery, and had an agenda none of them could fully identify. "*Trust is an elusive thing*," Rip always said about Booker, a man he did trust, whenever he could.

"Dad, there's a Blaxer army out there. We're safe," Cira said, noticing Rip's nervousness.

"You're right," Rip said, but he knew they were *never* safe. Powers, too great in numbers to contemplate, wanted the Eysens, and they would continue to kill to get them.

"We're ready," Savina said, never once glancing toward the door; maybe because she had not endured what Rip and Gale had, or because she only cared about unlocking more of the Eysens' secrets, or because she simply didn't have time for fear. "As soon as the Cosega Sequence runs through these three," she pointed to the three lit spheres known as the "Virginia," the "Malachy," and the "Jesus" Eysens respectively, "we shift the Odeon chip." The idea was to use them to "jump-start" the fourth one, known as the "Leonardo," which had yet to illuminate since its discovery in an ancient Italian wall. "Once we start, it's imperative the Sequence is not interrupted. The consequences of a pause could be a rupture, and . . ."

"How will it obtain the power?" Gale asked, already figuratively holding her breath, not wanting Cira to hear about just what a rupture entailed.

"We're counting on the connection," Savina replied while adjusting digital controls on a touch screen. "It will search, and then create a kind of storm with the energy it acquires in the shift. The dark sphere will connect with the source of the power—something we still haven't identified—and hopefully initiate."

They had been through this before, and Gale knew that the "source of the power" was the real wildcard. Whatever had enough energy to retain a complete account of everything in the universe, while maintaining a charge for at least eleven million years, could also destroy them—a rupture was akin to a core meltdown of a nuclear reactor. Savina had, in fact, theorized that some form of a nuclear reactor was at the center of each Eysen, but had warned them, "It could be something far more powerful, something we cannot begin to understand."

"Starting the final countdown," Rip said. "Five, four, three . . ."

THE SKIES and seas were still dark when the first Varangians came ashore. The special ops unit took their name from "The Varangian Guard," a band of Viking mercenaries who'd become highly paid bodyguards for a Byzantine Emperor in the tenth century, and soon transformed into an elite fighting unit, serving as the protectors of Constantinople for more than two hundred years.

Booker Lipton's private army, the Blaxers, were stationed around the island, relying on early-warning detectors, their remote location, and secrecy as the first lines of defense. They had no idea that all three had been usurped, and by the time they were alerted, the island had already been breached. More than half of the seventy-two men and women charged with protecting the Eysens and the people working on them, were now dead.

TWO

Terminus Clock: 121 Days Remaining

AT THE EVE of the end of the world, Trynn stood on what, in his opinion, appeared to be a primitive bridge constructed of concrete-like material and reinforced with a polished metal. Something about the spot seemed to connect two worlds, two times, two potential outcomes. His presence there might well determine which outcome came to pass.

He looked around at the solid structures which surrounded the span and imagined this must have been what it was like to live in Rip's time. He missed the light and gleaming rays of the Cosegan cities. Living in exile during such dangerous times, he missed much more than just the light.

A bridge on the outskirts of a Havlos port city seemed an odd place for a meeting, especially one this critical, but then his appointment was with an odd person—a gristly Havlos military leader called "Jarvo."

Jarvo wasn't the ruler of the Havloses; no one person had

held that position for thousands of years. Currently, there were seven different independently governed sections of Havlos lands which remained divided and competitive, much in the way that the Far Future countries such as the United States, China, Russia, and other nations, vied for supremacy and advantage over their neighbors.

However, one thing did unite Havloses-- their hatred for the Cosegans. Jarvo was the man they had chosen as a kind of supreme allied commander to lead the fight against their vastly more technologically advanced foes.

"The great Cosegan scientist, inventor, engineer, futurist . . . and Eysen maker," Jarvo said, greeting Trynn with a kind of grandiose introduction as he waved off his entourage. "Some warn me that you are a spy. Others claim you're responsible for all the ills of the world. Still more say you are the key to winning a war against the Cosegans." Jarvo glared at him, yet there was a hint of a smile playing on his lips. An angry one, but it was there nonetheless. "Well, Eysen maker, which is it?"

Trynn surveyed the rough looking man, still growing accustomed to the raw appearances of the Havloses compared to the Cosegans, who were far better at maintaining their health and youthful beauty. Havloses' average life expectancy, at just over one hundred years, was a fraction of what Cosegans enjoyed. Although he looked like a hard man, cruel and loud, there was something else about Jarvo, Trynn observed a great intelligence in his eyes. It may have been cloaked by his scruffy, stubbly face, patchy bald head, and leathery skin, yet it seemed obvious that Jarvo was far more than a brute.

"I assure you I am none of those things," Trynn replied.

"Then why should I maintain your asylum, risk our half of the planet, when you can cause nothing but trouble?"

"I'm doing just the opposite. I'm trying to save humanity from extinction."

Jarvo scoffed. "Yes, I know of the Terminus Doom. We have all been rattled by your tales of the end of the world. Whether it is true or not, I am still unsure."

"Unfortunately, it is very real."

"Yes, so you say . . . and a condemned man would say anything to save himself, would he not, Eysen Maker?"

"I can show you proof."

"Proof that you conjure in your crystal ball? That is no proof." Jarvo punched Trynn's upper arm.

"Whoa," Trynn coughed, recoiling in pain. The force of the blow surprised him even more than the action itself. It felt as if he'd been clubbed.

"*That* is real," Jarvo said, holding his fist as if he might do it again. "You felt that physically. The pain. The nerves in your arm screamed to your brain for help."

"It hurts like a wrench," Trynn complained, rubbing at his arm. "Why did you do that?"

"So you could understand the difference between your fuzzy forecasts and what is actually happening. In this case, immediately after my fist connected with your arm, the sensory nerve fibers in your peripheral nervous system produced a chemical response which determined the sensations applicable to this blow."

"Pain is the response!"

"Correct," Jarvo replied. "Special pain receptors fired off. The biology is quite sophisticated. Those nociceptors, activated since the impact, caused the tissues in your arm to compress. All of this occurs in the instant after contact. Impulses race through the nerves into the spinal cord, where it is carried to your brain."

"And your *point*?" Trynn asked, acutely annoyed.

"My point, Eysen Maker, is coming. But your patience, or lack thereof, is something you should be careful about. You are a guest here."

"Forgive me," Trynn said sarcastically.

Jarvo squinted back at him, as if contemplating killing the Cosegan scientist with his bare hands. "The spinal cord is critical to this," he continued. "It hosts an incredibly complex network of intertwined nerves, transmitting an incalculable variety of signals to and from the brain at any given moment. The flow of sensory and motor impulses is constant."

"Why are we discussing neurological anatomy?"

"You tell me," Jarvo said, and then continued as if Trynn was an errant student, and he the professor. "Reflexes come into play—their origin, the dorsal horn within the spinal cord, which simultaneously sends impulses to the brain and moves them to the area of injury. You see?"

Trynn nodded, but still had no idea *why* this topic was relevant to anything they were involved in.

"It wasn't your brain that made you yank your arm away from the power and impact of my muscle's assertion. The dorsal horn had already sent that urgent command. But moving wasn't enough. The brain must act beyond those simple reflexes. The tissues in your arm need to be healed." Jarvo paced around Trynn as a boxer does when he has an opponent on the ropes. "And what about fight or flight? Are you going to challenge the man who attacked you? Then your brain must decide what just happened, why it did, and keep a record of the incident for future reactions."

"It was a test?" Trynn said, rubbing his arm, an appalled look on his face.

Jarvo nodded. "Inside the brain, the thalamus directs that pain signal to a few more areas to be interpreted. The cortex decides where the pain came from and classifies it based on prior experiences with pain."

"An analogy?"

"The thalamus moves this information to the *limbic system*," he said, as if describing a lover. "Are you familiar with the limbic system?"

"I am," Trynn said, wishing he were somewhere else.

"Yes, I'm quite sure you are, Eysen Maker. The brain's emotional center. Your thoughts of Shanoah are there often—worry, tears, regret . . . fear."

He glared at Jarvo. The mention of Shanoah unnerved him. The man knew too much. He wanted to scream, but remained burdened by his silence.

"Every sensation you encounter creates a feeling, which in turn generates a response," Jarvo continued. "In this case, as soon as my fist hit your flimsy limb, you began to sweat, your blood pressure rose, heart rate increased, then confusion, irritation, and hatred clouded your brilliant mind . . . and all this happened because I decided to punch you. It is *real*, Eysen Maker."

"What?" Trynn asked, although he finally knew what Jarvo was talking about.

"War. I am going to end the arrogant Cosegan civilization and save the world from their reckless use of technology." He inched closer to Trynn, threateningly, as if he might hit him in the face this time. "How can a Cosegan like you save us, when it's Cosegans who are the ones causing the Doom?"

THREE

Inside the ultra-secure building, behind the vault-like door, the Eysen lab was a kaleidoscope of churning lights and spinning stars. "It's as if the Big Bang itself has engulfed us," Gale said, giddy with excitement, concern, and a host of other emotions simultaneously surging through her.

But no one heard her. The flashing power of the spectacle was too much for their mortal senses. All they could do was watch.

If they had no idea what the others inside the room were doing, they were extra clueless that outside the thick walls of the lab building, a war was being waged.

The moonless midnight sky was ready-made for an attack. The Varangians, unlike their Viking namesakes, came with high tech weapons and equipment that bordered on science-fiction. A laser weapon cleared the bunkers on the beach, where anti-aircraft guns had been ready to defend from sea or air. From there, the mercenaries utilized advanced night vision and laser-sighted Magneto Hydrodynamic Explosive Munition, or "MAHEM" weapons, which used a magnetic flux generator to fire projectiles without the need for chemical explosives. The dark, breezy air suddenly filled with alternating red and blue beams flashing in a sporadic, deadly light show.

The Blaxers took heavy casualties as the Varangians used the efficient MAHEMs to send large molten metal pellets with precise targeting. Even the island's armored vehicles were no match for the sophisticated weapons.

"Release the bees!" a Blaxer commander ordered.

A section of hillside opened and more than a thousand Hybrid Insect Micro-Electro-Mechanical System, or "HI MEMS", flew out like a lethal swarm of locusts. The weapons, in the form of bugs, could be silent or emit an eerie buzz. In this case, they'd been set to sound like the evil cloud of death they were. Like fireflies, the HI MEMS each flickered with a micro LED light.

"What the hell?" a Varangian swore, swatting at the HI MEMS as if they were mosquitos. And although mosquitoes kill more people every day—more than a million a year— than sharks have in an entire century, the HI MEMS were far more dangerous. Nano technologies had been implanted into the insects during their larval stage. Deadly electro dart stingers, infused with poison, cameras, and tracking devices, gave the killer bugs the potential ability to wipe out entire cities if their numbers were high enough.

Varangians began dropping onto the damp, verdant ground as the HI MEMS found easy targets in their exposed flesh. Their venomous stings caused near instant paralysis, and left the victim gasping toward a cold, shaking death within ten minutes. Booker did not want his people fighting the same enemy twice.

INSIDE, the spectacle of the Eysens continued as Leonardo's sphere came to life.

"It's him!" Gale shouted. The great master's image was projected to life-sized proportions, making it seem as if he were standing next to them.

Cira reached out and touched the holograph, and he turned and smiled at her. So realistic was the rendering that later they would speak of the change in temperature, and even a musty odor that entered with him.

Although he didn't say anything, his attention upon the sphere that once belonged to him took them all into his life. The lab had suddenly transformed into a narrow cavern.

"This is where he found it," Rip said, hardly loud enough to be heard. "We're seeing him discover his Eysen."

Leonardo da Vinci stood before the glowing orb and stared into eternity for the first time.

"Oh my god," Savina breathed as they all watched the Eysen show the amazed genius views of the world that none of them had seen before.

Then Leonardo moved and blocked their view of what he was seeing. However, the look on his face was one of sheer terror. At one point the master staggered, as if overwhelmed, like an old and feeble man in a battle, even though he was only twenty-four at the time.

"What is he seeing?" Cira asked in a tone that mirrored the fear in Leonardo's eyes.

"I don't know," Rip said.

"A man from the sixteenth century might be afraid of all kinds of things from our time," Gale said, trying to protect Cira. "Maybe he's seeing the atomic bombs dropping on Japan."

Rip was desperate to find out what Leonardo was seeing. He knew it was important. He worried it was the end.

"*È l'universo che controlla l'umanità*," Leonardo whispered in the silence of the cave as he watched, enraptured by the visions revealed in the Eysen. "*E questa sfera magica deve provenire dalla mano di Dio,*" he gasped, "*sebbene rappresenti ovviamente l'opera malvagia del diavolo.*"

"What did he say?" Cira asked.

Savina, the only one who spoke Italian, hesitated before responding. "He said, 'It is the universe that controls humanity, and this magical sphere must be from the hand of god, though it obviously depicts the evil work of the devil.'"

FOUR

THE PROSPECT of war between the Havloses and Cosegans was very real, and Trynn knew it would hasten the Doom quicker than any other circumstances. On the surface, one might assume the Cosegans would be swiftly victorious over their primitive neighbors. However, the Havloses had engaged in war, amongst their seven sections, on and off for tens of thousands of years. Presently, they were in one of those periods of fragile peace, although tensions had been growing, as they always did. Then the prophecy of the Terminus Doom and the urgent and dangerous reactions by the Cosegans united the seven sections for the first time in millennia. Havloses hated Cosegans, especially Imazes, but there was an exception to this disdain that Trynn hoped to exploit in order to prevent a war that would end it all.

The Havloses liked the Etherens. Everyone did.

Trynn knew Jarvo was not a man to anger or ignore, so he continued to listen as if interested, but his mind was distracted by a view he'd seen in the Eysens; something during the Far Future, something about Shanoah, the great love of his life, and the leader of the Imazes. She might die to save them all. He wished she wouldn't go, but death was assured if she didn't, and not just hers, but everyone's.

Jarvo, still rambling, brought Trynn back to the current crisis. "Images of the so-called future inside a ball of light," Jarvo said, while moving his hands as if they contained an orb. "That is nothing more than entertainment."

"There is nothing entertaining about those images," Trynn said, rubbing his arm, knowing it would bruise badly. Normally, he would use methodical mental healing efforts on the cells, but that kind of concentration was impossible while in the midst of a conversation with Jarvo. It would have to be done later.

"Stop selling the future, Eysen Maker," Jarvo sneered. "You ask for help, yet your own people have shunned you. If everything you say, all these wild predictions . . . or are they prophecy . . . regardless, if they were all true, why would the Cosegan Circle seek to imprison you?"

"They don't—"

"When I was a boy, everyone knew Cosegans did not have prisons. Only us primitive Havloses would lock up their own kind. Oh, I'm sure you know that the occasional Cosegan troublemaker would need *'correction'*, so what did your wise and pretty leaders do?"

"What does this—"

"Cosegans are too good to build prisons. Instead, they banished the non-conformists . . . to where, you might ask. They sent the worst of their people to live with us in what they clearly think of as a penal colony. Is that how you view us? As barbarians? Criminals?"

"No. I do not."

Jarvo studied him carefully. "Maybe you are sincere. Perhaps it is because you know that if the Terminus Doom is real, it was not caused by the Havlos barbarians. It was brought upon all of humanity by the high and mighty Cosegans."

"You seem obsessed with blaming us for the Doom, and yet everyone has contributed to this apocalyptic disaster—Cosegans, Havloses and those who come after us."

Jarvo shook his head. It was unclear to Trynn if he was disagreeing, or just disgusted.

"I will allow you to remain in Havlos lands, but you must be extremely careful. You will be watched. Everything you do will be recorded, scrutinized . . . I will know *all*."

"The only thing I'll be doing is trying to prevent the Terminus Doom."

"Yes, of course that is what you will be doing." Jarvo raised a brow skeptically. "There are many ways to prevent the Doom, are there not?"

"There are," Trynn agreed.

"The possible solutions are limitless, am I correct?"

"You are."

"And if you see inside your little magic orb that a thousand Havloses need to die, or even a million Havloses must be exterminated to stop the Doom . . . you will seek to make that so, would you not?"

Trynn looked into the powerful man's gray eyes, knowing his fate, and therefore that the fate of all humanity rested in his answer. He replied truthfully. "Yes, I will work to put into action any course that would save all of humanity, regardless of cost."

Jarvo's face filled with anger, his eyes flashing rage. Trynn feared he was about to be snapped in half by the battle hardened man. Instead, Jarvo's expression eased. "I am not surprised you feel that way, but I must admit I am surprised by your candor."

"The Doom is real. We have little time left to navigate."

"I suggest if you encounter such a *solution,*" he said the word as if it were a horrible lie, "that you find another way, because, as we have already established, there are limitless possibilities, and harming Havloses, even though there are many of my people that I really don't like much, is unacceptable, and it will not be tolerated."

"I understand."

"So do I." Jarvo pointed to his eyes and then to Trynn. "You have made many mistakes, Eysen Maker. Your errors have upended your life, taken the world to the brink. All that you have done has brought you here." He narrowed his eyes. "Don't underestimate me. For that would be your *last* mistake."

FIVE

Zunt, zunt, zunt . . . the loud repetitive buzz, along with alternating red and blue strobe lights, alerted Rip and the others that someone wanted their attention on the other side of the vault door. The system had been designed after an incident at another one of their research facilities when Savina, lost in an Eysen takeover, did not respond to ringing door chimes for more than three hours. Sensory overload made it nearly impossible to notice anything other than what the Cosegans were presenting.

Gale tore herself away from the enchantment and tapped the touchscreen controls. A monitor displayed the exterior of the door. Upon seeing Donner, a Blaxer who had kept them safe for several years, she enabled audio.

"Gale, the island is under attack. We must evacuate immediately!"

"How bad is it?" Gale asked, his words gripping her stomach, forcing her to recall previous narrow escapes, particularly from Fiji, when they'd almost lost Cira.

"It looks like they're going to take the island. We don't have much time."

Gale clicked the touch-screen controls and brought up the interior lights to signal to the others that the event was over. At the same time, she cycled through the exterior cams positioned around the island and saw the horror unfolding. "Rip, look at this!"

The urgency in her voice brought Rip back across five centuries, where he was still trying to see what Leonardo had seen. Reluctantly, he joined her at the monitor. "What's wrong?" Then he saw. "Oh no . . . it looks like a sci-fi battle out there. Who are they?"

"Does it matter?"

"It may make a difference in how we escape."

She looked at him as if escape was a crazy idea. Gale grabbed Cira.

"It looks rough out there," Rip said to Donner through the relay. "Is it really safe to come out?"

"I wouldn't say that," he responded. "But coming out is a better option than being trapped in there when the island falls."

"This room is a fortress," Rip said. "We've got two week's worth of food and water. No one can get in here."

"You've got four Eysens inside," Donner said. "They'll figure out a way to get in."

Rip looked back at the monitors and studied the invaders, with their lasers and high-tech body armor. "They might have something that could—"

"We've got to go *now*," Donner interrupted.

Savina was still lost in Leonardo's cave, contemplating crosscurrents of Eysens, developing a mental plan of how past viewings could be used to enhance the power of the Eysens they already had, and used to help locate the ones they did not.

"What is the escape plan?" Gale asked, knowing there were always dozens of procedures in place to get them out. Blaxers took into account *every* contingency to protect the Eysens. However, what she really meant was did they have an evacuation strategy to deal with exactly what was going on now. Quickly viewing multiple cams throughout the island once again, seeing the lasers' lights, glowing drone swarms, and the eerie night-vision-green silhouettes of so many soldiers, she did not understand how it would be possible to escape. "Is there even one?"

"Yes," Donner snapped. "If we can time it right."

"What about the ships?" Rip asked, speaking of the evac vessels surrounding the island at all times.

"Three are triangulated and standing by."

"Three?" Rip said. "I thought there were five?"

"Two are unresponsive," Donner replied in a detached tone.

Gale looked at Rip. "If whoever is attacking has already taken out two heavily armed ships that were meant to protect the island . . . that was how we were supposed to get off in the event of a catastrophe . . . how can the other ships be safe?"

"They can't," Rip said.

"We've got to go, *now*!" Donner repeated impatiently.

"I think we should stay in the room," Gale said.

"No!" Donner insisted. "Do not underestimate Booker."

"Booker is a thousand miles from here."

"Booker is everywhere," Donner corrected. "He will solve this."

"He isn't god," Gale shouted.

"I think we should leave," Cira interjected. "I don't want to be trapped in here like a treasure chest at the bottom of the sea that everyone is trying to pry open."

"We will protect you," Donner said.

Gale manipulated the camera controls and panned out

from Donner's image to view more of the surrounding area, making sure he wasn't under duress, that it wasn't a trap. The nearby cameras showed a narrow lane in which they might get through.

Donner answered someone talking in his ear, then turned back to the camera. "Gale, Rip, it's now or never. Let's go."

Savina, still oblivious to the light being on and all the commotion by the door, did not answer the first two times Rip yelled her name.

Cira ran over and grabbed her arm. "Savina, the enemy is on the island."

"Who is the enemy?" Savina asked, startled and dazed.

"The people who want the Eysens!" Cira shrieked. "Kalor Locke's army!"

SIX

On another part of the island, Blaxers manned "the final station," a place of last resort for Rip and the others in the case of every catastrophe.

"This is the only chance they have to escape," Stade, a long time Blaxer, said. He'd been on Rip, Gale, and Cira's personal protection detail for the past five years. "I don't know who this phantom army's working for, but if they get here . . . " He looked at another man. "We're the last line of defense."

"If they get here," the other one said, "there are too many of them."

"What kind of intel do they have to even *find* this island?" Stade asked.

"The vault is going to fall!" the other shouted after getting a report in his earpiece.

"Then we need to go there right now," a third one said.

"We *cannot* abandon this post," Stade said emphatically, adjusting his night vision goggles. "This is the only way Gale and Rip can escape. Reinforcements won't be here in time." It was a difficult call for Stade. The former Secret Service agent had protected two presidents and their families. All his training and instincts told him to get to the vault, secure the family, but if they lost this position, there'd be no way off the island.

"They're going to die in an ambush on the way," the second one argued.

"We have to go or they won't be alive to get the chance to escape!" the third one yelled.

"*No*," Stade insisted. "We have our orders for a reason."

Before the argument could go further, twenty-six armor-clad, laser-weapon wielding Varangians crested the ridge above Stade and the other five Blaxers.

The ensuing firefight was swift and vicious. Stade suddenly found himself the only surviving Blaxer facing seven remaining Varangians.

"Outmanned . . . outgunned," Stade hissed as he wedged himself behind a small boulder against a volcanic cliff. "Stuck between a rock and a hard place." With the inconceivable task of taking out seven futuristic soldiers, the veteran Blaxer reviewed his objectives.

Hold the position, kill those seven slimeballs, get one of their laser guns. Then, if I'm still alive, assist in evacuating Rip, Gale, Cira, and Savina out.

"Nothing like doing the impossible," he whispered to his fallen comrades.

Stade was desperate to avenge the deaths of his friends, but knew not to let that cloud his judgement. He also wanted to capture a laser weapon so Booker's team could reverse-engineer it. However, mission one was holding the position so Rip and the others would have a chance to escape with the Eysens.

Stade suddenly realized he still held one advantage—the water.

He quickly and quietly slid into the deep pool they had been protecting and swam over to the "Mexiscape." The advanced submersible could hold eight passengers, and was one of the many contingencies Booker had designed into the island. But the submersible wasn't a routine backup plan, it was the *last* one.

If Rip and Gale get this far, Stade thought, *the Mexiscape is their only hope.*

As a Blaxer commander, he'd been trained to pilot the underwater vessel in the event that its autonomous controls failed. That also meant he had more than a working knowledge of the Mexiscape's defense capabilities and propulsion systems, both of which he planned to modify.

Stade put his plan in motion while the Varangians scoured the high ground, looking for any movement. A few minutes later, he climbed a steep volcanic cliff, just as the Mexiscape's propulsion system spun into the direction of the remaining Varangians. The adjustments he'd made transformed the vessel's dynamic navigation assisted energy drive into a high-pressured water cannon.

As the columns of focused seawater rotated across the now drenched area, it knocked the surprised mercenaries off their feet. Stade fired his modified Vector submachine gun and picked four of them off before the last three were able to recover.

The water was also wreaking havoc with the Varangians' lasers, but Stade quickly discovered they had conventional weapons too as a high caliber round cut into his gut.

He returned fire, winging another one as he and the water cannon went in for another round. In the mayhem, he crawled over to the bodies of the fallen enemies and stripped them of three laser weapons and a backpack. The Varangians still had difficulty fighting through the onslaught of water. The "storm" allowed Stade to take out two more, but his wound was weakening him.

"One left," he groaned to himself, wondering if he might actually survive this. He tried twice to use the laser weapon, but couldn't quite figure it out. There were several "buttons", and none of them seemed to work. *Must be the water.*

He painfully dragged himself through the mud and wet vegetation. Trying to escape back behind the water line, Stade suddenly found himself looking up at the last man standing.

"You will die this time!" the Varangian growled through gritted teeth as he raised his gun.

Stade had no time to aim or escape. Instinct and desperation took over. His fingers squeezed and pushed at one of the long weapons he'd confiscated. A bright red beam lit the darkness and instantly sliced through the Varangian. The stunned man was dead before his scorched body dropped onto the wet ground.

Stade stumbled to his feet, but collapsed again. He struggled down a slope and reached the Mexiscape. The process of shutting off the water and loading the weapons and materials inside was a monumental task in his injured state. Scanning the area for trouble, Stade closed the hatch, checking that it was still secure. He rested a moment and looked back up the hill, wondering how soon more would come.

It'll be better if I'm defending from the high ground, he thought. *One more climb. You can do it.*

After three or four feet, he could go no further. "Damn," he said, taking two last breaths before his heart stopped.

SEVEN

It had not been easy for the Arc to get to High-peak undetected. Her rival, Shank, had teams searching for Trynn's former secret Eysen facility, but the underwater laboratory had eluded him. Shank was certain the Arc knew the location, he just couldn't prove it.

"Status?" the Arc asked her head of security as they arrived. For nearly a century, as the ranking member of The Circle, the Cosegan's governing body, she'd ruled her people in a continued time of prosperity—until the revelations of the Terminus Doom derailed everything.

"No signs of detection," he said.

She nodded. "Good." The Arc relied on him and believed they'd been successful in losing Shank's surveillance. Shank, also a member of The Circle, had access to most of the same resources she did.

The Arc allowed herself only a moment to enjoy the massive windows surrounded by the underwater world, including giant fish of amazing colors. She would have liked to linger and get lost in the serene beauty, the calmness of the ocean's depths, but there were too many urgent matters needing immediate attention.

Markol greeted her in an open section made entirely of glass between the entrance module and the main labs. He had been Trynn's top apprentice, before Shank recruited him to pursue a divergent Eysen strategy. Then, as the Doom grew closer, in the waffling of Cosegan norms, the Arc had had Markol arrested and imprisoned here at Trynn's secret former lab. To an infuriated Shank, the Arc's move against Markol was the final reason to dethrone her.

The Arc looked into Markol's eyes, always searching for a reason to place so much faith in him. *Something was there,* she thought, *perhaps enough . . .*

Markol led her into what used to be Trynn's Room of a Million Futures. Gone were the specific views of Renaissance era Italy, the Biblical middle east, Middle ages France and England, Rip and Gale's United States—the inserted Eysens Trynn was managing and the yet-to-comes. Markol had been unable to tap into those precise times. Yet among more than twenty-thousand holographic projections, he could see the evolutions of the Far Future, and he used it to attempt to track Trynn.

The Arc looked into the moving images and shuddered. It always overwhelmed her. "Are you ready?" she asked impatiently.

Markol's voice cracked in his affirmative response. The woman intimidated him. Her powerful stare, firm speaking tone, and commanding presence often masked a raw beauty, but Markol always felt her force. The Arc's exact age would be hard to determine, particularly with the Cosegan's measures of time, but certainly it was many hundreds of years. However, if a modern human had seen the luster of her smooth cocoa skin, the awareness and vibrancy in her large dark eyes, and the intensity of her stare, one might easily guess the Arc to be in her thirties.

"There are risks," he said carefully.

"Anything new since our last laborious discussion of the matter?"

He shook his head tentatively, wanting to say, "*There are new developments every single second, that keeping up with the potential spiraling ramifications of each move and its resulting minutes of change could take a lifetime,*" but instead he said, "It's the same."

"Then proceed," she said, as if each moment they waited the end of the world grew closer—which, of course, was frighteningly true.

The Arc had kept The Circle in the dark. Most of the collection of wise elders trusted her. However, there were those loyal to Shank and Jenso, another Circle member and powerful woman in her own right, bent on removing the Arc. They questioned her abilities to lead them through this crisis and, in her quietest moments, she also wondered if the Cosegan's could survive the Doom, but she was certain that it would only be possible if she were in charge.

As the Arc stood next to Trynn's former student, who had once been sponsored by Shank, she felt his connection to the two most important people in her life. Continuing to study the scientist circumstances had forced her to put so much faith in, the Arc desperately hoped Markol could somehow do what Trynn had been unable to accomplish. She glanced up at the Terminus Clock. *One hundred twenty-one days remaining.* "Millions of years of human history, both known and unknown, come down to one hundred twenty-one days," she said.

Markol nodded, though he wasn't really listening. His

concentration was on the images of a Million Futures, and the answer to a single question. *Do we survive?*

However, the Arc was more worried about the next one hundred-twenty-one hours than she was about the next one hundred twenty-one days. Shank had large contingents of Guardians searching for Trynn, Eysens, and Globotite, not to mention High-peak and Markol. She could not allow him to find any of them.

The Guardians, as close to police or military as the peaceful Cosegans needed, worked at the direction of The Circle. Their ranks included those with the best physical attributes, and minds suited for investigation, enforcement, and tracking. She had her own loyal Guardians, but knew that with one slip, they would turn and come for her.

"Are you ready?" she asked again. "Is this going to happen today?" She was nervous being there, wondering if Shank's Guardians would burst in at any moment in spite of the cautions, security, and secrecy. If they found her with Markol, she would indeed be in deep trouble, but if she wasn't there when it happened, she would at least still have a chance. That was why she had been so crazy to come there, and yet she could not leave the critical decisions to someone as young as Markol, someone who had already committed the unthinkable act of murder at Shank's behest.

"Everything looks good," Markol said. "They are cast."

He pulled up another viewer. It showed a group of Cosegans traipsing through a swampy area. Their sophisticated equipment told them where to stop down to the precise millimeter. Markol confirmed the exact readings with the target placement. "They call it Florida," he said.

She knew by "they," he meant those in the Far Future. "Say hello to Trynn," she whispered to the live images streaming in from "Florida."

He thought the statement odd, but ignored it. “Go . . . now!” he said. The command left his throat dry. “It’s done.”

She sighed. “That was far simpler than Trynn made it out to be . . . Turns out *anyone* can insert an Eysen into the Far Future.”

EIGHT

Donner, wishing he could open the vault door, tried one more time to convince them. "We've got to get you out of here!"

"We're coming," Gale said, keeping her eye on the screen showing the wide view as her hand moved to key-in the sequence that would open the massive door.

Rip, packing up the Eysens, warned Savina. "Hurry!"

Gale's blood-chilling scream shattered the tension in the room. Rip ran to her and was sickened by the image.

Donner had been virtually cut in half by a laser. They watched several more Blaxers die in similar ways.

"They're coming," Rip whispered, trying not to upset Cira.

"It's Star Wars and Hell out there!" Gale exclaimed. "We can't go now even if we want to."

"I want to!" Cira yelled, having seen the invasion headed their way. "I want to get off this island! I want to get out of here!"

"We're safe inside," Rip said. "They can't get in. It's built to be an emergency fortress. Booker planned for trouble."

"I don't think he was counting on terminators from the future," Gale said, pointing back to the monitors. The tech-armor-clad Varangians shooting lasers definitely gave off the impression of an apocalyptic science fiction movie.

"There's got to be another way out," Savina said. "Gale's right, it won't take them long to get in."

"They may just blow up the whole building," Cira said. "With us trapped in it."

"No," Rip said, "not with four Eysens in here. They're coming for the Eysens, not us."

"He's right," Savina agreed. "These cretans won't risk destroying the spheres."

"The Eysens have survived eleven million years," Cira said. "Maybe they can't be destroyed. Maybe they know that. Maybe the Eysens are the only thing that would survive an explosion."

"We've got to escape before we find out," Gale said.

"The power," Savina said, quickly searching the corners and ceilings of the room. "How does the power get into the lab? There must be conduits entering the building. We're talking massive amounts of energy required. Maybe we can get out." She searched the computer for building plans and engineering schematics. "Here it is. There's a panel behind that console."

Rip began pulling panels. "Cira, get me the tool kit."

Gale continued watching the monitors. "There are lasers being fired in the distance, that means there must still be Blaxers alive out there. Maybe they can fight them off."

Cira brought her father more tools and soon he had a large panel removed and had cleared the initial area of insulation and brackets. "The conduit is too thick, we won't fit."

"It's going to come to a terminal box outside, about twenty-three feet from the building," Savina said. "Gale, can you see what the area looks like?"

Gale panned the camera views until she found it. "The terminal box is mostly concealed with vegetation and no one is anywhere near it."

"So if we can get through, we could make it into the trees," Savina said.

"As long as it stays clear."

"Then we have a chance," Cira said.

"We've got to get the cables out of here," Rip said. "Tell me which ones I can cut . . . one of these is probably keeping the vault door closed."

"Even when we kill the power, there'll be a backup." Savina looked over. "Although, they can override that in about fifteen seconds, but then they still have to get it open mechanically, maybe another fifteen seconds."

"We've got four hostiles outside the door," Gale said. "They've brought some kind of equipment."

"Which colors?" Rip yelled.

"Yellow, cut the yellows," Savina said. "No, wait, do the orange first."

"There *isn't* any orange."

"Strip the metal shielding. Should be underneath."

"With what?" Rip looked at the ten inches of woven cables and wires. "We don't have time."

"The orange should be wrapped in a silver shielding with blue lettering . . . "

"They have some kind of laser saw," Gale shouted.

"They're using Cosegan technology against us," Rip said, mostly to himself.

"Cut them!" Savina barked.

Rip pulled and started to cut. Sparks shot out. The force of the jolt sent him backward.

"Dad! Are you okay?" Cira cried out.

"Yeah, I think," he said, a little dazed. "Savina, we need to kill the power."

"There should be enough room for you to get to the end of that wall," Savina said, still looking at the plans. "Then you'll be in a maintenance shaft."

"But we can't get there until we cut the power and I can yank out the rest of the cables."

"Only the big one blocks the exit. You three go first," Savina said. "I'll stay back and kill the power once you're there. Otherwise we lose the door lock."

"You go with Gale and Cira," Rip said. "I'll stay and do the power."

"No," Savina argued. "You protect your family."

"I'm not leaving you back here to die!"

"I'm not going to die," Savina said. "I'll have thirty seconds. I could run to the beach by that time."

They both knew that wasn't true, but she was smaller and more agile than him, that gave her an advantage. Savina might be able to get out a few seconds quicker than Rip, and he did have his family to think about. Still, the idea of letting her sacrifice her life for his . . .

"There's really no choice," she said. "I'm not leaving, now get out."

"Go!" Rip yelled to Gale and Cira, who each had a case containing two Eysens. "I'm right behind you."

Cira, still nervous about the sparks, didn't want to go first, so she followed Gale. Soon they disappeared into the narrow shaft.

"Now you," Savina said. "Yell back when you reach the block. I'll terminate the power, and then I'll fly in after you."

"Don't waste a second," Rip said, staring at her as if he might never see her again. Their eyes shared an hour long conversation in an instant.

"See you soon."

"Yeah," Rip said, as he turned and crawled into the shaft. Squeezing into the tight space was almost impossible, but somehow he twisted enough and soon caught up to Gale and Cira at the block. "Now!" he yelled back.

Savina cut the power, and everything went dark.

NINE

MARKOL STARED into the Million Futures. “It’s starting,” he said. “Finally we can work in the Far Future.” The confidence in his voice did not match that of his words.

The Arc understood. She had followed enough of Trynn’s work to know a *lot* could happen in the eleven million years between an insertion and a recipient recovering a sphere. “Are we certain the recipient is the right choice?” She had asked this before, but now that Markol had pulled the trigger, and the insertion team had laid an Eysen in place three thousand miles away, she had to ask it again, even if she had no idea if it was possible to reverse the risky move.

“I’ve run it every way I know how. I’ve used it against the same protocols Trynn has been using.”

She raised a brow at him. “How did you get those protocols?”

“I took the data from the four insertions he has already done, then we isolated all the synch ops and defined parameters and fixed criteria.”

"Then this isn't anything direct, not based on any kind of source material."

"No, but I thought you understood. We've just reverse engineered it."

"A narrow method," she said disapprovingly. "Without his structure . . . you can't know what you don't know."

"How else would you have me do it?"

The Arc thought of her spies, thought of using underworld connections in the Havlos lands to attempt contact with Trynn, but she knew he would never approve of the operation. Even Markol had told her that the dangers multiplied with each insertion, the exponential growth of complications as millions of years of incidents, lifetimes, experiences, and cross-currents overlapped with each other. The ramifications were staggering, and way beyond human comprehension. Only a series of the most powerful Eysens could begin to decipher such a tangled web.

"Who is the recipient?" she asked.

The question surprised Markol, since the name couldn't possibly mean anything to her. Even if she had studied the Far Future, this recipient was no world leader, religious figure, or great explorer.

"Give me the name," she demanded.

And as he did so, he could tell by the recognition on her face that she *did* recognize the name, and Markol didn't know whether to be impressed or afraid.

After a minute or two spent lost in deep thought, the Arc spoke in an ominous tone. "Then I assume the sphere is going to what those in the Far Future refer to as the 1970s?"

Again, he was surprised by her knowledge. "That's correct, 1974."

She nodded, as if this made sense to her. "Then let's make sure he gets it."

But Markol didn't even hear her. There was already trouble. He could see it in the Far Future—cracks appearing in the facade of what had been there before. The image of Haung's face invaded his mind yet again. The man he'd killed across eleven million years had haunted him since the moment he'd turned the Eysen on that innocent Far Future inhabitant.

"Our Eysen looks different from the ones Trynn produces," the Arc said, studying the silver sphere.

"It's the latest model," he said absently. "Does not require a casing."

She recognized the elongated triangle as the Cosegan symbol for Eysens. The typical rendering of the Eysen symbol was the elongated triangle breaking through a circle, but when used on an Eysen, the triangle was used alone, since the physical sphere replaced the circle.

The Arc wondered what those in the Far Future would do if they had access to all the knowledge the Cosegans had harnessed. *It would be disastrous,* she thought. *The Havloses are a prime example of too much knowledge being dangerous in the hands of a less evolved people.*

Cosegans knew better than to manipulate genes in the laboratory to produce enhanced humans. They did it with their minds. They could also identify those whose bloodlines gave them specific abilities, mental and physical. Most of the latter became Guardians.

Shank thinks he's infiltrated the Guardians, that they will follow him in the event of a revolution, she thought. *He doesn't know what I know.*

The Arc was not underestimating Shank, but believed *he* was underestimating her. She looked into the Million Futures and wondered if she would prevail. *Can I see it there?*

A chime on her strandband told her it was time to leave. If

Shank somehow found her with Markol at Trynn's former base of operations, he would have the proof he needed to destroy her once and for all.

"I must go," she said, glancing at the Terminus Clock. "What's happened!"

Markol, who had been lost in the Far Future, exploring every new dynamic change, had no idea what had upset the Arc so much, and shot her a puzzled expression.

"The Clock, you fool! It's plummeted to just nineteen days!"

"I must have missed something," he admitted in a panicked voice.

"You'll kill us all!"

The Clock ticked down to eighteen days.

Markol stared again into the future views, wondering what had gone wrong, his mind racing, throbbing painfully, trying to grasp every ramification of the insertion. Huang's face again flashed in his mind. His mouth went dry as he attempted to understand the potentially endless moves.

How does Trynn juggle all the Eysens? I can't even handle one.

He realized the rumors must be true. There *was* a mind-enhancing drug, he'd heard other Eysen Makers speak of it. He didn't know what it was called, or where to get it, but it was real. It *had* to be, or there would be no way to fathom the effects of an Eysen in the Far Future.

"I have to leave," the Arc barked, bringing him out of his fear-induced mental thrashings. "But you fix this, Markol. You get that Clock back above a hundred days—*well* above. Do you understand?"

"Yes," he stammered. "I'll figure it out."

The Arc stormed away, seconds before the Terminus Clock

ticked down to seventeen. Markol looked back and saw the fire raging at the insertion point. Eleven million years into the future, the Eysen he'd just inserted lay unfound, engulfed in flames.

TEN

The blackness closed in on Rip, Gale, and Cira like an evil assailant strangling them in an icy grip.

Cira stifled her own scream so it came out as a muted, groaning gasp.

"Stay calm," Gale whispered, as much to herself as to Cira. The two Eysen cases made navigating the cramped shaft even more difficult.

"Give me some glow," Rip said quietly. "I think I know where I am, and what to cut, but we'd better be sure."

Gale held her phone out, its display illuminating the shaft enough to see a couple of feet ahead. They didn't want to use the flashlight in case its brightness could be seen on the outside.

Rip used the cutting tool like an expert, but luck was also with him. He hit the right sections in the correct order and the hydraulics snapped through the large cables without electrocuting him. Gale and Cira helped pull the lines out of their way, pushing them off into a small cavity.

Rip stole a quick glance back, hoping to see Savina, then pried loose the rest of the blockage.

"Still pretty narrow," he said, unsure if he'd be able to squeeze through.

"Let's try," Gale said.

He hesitated.

"She'll come," Gale told him softly, though her voice wasn't as certain as her words.

"I'm not as sure as you."

"We've got to keep moving, or her sacrifice—"

"I know."

The last thirty feet seemed endless. They moved in almost total darkness. Gale produced her cell phone again at the end.

"I hope it's hinged," Rip said, pushing on the cover. "Damn . . . it's screwed in from the outside."

"Use the cutter."

Rip, realizing, to his surprise, that the tool was still in his hand, forced its head into the area where the screws protruded through the composite covering.

"It's taking too long," Gale said.

"Why isn't Savina here yet?" Cira asked.

Rip, too busy concentrating on working the tool, trying to degrade the screw mounts, didn't respond. "I think I can kick it out now."

"Won't it make too much noise?" Gale asked.

"I don't know what else to do. There isn't enough room."

Cira and Gale shoved the Eysen cases into another narrow side cavity, then crawled backwards to give him more space. Wedged into the tight tunnel, it took him two tries before the panel broke. Rip held his breath for a moment, waiting for their killers to come. When they didn't, he worked his way out of the large junction box and looked around. The foliage was enough to shelter him from view, especially in the darkness, but he still expected bullets.

After a few long moments, believing it was clear, he whispered for Gale and Cira to join him. They pushed the Eysen cases out first, then he helped pull them up.

"The residence is burning," Gale said, staring out toward a section of the island near where they had been staying, now engulfed in flames.

Angry shouts and sporadic gunfire filled the night air.

"Look!" Cira pointed to the hot glow of lasers not too far away.

"There are still Blaxers fighting," Gale said, feeling the familiar pangs of guilt as she thought of the men and women fighting to keep her and her family alive, protecting the Eysens.

Rip stared into the black mist of the tunnel they had just exited. He saw no sign of Savina. The three of them dashed across the open area into a denser stand of trees.

"The fires will provide enough light for us to see for now," Rip said. "But when we go much further, we'll have to use the flashlights."

"Where are we going?" Cira asked.

"The Mexiscape," Gale replied.

With the dim lights from their phones, they moved cautiously through the trees, Rip in the lead, Cira next, and Gale close behind.

"What the . . . " Rip hissed as he stumbled over the bloody, black-clad body of a Varangian. He stopped, looked around, and saw two more. "Looks like a battle," he whispered, taking a pistol from a man's leg holster.

"There could be more, still alive," Gale cautioned softly.

"Over here." Rip motioned, dashing into a small ravine. They followed. The three of them crouched behind a cluster of trees, listening.

Somewhere close by, a twig snapped.

"What was that?" Cira whispered.

"Someone's coming," Gale said.

Rip pointed the pistol toward the rustling of footsteps as they grew closer. At the last second, he turned on the bright flashlight and saw Savina. His hand shook. He had almost shot her.

"It's Savina!" Gale said in a loud whisper.

Savina almost dove into them. "I didn't know if . . . "

"We all made it," Gale said.

"Still a ways to go," Rip reminded her. "We don't know how many are between us and the Mexiscape. Hell, the vessel may even not be there anymore."

"I don't want to stay here," Cira whimpered.

"We're not, honey," Rip assured her. "Let's go."

He aimed the pistol out in front as they followed. The closer they got to the island's inner lagoon, the more bodies they found.

"It looks clear," Rip said, standing above the slope. "I can just make out the silhouette of the Mexiscape."

They scampered down until reaching one body whose face was too familiar.

"Oh, no . . . " Gale breathed, holding back tears. "It's Stade. He was such a good man."

"We owe him our lives," Savina said. "Looks like he defended the Mexiscape until the end."

Once they were all aboard the small craft and found the stash of sophisticated weapons inside, their awe for what Stade had done grew even more. "These are Cosegan weapons," Rip said as Gale started the engines. "He must have wanted us to see them . . . or use them."

"Where did they get Cosegan Weapons?" Cira asked.

"Don't know," Rip replied, the possible reasons already leaving dread gnawing at him.

"Whatever the answer is," Savina said quietly, "it's a scary one."

ELEVEN

The "Cry," a floating vessel used for conducting and monitoring Eysen experiments into the Far Future, had been named for what Rip called Trynn: the Crying Man. The mammoth ship was one of several Trynn had long ago repurposed. Like the others, the Cry had the ability to stay at sea for months at a time, and could conceivably remain submerged for years. Since fleeing his former facility, High-peak, it had become Trynn's main base of operations.

He stood in one of the lower cabins, a massive room filled with incredibly advanced equipment, and looked into his fixed point—a glowing, holographic, laser data view used in the tracking of Rip's life.

"It's deviating," he said, trying not to panic.

Nassar, Trynn's recently elevated apprentice, asked the question many had tried to understand before. "Why does the archaeologist matter so much?" The apprentice had studied the Far Future and knew that the prior recipients—Nostradamus, Leonardo da Vinci, Jesus, and the others—were among the greatest people to ever live in the Far Future. Although Rip was at the top of his field during his lifetime, other than discovering the Eysen, he was not *remotely* comparable to the previous recipients.

"The archaeologist is the actuality. He discovered us. He connects the Cosegans to the Far Future, and that continuity is our only chance to defeat the Terminus Doom." Trynn looked back at Ovan. "We can't lose this sphere."

"I'm looking," he said.

"How can we lose it?" Nassar asked, gazing into the display of the insertion team.

"They aren't going to lose it," Trynn answered.

"We're talking about eleven million years," Ovan replied to the apprentice with more patience than Trynn could muster under the circumstances. "There are trillions and gazillions of variables across that time. If the wrong person discovers the Eysen at the wrong time, if it's even off a few *minutes*, everything will spiral out of control."

"But you've done it before."

"Each time it gets worse," Ovan said. Trynn began calculating math equations. "It's not just coping with the infinite variables which exist preceding an insertion. The Eysen itself introduces all of eternity into eternity."

"Sounds mind-boggling." The apprentice looked at Trynn with fresh awe that the man could somehow keep it all straight, understand the consequences of the consequences. He didn't know about the Revon. "But I still don't understand the archaeologist," the apprentice said quietly to Ovan, afraid to break Trynn's concentration.

"The idea is to embrace the archaeologist's life. We can't do it with somebody as famous and remarkable as Leonardo or Jesus. We need people like that to amplify the impact of the Eysens. The importance of their lifetime does that for us, reverberating through history in both directions. However, with a man like the archaeologist, we can erase his life and it will hardly be noticed."

"But he's already found his Eysen. He has accumulated other Eysens."

Ovan nodded. "Yes. We are using that. There is only one solution. Once we get the Far Future precisely as it needs to be to stop the Doom, at the exact moment Trynn pushes that switch, it will lock everything into place."

"And, once and for all, that will stop the Doom?" Nassar asked.

"That is the hope."

"How many chances do we have with the switch?"

"One," Trynn said, now joining the conversation. "Everything has to be perfectly aligned. We get *one* shot."

"And the archaeologist?"

"If we get it right, he will never be."

Nassar frowned. "Does he know that?"

Ovan shook his head.

Nassar didn't know what to say.

A loud siren suddenly blared through the tense silence in a series of irritating alarms.

"The Terminus-Clock warning!" Nassar said. They all looked up and saw the days remaining had plunged to just nineteen.

"What just happened?" Trynn exclaimed, looking around as if everything might be on fire.

"What was it at?" Ovan asked.

"One-twenty-one," Nassar said. "Have we ever had a hundred point crash?"

"It's eighteen now!" someone yelled.

"This could be the end," Nassar said. "Seventeen."

Trynn, choking on dismay, looked again at the Terminus-Clock.

"What could've possibly run the Clock down so fast?" Trynn exclaimed as he rifled through the windows into the Far Future, searching for cause and effect. "There are whole eras in the Far Future suddenly in turmoil."

"I'm scanning, but can't find the source!" one of his assistants yelled as crisis mode took over.

"Was anyone doing anything?" Trynn asked.

"Negative, everyone was monitoring and tracking," someone replied.

"This is seismic," Trynn said. "Something *made* this happen."

"Agreed," Ovan said, his face filled with concern as he watched the Far Future views transform. "This is no nominal shift."

"It's not even a shift," Trynn said, pointing at the searing images. "It's a ripple . . . ten thousand ripples." He checked the Clock again. They'd lost another day. "We've got to find this. We need an origin point."

Ovan nodded, his expression that of a man drowning in worry. "If we don't reverse this quickly, the Clock is going to unravel to zero."

"At the rate we've been losing days," a technician said, "we may have less than an hour left to find out what happened."

"These patterns share some of the characteristics of the anomaly results we usually see after an insertion," another technician said, "only magnified by ten thousand."

Trynn studied the patterns from the events, realizing she was right. "Quick, run a summary overload. See if you can find commonality in the insertion data."

"Even if we confirm any of this," a technician began, "we still won't know where it's coming from."

"Could it be an echo from one of our insertions?" Ovan asked quietly. "A time echo?"

Trynn's eyes widened, as if that would be the worst news he could imagine. "I hope not." Then he whispered to his assistant to look for echoes.

Ovan ran from the room, heading to his private office to check his research.

"Where are you going?" Trynn yelled after him.

Ovan pretended not to hear. He didn't want to answer until he'd verified his theory about the cause of the drop, and learned just how catastrophic things had become.

TWELVE

A NATURAL UNDERGROUND WATER CHANNEL, modified by a Booker-owned marine engineering firm, led out to the sea. The Mexiscape, a highly advanced autonomous underwater vessel, navigated the tight spaces with only inches to spare on either side.

"The tolerances are a little slim," Savina said, looking out of a porthole, its curved glass making the rock wall appear even closer.

"Glad *I'm* not piloting this thing," Rip said. "We'd already be sunk."

"How do we know the bad guys won't be waiting for us when we come out in the ocean?" Cira asked.

"One, they don't know we're on the Mexiscape," Rip said. "Two, even if they *did*, they don't know where the channel goes. And three, there are three heavily armed ships out there waiting for us."

"The ships know we're coming?"

"Yeah, the Mexiscape automatically alerts them."

"Can't we call them on that radio?" she asked, pointing to the communications equipment.

"It's only for emergencies."

"Isn't *this* an emergency?"

Rip laughed. "Yes, but . . . a different kind of emer—"

The Mexiscape suddenly listed as it emerged from the channel into the open sea, jostling its passengers.

"What was *that*?" Cira yelled.

"It's another submersible," Savina said, looking out one of the small port windows. "Bigger than ours, and I don't think it belongs to Booker."

"Why not?" Gale asked, trying to get a view.

"It looks like they're going to ram us!"

"Can we override the autopilot and dive?" Gale yelled.

Rip grabbed the controls and tried to recall the brief training session he'd had on how to take over from the autopilot. Even after all they'd been through, he's never actually believed they would have to use the Mexiscape. *But here we are,* he thought, frantically scouring his mind for the necessary steps. "I don't remember how to do it!"

"It doesn't matter," Savina snapped. "It's too late!"

"What?"

"Brace for impact!"

Rip suddenly recalled the override code—a short combination of numbers beginning with Cira's birthday and ending with the date he'd discovered the original Eysen—the same day he'd first met Gale. Halfway through punching in the digits, the Mexiscape listed hard again before completely rolling.

Cira screamed as they found themselves upside down in complete darkness. "What's happening?"

"They hit us," Savina responded. "The collision must have knocked out the interior lights."

"What if the oxygen fails?"

"It's still active," Rip assured her as he saw the blinking indicator light come back to life. He reached up to the screen, hoping to gain control of the vessel.

Loud grating metal-on-metal sounds made their grave situation seem even more ominous.

"What is *that*?" Savina asked. "Are they trying to cut us in half?"

Rip responded, but the grinding made it difficult to hear each other. He tried to see the source of the attack, but everything outside the window was darker than inside. He finished re-entering the code while Savina managed to get the electrical system back on.

"Give us some exteriors," he said to Savina as the metallic noises subsided.

She got them on, but the outside lights were blocked. "That's not good!"

With the touchscreen now illuminated, Rip attempted to send the craft higher. "If we can get to the surface, we can swim for it. The island is still close."

"The island is full of people with guns," Cira reminded him.

"It's also got oxygen," Rip said. "Why aren't we going up?"

"They've got us," Savina said.

"Got us?" Gale echoed.

"Look." Savina pointed outside, where the glow of the projection lights had finally lit enough of the area that they could see they were now entering a larger craft. They had been captured.

"We've got to jettison the Eysens!" Rip yelled. They knew all the cases could float, and were equipped with locating beacons, but the idea of sending the four precious Eysens into the vast ocean was terrifying.

"We can't," Savina said.

"Booker will find them," Rip countered, knowing they could not be allowed to fall into the hands of their attackers.

"No," Savina said. "We're out of time!"

THIRTEEN

Jarvo stood in the Havlos War Room, a command center the size of a sports stadium, filled with teams of people monitoring every scrap of technology and weaponry the Havloses had access to, which was considerable. The Havloses may not have the super advanced engineered equipment and "magical light" applications of the Cosegans, but they were far from backward people.

"What's the latest on Guardian movements near the borders?" Jarvo asked a subordinate.

"They continue the steady buildup," the man replied.

The Havloses had a special division similar to the CIA and other intelligence agencies of the Far Future that had been spying on Cosegans for centuries. And although Havloses had not explored the outer reaches of the universe, they did have orbiting weather and communication satellites that had been modified to monitor the Cosegans. While their sophisticated neighbors were peace-loving, science-pursuing people who believed their superiority meant war had been relegated to ancient history,

Havloses were always expecting that war with the Cosegans would one day come.

"Any indication they've detected our submarines?"

The man checked an overlay comparing Guardian deployments to paths and trajectories of the Havlos underwater assets. "None."

"Good."

Giant screens and streamlined computer equivalents projected content data and images. The War Room housed more than a thousand personnel, whose sole mission was monitoring and strategizing. They were experienced military professionals, combat veterans, something the Cosegans did not have.

Even with all that, Jarvo spent hours watching the Cosegans on his own. He knew them completely, and had memorized all their important strategic practices. He liked to believe he could anticipate their every move.

"They seem to be expecting trouble," Cass said. The petite Havlos was Jarvo's right hand, and what he responded to automatically with anger, she applied an understanding that could have been called empathy in a different setting, as she had an uncanny ability to put herself in another person's shoes.

"They're expecting us," Jarvo said, not taking his eyes from the screens depicting Guardian trainings on a scale, and of a type, not previously seen.

"But they don't really *believe* it," Cass said.

"Some of them do."

"And do you?" she asked, already knowing the answer but wanting to stir the fresh debate with her superior. She was one of the few who could truly challenge him on that topic.

"Cosega will fall!"

"Then war is unavoidable?"

"War? Of course there will be war," Jarvo said, as if she might have been making a joke. "I will see to it."

"We've avoided war with the Cosegans for millennia," she said in a gentle way that, for some reason, always seemed to put him at ease. "It doesn't seem to be sensible when we're all facing the Terminus Doom, to finally engage them in conflict."

"It is precisely because of this timing that *now* is when we must act."

"But you know of the theories that the conflict between our people is what might be precipitating the Doom?"

Jarvo scoffed. "Of course."

"Perhaps that is reason enough to act with an abundance of caution."

"I am acting with abundant action."

Cass smiled. "I'm sure you are." She revered Jarvo, and she knew, contrary to perceptions, that he was not a reckless man. He possessed the ability to sort and consider thousands of details simultaneously. In war, especially one with Cosegans, that skill, as well as others he possessed, made him uniquely qualified for the position he had obtained. His strategic military mind was unrivaled among Havloses, and his knowledge of Cosegans was befitting his obsession with them.

"We will win," he said. "We will finally win."

"What will we win?" she asked almost mournfully. Cass's father had died in a Havlos war. He'd been a career military man, achieving their highest rank, the equivalent of what in the Far Future would be a five-star general. The war had been between the northern and southern groups in the farthest reaches of Havlos lands in a territorial dispute. The highly respected man had doted on his daughter, who was just eighteen when he was lost in battle.

Cass immediately followed in his footsteps and joined the military. Prior to his death, she had planned a career in diplomacy. It wasn't so much that she wanted revenge, as to understand *why* he had given his life to the pursuit of territorial pride and violence instead of his family. Instead of her. With her family connections and strong mind, Cass had risen far and fast. Jarvo had respected her father, and had since grown to respect Cass even more.

"Victory," Jarvo answered, as if it was the most obvious thing in the world. "Victory to shape the future."

With the Havloses at least temporarily and tentatively united, and the unsettling prospect of her former enemies now being allies, Cass took on the greater role of avoiding war altogether. "It means something else to you."

Jarvo was well aware of her stance, but it did not make him think less of her. On the contrary, he appreciated her resolve and counterbalance to his quest to unseat the Cosegan Arc and Circle as leaders of the world.

"We must seize the opportunity," he insisted. "They have failed."

She looked at him. For a moment, she saw her father, and she thought of the men who had killed him. Men who were now on her side. Cass shuddered. "It will not be easy."

"War never is."

"Like us, the Cosegans are running simulations, although they have far more powerful and sophisticated algorithms. Their actions seem to indicate no fear. They must see a path to defeating us."

Jarvo shook his head. "They are missing something, a detail that changes everything. An advantage we now possess."

"What?"

"The Eysen Maker."

FOURTEEN

Ovan entered the room, a worried expression on his face. "Something's not right," he said.

Trynn had seen something too, but couldn't place it. Hearing Ovan's words left a sickening urgency filling his throat that made it hard to swallow. "What is it?"

"I don't know yet."

"If *you* don't know, that means it's bad."

Ovan nodded.

While the others searched for echoes and cross complexes that one of their insertions may have caused, Ovan moved holographic displays based on the patterns he'd just seen in his office. He sailed through the fields, searching for an open cell injection, which would be a telltale sign another Eysen had been inserted into the Far Future.

Suddenly, Ovan's face went ashen. Trynn didn't notice because he was pursuing another lead, but Nassar saw Ovan's distress. "What's wrong?"

"There's too much curtailing energy in the Far Future. It no longer matches our inlaid numbers."

"Could one of the Eysens have somehow doubled?" Nassar asked. "The archaeologist has four of them now. We don't know what that kind of energy extrapolated across all the time . . ."

Ovan was way ahead. "Run a credit of magnified yield and give the presence of another Eysen."

Trynn shook his head. "No, equations won't work at a magnification gamut."

Ovan ignored Trynn and ordered Nassar, "Do it!"

"Look at that," Nassar breathed. The returning simulations showed every projection they had spinning in disarray.

"Open a window at High-peak," Ovan said urgently.

"Can we do that?" he asked, wondering why Ovan would want to look at their old abandoned lab.

"We should still have the settings."

A few minutes later, the images began coming through. "It's occupied," Nassar reported.

"Oh no . . . they did it . . . " Ovan's voice was laced with fear.

"What?" Nassar asked, still trying to understand what he was looking at in the images streaming from High-peak.

"Run the series," Ovan told the apprentice.

Nassar pulled open another holographic curtain.

Trynn turned to Ovan. "It's as if we put another Eysen into the equations. I mean, look at that. We've hit a huge offset."

"Exactly like another Eysen," Ovan said slowly.

"What's going on at High-peak?" Trynn asked, his brain catching up to Ovan's theory as he began looking into the images, then switching back to the data, and back again, until he finally saw it. "Oh, this can't be true."

"Why would they do an insertion?" Nassar asked.

Trynn did not respond. He wasn't going to speculate on who or why until he knew for sure a new Eysen was in play.

And yet, with each passing minute, it looked more and more certain that the only explanation was another sphere. "There it is," he said finally, in a soft, defeated tone Ovan barely heard. Then, as the overwhelming realization sank in, and his Revon-induced super-high functioning mind began processing the killer ramifications, Trynn moaned in primeval agony. "Nooooo!" He pounded his fists though the projected images. "He's killed us all!"

Ovan checked some readings on a nearby heads up display. "He inserted it into the time called 1974."

"Why then?" Nassar asked, sounding as if he might cry.

Trynn looked out suspiciously to his own people, but the bewildered looks he got back told him what he already knew. None of them had needed to help Markol. It was him who had taught Markol how to do the horrible thing he had just done. "Why, Markol! Why?" he screamed.

Everyone knew who Trynn was referring to as perhaps one of the top Eysen Makers, and Trynn's best former student.

"Why would Markol do this?" Ovan repeated Trynn's question, but then realized that Nassar had asked the more important one. "Why 1974?"

"Markol is sponsored by Shank," Trynn said.

"But Shank is vehemently *opposed* to our work with Eysens," Nassar said, confused. "He thinks insertions are suicide. Why would he try manipulating the Far Future?"

"Because the fool thinks he can stop us. And instead, they may have just ended humanity."

FIFTEEN

The Eysens were Rip's first concern, even more than their own safety. It had been an unspoken truth following them since they'd first fled into the Virginia mountains, trying to save the original Eysen. From that moment on, Rip and Gale had surrendered their futures to the fate of the Cosegans. Yet now, faced with imminent capture of themselves and the precious orbs, it had finally come down to nothing left to lose.

Rip took the laser weapon, for which Stade had given his life, and aimed it at the vessel's hatch. "They'll need to die before they get us or the Eysens," Rip said.

Another violent shifting while the vessel rolled.

"We're inside a bigger submarine," Savina said. The Mexiscape righted itself in a watery pool, lights from their craft showing they were in a small metal chamber approximately twice the width of the Mexiscape, perhaps three times as long.

"Maybe it's one of Booker's subs," Cira said.

They all knew it wasn't.

"The Blaxers will find us," Gale said.

"If there are any *left*," Rip muttered.

"Whoever it is, they must be quite sophisticated to be able to deploy something like this," Savina observed.

"Take one," Rip said, handing another laser weapon to Gale. "I believe these buttons fire it."

"The people on the sub might have the same weapons, right?" Cira asked. No one answered her. Gale just placed a hand on her daughter's back and then shouldered the weapon.

"It may be Kalor Locke, it may be the Foundation," Savina said, recalling the people she had once worked for, wondering if it was them or some other nefarious group wanting the unlimited power granted by the Eysens.

"Someone's coming!" Cira said, looking out the window. "There's a big door sliding open."

"Should we wait for them to force our hatch open, or should we go out blasting?" Gale asked.

"I don't feel like being cornered in here waiting to be shot like fish in a barrel," Rip said.

Cira stifled a cry.

Rip opened the hatch.

"There's four," Savina warned as Rip and Gale slipped out. Fortunately, the Mexiscape was between them and the oncoming men.

Rip silently counted, *one, two, three,* then rose above the edge of the vessel and fired. Amazingly, the lasers instantly crossed the void. Surprised to be attacked by advanced weapons, it was a fast slaughter. Two of them fell dead as incredibly accurate lasers sliced them apart. The third, badly injured, was no longer a threat. The fourth returned fire, but by now Gale had also gotten a shot off and ended the last man.

But three more appeared behind the fallen. Rip and Gale may have been able to hold out longer, but another dozen men poured out of an opening on the other side. Rip and Gale, finding themselves suddenly surrounded, while at the same time Rip's gun failed to fire, dropped and dove back into the Mexiscape.

"We really don't need you alive," a man yelled. "All we want are the Eysens, so it's up to you. Surrender now, or die."

Rip and Gale exchanged a quick glance.

"Are they really going to kill us?" Cira asked tearfully.

"We're outnumbered, outgunned, and trapped on a submarine in the middle of the ocean," Savina said. "No choice."

"You won't kill us if we surrender?" Rip yelled.

"Nah," the man said. "We don't need the mess. I hate cleaning up after a massacre."

THEY WERE ESCORTED down the narrow corridors into a small holding room, grateful they had been kept together, distraught that the Eysens had been taken from them.

"Who's in charge?" Rip demanded as the man was leaving. "I want to talk to whoever is responsible for this."

The man shut the door behind them without responding.

"Do you believe him? Was he telling—" Rip began, but Gale silenced him with her eyes, not wanting to upset Cira further. Gale had already reasoned that Rip and Savina were the only two they might possibly want alive, and hoped Cira had not figured out the same thing.

Hours passed and no one came. Rip exhausted himself looking for ways to escape, but nothing presented itself. His thoughts continually turned to Leonardo Da Vinci and the images the great master had seen in his Eysen. He had the strange feeling that if he'd only been able to figure out *what* Leonardo had seen in the Eysen in that cave so long ago, he might not have lost the spheres. A chill went up his spine as Da

Vinci's words echoed in his mind . . . *It obviously depicts the evil work of the devil.*

"What do you think they're doing with the Eysens?" Savina asked.

"I wonder if the Eysens are even on board anymore," Gale said.

"We haven't surfaced yet. I would think they would need to get up top before they could transfer them somewhere."

"Whoever it is must already have an Eysen," Rip said. "Which means Kalor Locke."

"Why do you say that?" Cira asked.

"Because they're using Cosegan technology against us. Lasers, advanced underwater operations, who knows what else . . ."

"And tracking," Gale added, wondering how they'd been found. "With five Eysens, he could take over the world."

"It's not necessarily just Kalor Locke," Savina said. "Don't underestimate the Foundation's abilities."

Rip thought the Aylantik Foundation's Phoenix Initiative was a misguided attempt to engineer a controllable plague in order to avoid an all-out extinction event. The problem, aside from it being done secretly by a self-selected body of wealthy elites, was that the Aylantik Foundation would choose *what* portion of the population died, and *when* they would die. Phoenix was about controlling the crisis. Out of the ashes, a single government could be created to rule the survivors. With Earth as a singular nation, and the massive reduction in population, the Phoenix Initiative fulfilled Clastier's Death Divinations and left a new kind of dystopian society in its place. Rip wondered how it was related to the Cosegan's Terminus Doom. He knew it must be connected.

"The Foundation is an old enemy. Kalor Locke is a new

enemy," Gale said. "I'm not thrilled about facing either of them."

"But Locke is far more dangerous than the Foundation," Rip said. "Because we know much less about him, and because he has an Eysen . . . maybe more than one."

The conversation seemed to overwhelm them at that point, and silence took hold. Hours more went by, and eventually they fell into fitful sleep.

"WE'VE BEEN on board sixteen hours," Rip said, as Gale woke up. "We could be anywhere by now."

"Why doesn't someone come?" Cira asked. "At least to bring us food. I'm thirsty."

Gale didn't respond, pulling Cira close instead. She recalled years earlier being on a different submarine, owned by Booker. Cira, temporarily blind, had been left in a Fiji hospital, and Booker's people had drugged and tricked Gale into leaving her behind. She had felt more trapped then. At least now she was with Cira and Rip. And she had hope. *Maybe Booker has a sub on the way.*

A couple hours later, the sub shifted. "What's happening?" Cira asked.

"Seems like we might finally be surfacing." Gale replied.

The door to the holding room opened. "This way," a burly man ordered.

"Where are you taking us?" Rip asked.

"You wanted to talk to who's in charge. Now's your chance." He laughed. "Careful what you wish for." He laughed even louder.

SIXTEEN

Trynn gazed upon the collapsing images as if watching the death of a loved one. "All stability in the Far Future is gone."

"We have to stop the Far Future manipulations," Ovan said. "At least until we figure this out."

"Figure it out?" Trynn echoed incredulously. "I don't need to figure anything out, he's just crashed the universe!"

"We can't give up," Nassar said shakily.

"You have no idea the ramifications of what has just happened!" Trynn blasted. "*Give up?* There is no *up* to give! We're buried."

"What if we find out where it is?" Ovan asked.

"What good will that do?" Trynn said. "He's already done it."

"We can insert another Eysen to offset his 1974?" Ovan suggested.

"We have to try," Nassar pleaded.

Trynn's head was spinning. He could not stop the exploding stream of scenarios playing out in the Revon haze. *I don't have enough Revon for a duel with Markol in 1974, to do another insertion, or any of it . . . There probably isn't enough Revon in existence.* Dreemelle's face flashed in his mind, providing a moment of calm, then a new wave of panic. She had warned him of the dangers to his cognitive performance. How much time did he have left until he was a brain-dead vegetable?

"Trynn?" Ovan said.

"We don't have enough . . . "

"Enough what?" Ovan asked calmly.

"We don't have enough . . . Globotite."

"We'll just have to get some."

AN HOUR LATER, a rag-tag team had been dispatched, but Trynn knew their best chance lay with his daughter. Mairis had proven incredibly adept at locating the elusive mineral.

"I'm heading back to Solas," Trynn told Ovan.

"To make a play for the Arc's Globotite stash?" Nassar asked, overhearing.

"Maybe," he replied, but Ovan knew it was for another reason.

Shanoah. She would be leaving the following day.

"The tracking on Markol's insert has shown something very interesting," Nassar said, missing the exchange of knowing glances between the two men. "It seems that the different Eysen models adjust the variables far more than previously thought. Each produces slightly unique requirements, affecting the outcomes, and, of course, those effects get magnified over the millions of years."

"Another complication," Trynn muttered.

"Or another piece of the puzzle," Ovan added optimistically.

"And there's something else . . . " Nassar said.

Trynn met Nassar's stare, giving his student the chance to impress them.

"There may be a way to use those imprints to counter Markol's insertion."

"Go on," Trynn said skeptically, but willing to hear out anything that might help.

Nassar didn't need to explain the manufacturing process to the greatest Eysen Maker who had ever lived, but he did so anyway.

"The lasers, of course, are precise in each Eysen, but there are hundreds of rare earth, rare air, and rare space minerals. Even with our exact measurements and content analysis, there are natural differences we can't account for."

"Yes," Trynn agreed, "particularly those obtained from asteroid mining. They are always the most inconsistent."

"Right, so, even between the generational changes we make in engineering and design as we improve the Eysens' basic performance, we have these variables. Globotite is the most important ingredient, and even its consistency levels make minute changes which, over time, are magnified to significant."

"We know all this."

"Sure, but it is those unique differences—like a human fingerprint, a specific strand of DNA—we can *track* those changes. We can know what consequences Markol's sphere is responsible for."

"And we can react specifically to it," Trynn said, genuinely impressed. "Good work!"

Nassar inclined his head in thanks. "I can set up an AI to track the special pressing machines. Since they work similarly to how coal is compressed into diamonds, there will be another imprint in that process."

Trynn thought of the Globotite. No Eysen could be built

without it, perhaps the only ingredient that had no substitute. The hard crystal unibody sphere was produced by the pressing machines, which then spun the spheres using the same formula as the formation of stars. "The insertion of a never-ending power supply relies on two things," Trynn said, taking over the conversation. "Globotite *and* solar manipulations. Those solar patterns are not only trackable, they are predictable! We may be able to stop Markol from the future."

"We can use the archaeologist," Nassar said.

"No." Trynn shook his head sadly. "The archaeologist must be kept far away from Markol's sphere. For this, we'll need someone else. Someone very, *very* special."

SEVENTEEN

RIP LOOKED down the cold metallic corridor, a grid stair-ladder at the end. "We're going up?" he asked, worried they were being led to an execution. To be tossed in the ocean. Shark food.

"The boss is waiting for you on the ship."

"Ship?"

"Unless you want to stay with us on the submarine."

"No, thanks."

They followed the man to the steps, four additional armed agents behind them. Soon they emerged from a hatch near the conning tower. Rip inhaled deeply, happy to be in the open air. The sun was close to setting. He scanned out over the horizon in every direction, but saw no trace of their island—or *any* land, for that matter. No sign of help. The only other thing for a million miles was "the ship," which was really a mega yacht.

A metal plank with thin railings extended from the massive white floating palace.

The plank took them onto the yacht's stern. Rip was relieved that the four of them were now off the sub, figuring their chances of being killed had been reduced. Still, he worried that Kalor Locke, someone from the foundation, or whoever else was behind this evil operation, was planning to use Cira and Gale as leverage to make him help them with the Eysens.

Standing on the aft deck, Rip glanced up and saw a man staring down from amidships glass enclosed area just below the bridge.

"Who is it?" Gale asked Rip.

"You'll find out in a minute," the man who'd brought them from the sub replied.

They entered the large room. The space was about the size of a basketball court, and appointed with modest luxury—white leather furniture, a blond wood floor, gold accents—but was clearly designed to not interfere with the 360 degree views. The glass had very few visible supports. Rip noticed an empty helipad just below and wondered if someone else would be joining them.

The person they'd seen through the window from below now took his attention. The rough-looking man frowned at them, as if he'd been expecting someone more formidable.

This guy's a thug, Rip instantly thought. *He actually has a scar on his cheek.* Unshaven, sunburned and mostly bald other than some gray and black spiky hair, the thug persona fell apart with his yellow cargo shorts and bright pink golf shirt. *This can't be the mythical Kalor Locke, or anyone bright enough to pull off this operation.*

"Well, well, well . . . Professor Gaines and his girly entourage," Scarface said, sniffing. He gave them a mocking smile. "'Course we all know the real brains of the group belong to the lovely and equally brilliant Savina."

Rip said nothing, but noticed the two sealed Eysen cases sitting next to the man.

The garishly dressed guerilla seemed irritated that his comment had not elicited the expected reaction, and he stared out to sea for a moment, as if they were no longer there, a sour expression on his face.

"We wanted to see someone in charge," Rip said in a condescending tone, exaggeratedly looking around as if someone more important than this dunce might appear.

The thug smiled, making his scar appear larger. "You're looking at him."

"I don't think so."

"Well, if I'm not in charge, I guess there's no one to stop these men from having a *very* good time with your wife and daughter, and then throwing their used bodies overboard for the sharks." He motioned to a man behind them. One of them grabbed Gale.

Rip turned to defend her. Another man shoved the stock of his gun violently into Rip's gut. Rip doubled over in pain, and the same man kicked his legs out from under him.

Another man began to drag Gale from the room. Cira and Savina were held back.

Rip rolled over on the floor, guns pointed at him. "Stop!" he yelled in a rasp, indicating a high level of pain.

Scarface waved his arm and nodded to the one who had Gale, then laughed as she shoved her way back toward the others. "My, it sure looks like your assumption that I wasn't in charge was incorrect, wasn't it?"

"Apparently," Rip admitted, stifling a moan.

"That's right . . . apparently," the man repeated. "But I'm not sure you're convinced. Perhaps if we take one of these Spartans—that's the laser weapon, we named it after the Spartans from Halo . . . I understand you were playing around with our toys . . . bad boy." He squinted at Rip and shook his head, as if scolding a dog. "Perhaps we cut off a foot or some other limb.

It's easy with the lasers. You might not need these?" He waved a fat finger at him.

A man advanced toward Rip and pointed the Spartan at his leg.

"He needs his legs!" Cira yelled. "Please don't!"

Scarface looked at her and smiled. "All right, I guess since you asked nicely. You might not believe it, but I have a daughter your age . . . somewhere. She might like it if someone cut off my legs . . . Anyway, we can let it go for the time being." He shook his head and the man with the Spartan backed off. "On your feet professor!"

Rip, still in obvious pain, stood.

"I don't own this ship, but now you know that I run it."

"Yeah."

The thug nodded, self-satisfied he had convinced the skeptic. "However, you are correct that I, too, have a superior, and he has requested the Eysens be brought to him immediately. So, that's where we're going." He motioned out to the ocean ahead of them. "But understand that there is an optional part to my orders." He smiled. Again, the scar grew. "I have to deliver all of these precious little crystal balls, but not all of you. You're a smart man, Professor. You must realize that Savina is the most important one out of you, and you might have some value, but your pretty wife and daughter, other than . . . " He paused and stared at them hungrily, as if they might make a nice snack. "Other than to solicit *your* cooperation without having to resort to Spartan, they are worthless to me, just taking up space. So I do hope you will prove your importance by turning one of these on for me."

Scarface walked over to the Eysen cases and lifted them onto a large glass table.

A massive explosion rocked the ship.

EIGHTEEN

Ovan and Trynn sat in the upper observation room overlooking the ocean. It was where Trynn often went to escape the distractions and think.

Below them, the constant chaos of the Far Future continued. Monitors gauged every effect on all time ranges, which crossed reviewed eras against all dates ahead with the newly added PAE system. These Present Approximate Errors divided each second in current Cosegan time and matched it with a past and future result. Holographic displays then showed changes related to "now" and "then" and vice versa. All movements were measured alongside the Terminus Clock. Simultaneously, other machines used that data and additional inputs to produce simulations on the likelihood of war between the Cosegans and the Havloses.

However, in the observation room, there was nothing but seven comfortable chairs, open space, and a panoramic view of the open seas.

"What do we do now?" Trynn asked, trying not to think of

the PAE system. With his Revon induced hyper-mind, he was finding that difficult to do.

"There is only one option," Ovan said in a tone as full of despair as Trynn had ever heard from his longtime friend and mentor.

"I just can't believe Markol would do this. I understand Shank would not know enough about the ramifications, but Markol *knows* better. I taught him."

"And you know there is a time when the student leaves the master. The dangerous time, because they try out all their newly gained knowledge while lacking the wisdom of experience. The consequences can be disastrous."

"That's putting it mildly."

"There may be another reason."

Trynn stared at Ovan and contemplated his words. "I don't need a philosophical lesson in *why* he did it. I need to figure out how we can reverse it."

Ovan gazed out at the choppy seas and shook his head. "It's too late to reverse. We have to complete the Egyptian insertion now, and use it to counter his blunders."

"Don't we risk even more by introducing yet another universe into the Far Future?"

"What would you suggest? That we give up the insertions and allow his to be the last?"

Trynn shook his head. "Once again, we are in a race with Rip."

Ovan frowned. "Yes, if the archaeologist reaches the Egypt sphere before we insert it, Markol will be the least of our worries."

"His insertion has caused this urgency. If we don't do Egypt immediately, Rip will make the discovery too soon."

"If we don't do it today, there may be no tomorrow," Ovan mused.

Trynn nodded. He watched seabirds landing on a rock a hundred yards from the shore. "Are you sure about this Pharaoh?"

"Egypt has been a crossroads for us. The Imazes, the Etherens—"

"And the Cosegans."

"Not yet," Ovan said.

"That's only because of this insertion. I grow tired of playing god with the future."

"That's who we are," Ovan said. "The gods to our future selves."

"Is there any other choice?"

Ovan shook his head.

Trynn sighed deeply, rubbing a hand over his face. "Make the preparations. I need you to oversee that."

Ovan looked at him as if questioning the words.

"I've got to go see Mairis and the smuggler," Trynn said, wincing. "We're going to need more Globotite . . . a *lot* more."

JARVO'S DEPUTY, Cass, studied the orders on her digital tablet. "If we do this, there is no turning back."

"Why would we *ever* turn back?" Jarvo said, thinking this was the craziest thing he'd ever heard.

Tired of all the arguments about how war could hasten the Terminus Doom, Cass went with something she knew Jarvo would care about. "We could lose."

"Ha." He stepped back, astonished, amused. "We won't lose!"

"What if we do?" She widened her eyes. "The Cosegans have been monitoring our internal wars for millennia. They know our tactics, our capabilities, our weapons . . . surely their

Eysens and mind-crystals can anticipate everything we will do."

"Only if they have all the information." His smug expression told her they did not.

"There is something their satellites cannot see?"

"We have been using sliver clouds to conceal our advancements."

She knew of the technology that filled the skies with biodegradable metallic-like particles known as slivers. However, she didn't see how that could be enough. "For how long?"

"Decades."

She nodded slowly, the realization that a war had been planned, or at least expected, for perhaps half a century rolling over her. "It's a foregone conclusion?"

Jarvo nodded once, sharply. "Yes, and we will win."

She found it hard to imagine that the ultra-advanced Cosegans could ever be defeated, and yet it was more difficult for her to believe that Jarvo would ever lose.

The two of them walked to the entrance that led to the large briefing hall filled with Havlos military leaders.

Just before stepping through, Cass asked, "What are you going to tell them?"

"Prepare for war."

NINETEEN

Rip instinctively moved toward Gale and Cira as the world shuddered around them. Gale was already pushing Cira onto the floor. Rip came down next to them. Savina lunged for the table with the Eysens. Scarface shoved her away. As the yacht listed from side to side, the other men ran from the room to fight the threat.

Machinegun fire, screams, shouts, and several more blasts echoed through the craft. In the confusion, Rip quickly crawled along the floor and managed to grab Scarface's legs, pulling him down. The two men immediately locked in a wrestling match, but the stocky captain, no stranger to violence, had the advantage.

Savina recovered and got to the open Eysen case just before it slid off the table. Closing and securing the cover, she went for the other case.

Steady bursts of gunfire continued splitting the air. "It's got to be Blaxers!" Gale yelled.

Canisters of smoke appeared on the decks below them.

Rip aimed for the scar and surprised them both by landing

a hard fist on his face. Outweighing and much stronger than Rip, Scarface took the blow as if it were a kiss.

Rip tried again, but this time he missed. Scarface swung his thick arm like a club. Rip rolled and got a knee into the man's groin. Furious now, the captain pulled a large knife from somewhere and plunged it toward Rip's throat. At the same time, Gale kicked the back of the thug's head. It was a weak attempt, as the boat shifted and sent her effort a bit off balance, yet it caused his knife to miss its target. Still, he cut a decent gash in the side of Rip's torso. Instead of weakening him, though, the injury made Rip even more determined, at least for the moment. With his new-found strength, in an upward thrust, he landed both fists under the man's jaw. The force of the blow slammed Scarface's head back into the floor. This time, Gale's foot connected dead center in his face. The captain reeled in blood and fury. His arms flailed as he grabbed Gale's leg.

Rip pounced on his arm, breaking his grip on Gale. He also found the knife and sunk it into the captain's side. Gale sent two more kicks into his neck and chest. The knife wound took the fight from the big man. He roiled in pain, then suddenly lay motionless.

Gale gave him another kick. Nothing.

Rip got to his feet and saw the first glimpse of another force. "They're dressed differently," he said, holding his side. "They don't have the same body armor as the attackers from the island."

"They don't look like Blaxers, either," Gale said, worried, as she inspected his wound. "You need stitches, and soon."

Rip checked to see if any of their captors were close by. "I hope they're here to rescue us, because it looks like they're winning."

Cira came over to check out his injury.

"What if they're from the Foundation? Or another rival group trying to get the Eysens?" Gale asked.

"They're definitely not Blaxers," he said, feeling as if his insides were boiling out through the deep cut. "We gotta get outta here."

"Dad, that's not good," Cira said, pointing to his still bleeding side.

"I think I'll live," he said, sounding tougher than he felt. He actually wasn't sure he would, depending on how soon he could get medical help. *You can't bleed forever*, he thought.

They watched as the two forces fought it out on the decks below. "Definitely looks like these new guys might win," Savina said.

"Where did they come from?" Gale asked.

"I don't see another boat," Cira said. "Maybe they came by submarine?"

"There's a helicopter approaching!" Savina said, now carrying the two Eysen cases. "Let's hope it's the good guys and not reinforcements for Scarface."

"Help me," the captain groaned weakly, blood puddling under him.

"Not much we can do," Rip said, also wincing in pain. "Who do you work for? Where were you taking us?"

"I'll tell . . . you if . . . you help me," he said, gasping.

Rip looked at Gale.

"I don't know how we can help him," she whispered. "Even if we wanted to, none of us are trained."

"We could staunch the bleeding," Rip said.

"Not me," Gale replied.

"Where should we go?" Cira interrupted, watching the battle below winding down.

"I think the best place is to maybe stay here," Rip said. "We can see everything that's going on. I don't want to go down into all that fighting."

Gale and Savina agreed.

"Please," Scarface repeated.

"We should be ready for whoever comes up here," Rip said, ignoring the captain.

Gale found two guns and they all moved behind the door. Cira grabbed a heavy lamp she planned to use as a club.

A few minutes later, it was all over.

"The new guys won," Savina reported.

"Then we're about to find out who they are," Rip said as the helicopter landed.

TWENTY

OUTSIDE OF NAPERTON, a small Cosegan coastal town, ten Guardians stood, leaning against a grid of light that made them invisible to anyone not wearing "scopes." Since Havloses did not possess such technology, the Guardians felt safe, even though intelligence reports indicated there was an increased possibility of enemy agents in the area.

The skies along the coast were clear, the breeze warm and fragrant from the blooms of a Flores bush that produced lemon-sized wild berries that tasted like chocolate and custard. A plant that would unfortunately go extinct in the Missing-Time.

One of the Guardians tested the strength of the grid, possibly a little nervous about the Havlos report. None of them had ever faced a real enemy. The reading verified its level of protection was at maximum, impenetrable.

Grids had originally been developed for the Planetary and Star Surveyors to shield miners in space mining operations. The Imazes had also used them for added protections against debris fields in space walks. However, with the increased hostilities between Cosegans and Havloses, the Guardians had co-opted grids as a defensive measure.

"Think there'll be a war?" one of the Guardians asked his female superior.

"No," she said. "Havloses are not that stupid. Why would they do something that would assure their own destruction?"

"Yeah," he agreed, but neither believed her words. They both knew it was impossible to understand the Havloses or begin to predict what they might do.

"The Terminus Doom," another added.

"He's right," the first one said.

The commander nodded, knowing he meant that the Doom changed things. "True . . . nothing makes sense anymore . . . Still, the Havloses must know we're their best chance at surviving the Doom."

"Again," the first one said, "they might be too stupid to know anything like that."

The commander did not respond. She was dead.

The other two who had been talking died a split second later.

Only the last surviving member of the squad even managed to reach his screamer gun, but he didn't have time to fire it before he joined the other nine in swift death. All ten highly trained Guardians were executed from a distance of nearly one thousand feet in less than two seconds. The "too stupid" Havloses had just achieved their first victory in a war that never should have happened. A war that would shape every human alive, and all the ones who would follow, in rippling repercussions that would imprint on the world for more than eleven million years.

THE ARC SCANNED the status updates on a hundred things. Each Guardian station was continuously monitored. Every report was analyzed by AI, which then merged and projected, in real time, based on interrelated outcomes of the infinite data available, all possible finalities.

"Imaze review," she said. Instantly, a flow of data and images filled the air around her. Satisfied, she moved onto Globotite holdings, Etherens, and, eventually, after reciting a long alphanumeric string, the happenings at High-peak played before her.

As she studied what Markol was studying, saw what he saw and read the thoughts he was thinking, she anticipated the danger in the Far Future. "It is much greater than he indicated," she said absently.

"What is?" her deputy asked.

"The catastrophe Markol has created."

Before the deputy could respond, the images slipped away, momentarily overwritten by a more urgent matter. The two women stood paralyzed by the scene playing out before them.

"Ten dead," the deputy said when it was over. "How did they penetrate the grid?"

The Arc did not reply. Her mind was already racing ahead. The number of dead did not matter, and, in the grand scheme of things, neither did the method of their deaths. She was, of course, also curious as to how the Havloses had bypassed the impossible-to-bypass, something even a Cosegan with all their technological advances should not be able to accomplish. The real concern, the matter of the future of humanity, lay in the realization that the war had begun. The end of her reign was very near, the last breath of the Cosegan civilization was close, and a cosmic order which had stood since the big bang, was all about to crumble in disastrous ruin.

TWENTY-ONE

THERE WASN'T ANYWHERE to hide in the all-glass room above the bridge. Rip and the others waited, tensely holding their weapons. Six of the "new guys," two of whom turned out to be women, approached the door. "There appear to be hostages," one of them said into his radio.

"We're armed," Rip yelled. Suddenly his bleeding wound didn't matter. "Who are you?"

"FBI," the man responded.

Rip looked at Gale. She shook her head. Savina also expressed her doubts by making a face.

"What's the FBI doing in the middle of the ocean, in the middle of international waters?" Rip yelled back.

"Apparently, we're saving you," the man replied.

Gale shook her head again.

"And who are we?" Rip asked.

"I'm not sure," the man said. He held up a camera and filmed them. "But we'll know in a few minutes." Then he said something else into his radio they couldn't hear. Seconds later, they heard him say, "Copy that," before telling his crew, "He wants us to sit tight for a minute."

At the same time, a slender, six-foot-three man with short blond hair, a perfect smile, and piercing eyes, sat on the helicopter, reading reports on a screen.

"We're sitting ducks," Rip said, frustrated.

Scarface moaned from the floor.

"There's no place to go," Gale said.

"Maybe they really are FBI," Cira suggested.

"If they are, all that means is they aren't going to kill us," Rip said. "We'll still lose the Eysens."

"That's worse," Savina said.

The tall man strode off the helicopter without stooping, glanced around at the bodies, assessed how many were his, and walked briskly to the hall outside the glass room. He resembled a combination of an angry marine and a Senate candidate, but lacked the temperament for either role. His men cleared the way for him to approach the door.

"Well, well, well," he began. "Looks like we hit the jackpot. Ripley Gaines and Gale Asher."

Rip recognized the voice even before the face registered. "Dixon Barbeau!" Rip said in a voice filled with a combination of relief, confusion, and fear. "How did you find us?"

"I wasn't looking for you."

"I don't know what should make us more worried," Rip said. "The fact that you found us at all, or the fact that you did it without even trying."

The stunning development did not completely ease Rip's mind. It wasn't great that these people truly were the FBI. As he'd just told Cira, even if they weren't taken into custody, they would certainly have to return the Eysen to the United States, where they would be turned over to the NSA or maybe even, eventually, to the Foundation.

"Put your weapons down Professor Gaines," the agent next to Barbeau said. "You are no match for the eighteen agents on this vessel. You saw what we did to the Varangians."

It was the first time they had heard their captors identified, but it still didn't mean anything. Only Rip had ever heard of Varangians, but not in this century.

Rip held his wound as blood oozed around his fingers.

"He's right, Dad," Cira said quietly. "Being in a glass room surrounded by all these people with guns . . . It doesn't matter who they say they are, we can't escape with a couple of guns and a lamp. All we can do is get ourselves killed."

"Wise girl," Gale said. "We don't need any more injuries."

Rip put the weapons down and walked to the center of the room. The others followed him. The door opened. Four agents came in and secured the area. One of them checked Scarface.

"He's dead."

Rip and Gale shared a glance. They had killed him.

Another agent noticed Rip's bloody side and called for a medic.

Barbeau looked at Rip. "The body count continues to climb . . ."

Rip nodded.

The medic entered the room and motioned for Rip to lift his shirt.

"Nasty gash," Barbeau said. "I guess we got here just in time."

"But *how* did you get here?" Gale asked. "*Why* are you here?"

"I've been tracking the Varangians for a long time."

"Who are they?" Rip asked, biting back a moan while the medic cleaned the wound.

"The Four Horsemen of the Apocalypse."

Rip narrowed his eyes. "A religious reference from you,

Dixon, seems a certain irony." But Rip immediately dwelled on the words Leonardo had uttered when first seeing his Eysen in that cave. The biblical prophecy suddenly seemed apropos.

"The Varangians are an incredibly lethal army," Barbeau said. "And they are in the employ of a very dangerous and ruthless man named Kalor Locke."

"We've heard of him," Gale said. "He's trying to accumulate all the Eysens . . . that's about all we know."

"I'm afraid I know quite a bit more," Barbeau said, glancing at the cases Savina still held in her hands. "Kalor Locke was once the director of the most secret government agency in existence. HITE handles technologies obtained from a variety of sources—anything unexplained, super advanced." He paused as he studied a laser weapon. "HITE acquires and controls things like this, whether created domestically, internationally, or extraterrestrially."

"Like Eysens," Gale said.

Barbeau nodded. "The agency apparently unknowingly got hold of an Eysen back in the seventies and didn't understand what they had. Someone else was in charge of HITE back then. Eventually Kalor Locke came on the scene and conducted a review of all HITE's holdings."

"And he came across an Eysen?" Gale asked.

"Correct again. During that process, the mysterious sphere came up. After additional tests, HITE analysts finally gained limited access into it, enough that Locke became incredibly intrigued by it and ordered more studies."

"Another Eysen," Savina whispered, looking out to sea as if searching for it. "Crying man lives."

TWENTY-TWO

TRYNN WALKED INTO THE DUSTOFF, a kind of seedy bar slash employment center for those working at the wharfs or going out to sea. It was a place where smugglers, pirates, and other odd characters gathered and schemed. In another lifetime, the cavernous space could've doubled as a warehouse. One could feel the plots and crimes being hatched in the thick, salty air.

Trynn spotted Mairis in conversation with a Havlos sailor. As he approached her table, the sailor gave him an annoyed look, as if to warn Trynn away from his territory. Mairis quickly stood up and hugged him. "Dad," she said, smiling.

The sailor's eyes turn up for a moment, as if deciding whether he really was her father while also gauging how easily he could take Trynn down. The sailor guessed the answer to the first point was yes, and the second might be no. He excused himself with the decorum—or lack thereof—one would expect from a pirate, and disappeared into the dark outer reaches of the Dustoff.

"Who was that?" Trynn asked, wondering if the sailor was a new source for Globotite.

She shrugged. "A guy who thought he might have a chance with me."

Trynn looked back into the crowd, but it was unclear if he was trying to get another look at the sailor, or was searching for someone else. "Where's our source? What's his name, Dirt?"

"It's Mudd," she said, laughing. "I warn you, he's quite a character himself."

"Everyone in Havlos lands seems to be a character."

She nodded. "Yeah but . . . Here he comes."

Trynn looked up and saw a man that looked like his name. He had a muddy complexion, brown, shaggy, unkempt hair, like someone who had been living out in the wilderness for a few weeks, and dark eyes.

Mudd gave Mairis a good, long hug. "I've missed you darling."

Trynn raised his eyebrows.

Mairis pushed Mudd off. "This is Trynn."

"Oh, the Cosegan," Mudd said, as if just noticing him, and in a tone that implied being a Cosegan was something unfortunate.

"Yes, the Cosegan," Trynn said, "*and* her father."

Mudd's face registered surprise. "Well then. I didn't know, but I'm glad you're here. I want to tell you about our marriage."

"What marriage?" Trynn asked, unusually surprised and confused.

"Mairis and I are getting married."

"*Really*?" Trynn said. "And I'm the last to know?"

"No, Dad," Mairis said, shooting a look at Mudd, "apparently *I'm* the last to know."

"It's not happening today," Mudd said, holding up his hands. "There's a lot still to do . . . invitations, ordering the cake

—I really love cake, the cake might be the second . . . no, the third . . . well probably the fourth best thing about a wedding. Anyway, we've got a few weeks to get all the arrangements made. I assume you will be there."

Before Trynn could answer, Mairis interrupted, "Perhaps you should ask me if *I'm* going to be there," she said, looking incredulously at Mudd. "I believe that's how it's normally done."

"Oh, baby, we wouldn't do it without you. It's going to be a *big* cake."

Trynn checked the Terminus Clock on his strand. "Listen, you kids can make your wedding arrangements on your own time," he said impatiently. "If we could get to the matter at hand?"

"Something more important than your daughter's wedding?" Mudd looked at him. "Man, that's cold."

"Globotite," Trynn snapped. "You told Mairis you would not get us any more unless you spoke with the end user. Well, that's me. Here I am. What do you want to speak about?"

"Okay, *famous scientist*, just what do you do with all the Globotite? Are you eating the stuff?"

"It's no concern of yours," Trynn said.

"Wait, didn't I just ask you why you needed it? Sure sounds like it's a concern of mine."

Trynn rubbed at his eyes. "I was being polite. What I should have said is, it isn't any of your business."

Mudd smirked back at him. "Wrong again. My business is selling Globotite, so . . . "

"Why do you care?" Trynn asked, trying to remain patient.

"It's in limited supply. Prices are out-of-control, and where you come from. it's a high crime to traffic the stuff."

"Your *point*?"

"Are you really manipulating the future?"

Trynn looked at Mairis. She raised her eyebrows and shook her head slowly.

"Can you get more or not?" Trynn snapped.

Mudd's smirk was gone. "There are other buyers, paying far more."

"Do you ask them what they want it for?" Trynn shot back.

"I do. They don't answer either, but I've heard rumors."

"I'll bet you have."

"Apparently someone's doing the opposite of you."

"What's that mean?" Trynn asked, confused.

"They want to use Globotite to change the past."

TWENTY-THREE

On board the Varangian's yacht, an agent handed Barbeau a computer tablet. Barbeau read the screen, checked the image, and then nodded.

Gale wondered if it was about them. Were they orders to take them into custody and deliver them to . . . who? Dixon Barbeau had saved them before, but he still worked for the US government, one of the many groups who sought the Eysens . . . and themselves.

"The sphere's mystery and perfection soon became an obsession for Locke," Barbeau continued. "Apparently, it's somewhat different from the one you found in Virginia."

"How so?" Rip asked, gritting his teeth from the pain.

"Rather than being housed in a stone casing, this one has some kind of metallic skin, making it more difficult to open. The diameter is also slightly smaller."

"Excuse me," the medic said. "Mind if I stitch you up right now?"

"As long as it won't hurt," Rip said. "Go right ahead."

The medic laughed. "It's going to hurt, all right."

Rip nodded, as if to acknowledge he had been joking about that part. "I appreciate it."

"So you were saying about Kalor Locke?" Gale prompted, hoping to learn as much as they could before they were arrested.

"Eventually Locke resigned from HITE. Suddenly, he was in possession of a fortune. We don't know what else he did or took from the agency, but apparently he was able to use the Eysen to accumulate vast sums of wealth, some of which he used to put together the Varangians."

"Did he name them for the Varangian Guard?" Rip asked, biting back pain as the medic completed the stitches.

"Yes, he did," Barbeau said, not surprised Rip knew of the Viking mercenaries. He'd had to research it himself when they'd first come across the name.

Rip explained to the others that the original Varangians were paid bodyguards for a Byzantine Emperor in the tenth century. "They eventually morphed into an elite fighting unit that protected Constantinople for at least two centuries."

"As you've no doubt ascertained, these new Varangians aren't Vikings," Barbeau said. "Locke has equipped them with mind boggling technology on his quest to obtain other Eysens."

"So you've been tracking him?" Rip asked.

"We were hoping to find him on board, but he manages to stay a few steps ahead."

"Cosegan technology can help him do that, too," Rip said.

Barbeau nodded. "I'm painfully aware. The bastard can see the future."

"Are you going to arrest us?" Cira asked.

Barbeau seemed surprised.

"The FBI isn't exactly our friend," Rip explained.

"We're not regular FBI," Barbeau replied. "If we were, we would have to take you into custody. Instead, as soon as they sent me your photographs a few minutes before I arrived, I contacted Booker. Some of his Blaxers will be here shortly to transport you somewhere else, a destination of your choosing."

"And the Eysens?" Savina asked hopefully.

"I don't think I want to compete with Booker for those at present, so you can keep 'em."

"So DIRT still works?" Rip asked, recalling Barbeau had been with the ultra-secret group buried in the Bureau.

He nodded. "There's only two people inside the FBI who know we exist."

"The director, and . . . ?"

"Not this new director," Barbeau said bitterly. "Just a couple of deep lifers."

"How did your people get here?" Gale asked.

"L-RUD," Barbeau replied. "Long range underwater deployment." He forced a smile, glancing again at the cases. "Booker and Locke aren't the only ones with super advanced technologies."

"Where does the budget come from?" Rip asked.

"Classified," Barbeau said curtly. "But DIRT has MONSTERS, and the current director of HITE is on our team."

Rip was also aware of the covert directive that allowed a credentialed official to call on the power and authority of every civilian and military asset of the US government. Most agencies had a MONSTER, "Mission of National Security Transfer Every Resource," point person, a highly classified post even within top-secret clearances. The MONSTER could access the assets of any agency, department, or military branch instantly, and often invisibly. The MONSTER structure had been put into place as part of the Patriot Act following the September 11, 2001 terrorist attacks. MONSTER, like so many other provisions, was hidden from public knowledge and withheld from Congress. Even within the government, the few who knew about it believed it to be a resource-sharing plan which could be used to cut through red tape in times of national emergencies and threats to national security. MONSTER had been created without input or oversight. Not even the President was aware of its full extent.

Rip silently wondered who exactly Barbeau was taking orders from.

"Where did Locke find the HITE Eysen?" Savina asked.

"Florida," Barbeau said. "Fort George Island."

"When?"

"1974." He pulled out a small tablet and fingered its screen. "March 27, 1974."

"Thank you," Savina said, committing his reply to memory, happy for the precise answer as she tried to figure out the sphere's origin and its original intended recipient.

Now less distracted by his injury, Rip stared at Barbeau. "I'm amazed to see you again," he said, shaking his head.

"Likewise," Barbeau replied. "We didn't know you'd be at the end of this road."

"Or that you would save us once again," Rip said. He held the FBI man's gaze. They had a long history together. "Thank you, my friend."

Barbeau nodded. He handed Rip one of the Spartan laser rifles. "Take this to Booker."

"Blaxers incoming," an agent reported. They all looked out the windows until they saw a pair of black choppers inbound.

A few minutes later, as they were boarding the helicopter, Rip thanked Barbeau again. "I guess this is farewell."

Barbeau slipped Rip a small computer tablet. "Unfortunately, we'll meet again."

TWENTY-FOUR

Shanoah met with the mission-chosen elite Imazes who would cross the boundaries of space, through the spectrum belt, into channels of time which would allow them access to the future. Inside the main hanger at the ISS, she stared into the faces of the men and women who, even by Cosegan standards, possessed incredible intelligence, were extraordinarily energetic, and physically conditioned to the levels of strength and stamina necessary to endure such a journey.

After addressing the full crew, Shanoah convened her inner circle to discuss the more specific objectives. While she spoke, Sweed, her right hand and second in command, worked silently, adjusting the parameters that would order the ignition sequence. The other Imazes affectionately referred to Sweed as Shanoah's sister since they shared similar appearances, often said and did the same things, and were generally considered interchangeable in most situations. The two also held the distinction of being the best Imaze pilots.

"Do we have any idea of the date we are going to try to get

to?" Maicks, a bald, dark skinned man, and the third pilot on the mission, asked.

Drifson, a slender, fair-haired man, responded, "Yes, a period of time those in the Far Future refer to as 200 BC." As the Imaze's chief historian, he knew more about the Far Future than any other Cosegan—with the possible exception of Ovan or Trynn. Those two had gained experience from extensive viewings of actual events as seen inside Eysens. However, Drifson's knowledge had been acquired from traditional studies. "We are going to the land they call China."

Shanoah had carefully explained their mission was to specifically protect certain people in the Far Future, which had surprised the other Imazes. Still, she was annoyed when one of them questioned her.

"How are we deciding which people get to live?" Lusa, the mission's tech officer, asked. She had known Shanoah for years. The pair had joined the Imazes in the same month, but Shanoah had quickly surpassed her in rank and time logged in space.

"They are descendants," Shanoah replied, her swirling emerald eyes narrowed.

"But surely there are millions of descendants, possibly even billions," Lusa said, smiling. She was not as pretty as Shanoah, but her radiant smile disarmed anyone. "How does one determine the lucky few? I mean, what criteria is he using to establish the winners and the losers?"

"He's using the Eysens." Shanoah smirked in return. "It's complicated."

"The circle has forbidden such work," Lusa said. "Unless it goes through the Enders, and I somehow doubt he's consulted them."

Shanoah shook her head. "We can't go in blind."

"Of course not, but the Enders have given us all kinds of specific missions. How are you going to ignore that?"

"The Enders are working with insufficient data," Shanoah said impatiently, ignoring the question.

"We may only get one chance," Sweed interjected, her gentle voice quickly easing the tension. "Shanoah is in command. We take our orders from her; not the Enders, not the Predictive League, not even the Circle."

"Of course, but we can question."

"Question, but not debate," Shanoah corrected, trying not to sound angry.

"Anyway," Sweed continued. "There is no denying that Trynn has seen more of the Far Future and better understands the effects of infinite scenarios that result from our potential actions. We're *all* working to stop the Terminus Doom."

"Trynn is a fugitive," Lusa said in a biting tone. "And his knowledge does not mean we have to ignore the Enders directive."

Sweed caught Shanoah's face flashing from fury to control. "The Circle issues directives," Sweed corrected her.

"Yes, but from recommendations *made by* the Enders. *They* are our best minds, not a single person." She folded her hands in her lap, pleased with herself.

"We are not allowed to meddle in the Far Future where it would affect history in either direction," Shanoah said. "However, we *can* do things that affect the Terminus Doom—that is our mission."

"Then why save these people?" Lusa persisted. "The Enders have not sanctioned that. It certainly seems like meddling."

"It is not meddling," Sweed responded. "Trynn is making observations."

"But we will be saving people, changing events," Lusa argued. "It's the same thing."

"Not exactly," Sweed said. "As Imazes, we have a different mandate; to act by any means necessary to save the Cosegan civilization. Once we pass through the belt, we are governed by our own rules in order to achieve that goal."

"And by the final directive," Drifson added coolly, like a wizard from some fantasy who knew everything, but spoke covertly.

The room fell silent. Each of them were painfully aware that the final directive meant if they found themselves trapped in the Far Future, unable to escape back into space, they were required to end their lives to ensure that their presence did not inadvertently interfere with the Far Future in a way that would precipitate the Terminus Doom. Each Imaze had taken an oath: "There are a thousand ways to die as an Imaze, but one rises above the other. A Far Future suicide."

TWENTY-FIVE

The plane landed at a small airport in Turkey. Rip, Gale, Cira, and Savina were greeted on the runway by a dozen Blaxers who quickly hustled the four of them into a large silver SUV. Two more matching vehicles completed the convoy while they rolled through busy streets. Rip glanced out the window as they drove past aged concrete low-rise buildings.

"Where are we going?" Rip asked.

"Booker wants to see you," a man in the front passenger seat replied.

"He's here?" Gale asked.

The man nodded.

"Maybe he wants to apologize for the security breach," Gale said.

"Booker never apologizes," Rip said, shaking his head. "Anyway, he kept us alive."

"Then why is he here?" Gale asked.

"Because he misses me," Cira said. The two of them had developed a grandfather/granddaughter relationship over the years.

"I'm sure he does sweetheart," Gale said. "But these are dangerous times for a social visit."

"Booker doesn't *do* social," Cira said confidently, raising her eyebrows to her mother, momentarily switching roles.

"Perhaps he has new information for us," Savina said, staring out the window as they passed a small open-air street market. Soon the scenery turned more rural, with only the occasional structure punctuating the passing landscape.

Fifteen minutes later, they pulled into a courtyard behind a modern villa tucked in the hills. Two black men greeted them. One was Booker, the other was a man they had never met.

Rip hadn't noticed, but they'd traveled through six rings of security to reach them—subtle, but sophisticated and comprehensive, the kind of defenses befitting the world's wealthiest man, particularly one caught in a seemingly never-ending power struggle for the future of the human race.

After pleasantries were exchanged and a hug for Cira, Booker introduced the other man. "Alik is a brilliant hacker from Leningrad."

The new Huang, Rip thought, thinking of his old friend. Savina and Gale were thinking the same thing. Huang's replacement. Their long-time chief IT specialist had been killed through an Eysen in a stunning attack by an unknown Cosegan weeks earlier. No one mentioned it.

"No black Russian jokes," Booker said. "Alik has heard them all."

Alik let out a hearty, infectious laugh that endeared him to the others quickly. "But I like a good joke," Alik said. "Humor keeps us healthy, especially in these tense times. It's easy to get too serious."

"Yes," Booker agreed dryly. "No reason to get all stressed out about the end of humanity."

"See? A very funny man."

"Anyway, Alik is one of the best there is."

"Booker is far too modest. I am the *absolute* best."

"But are you trustworthy?" Rip said through a forced smile, inadvertently holding his side where the knife had cut into him.

"No hackers are trustworthy," Alik said. "Especially not a Russian one."

"But you're different?" Gale asked.

"Booker has my wife and children locked up," he said in a serious tone, a matching sad expression on his face. "He says he will kill them if I don't cooperate."

Cira and Gale looked at Booker, astonished.

Booker smiled. "I do what I have to do." He noticed Rip's hand at his side.

Alik laughed. "A joke! I wish he had my wife. I've been looking for a wife. Apparently not many women are interested in Russian hackers."

Savina said something in Russian. They both laughed.

"I've brought Alik up to speed, and given him access to all Huang's files," Booker said. A Blaxer entered the room and nodded to Booker, as if indicating an assignment had been completed. "How are the efforts going to get ahold of Crying Man?"

"We are nowhere with that," Rip replied, motioning toward their two secure, digitally locked, custom-made cases, each containing two of the four priceless Eysens.

"We don't even know if he's alive anymore," Savina said.

"Yes," Booker said, looking at the cases. "Eleven million years . . . anything could've happened."

"We've seen several references to what Cosegans cite as the 'Missing Time'," Rip began. "That's apparently what they call the period between the end of the Cosegan civilization and the beginning of ours."

"The theory is," Savina said, "that whatever catastrophe

they are trying to prevent, which they referred to as the Terminus Doom—"

"Terminus Doom," Booker repeated, "that does sound ominous . . . world-ending . . . What is the actual event?"

"We have no idea," Rip said. "Some equivalent of nuclear annihilation, a catastrophic meltdown, a ravaging plague . . . Whatever it is, it has to be something man-made. There's nothing in the geological record—asteroid related, volcanic activity, earthquake, polar shifts—*anything* that would've wiped out a civilization . . . especially one as advanced as theirs."

"But they were a peaceful people."

"As far as we know," Rip theorized. "However, in creating Eysens, they were playing with some pretty powerful forces. Maybe they went a step too far."

"Let's not forget they appear to have transcended time in multiple ways," Booker added.

"Maybe not multiple ways," Savina interrupted. "Everything comes through the Eysens."

"That all depends on if the Imazes made it here or not."

"The Imazes?" Alik asked. "I'm a little vague there."

"We all are," Booker said. "However, based on conversations Rip has had with Crying Man, the Imazes were a select group of Cosegans who didn't believe the Eysens were the way to prevent the Terminus Doom. Instead, they went looking for answers in outer space."

"And we believe," Savina said, taking over the thread, "that they may have found a way to visit their future . . . and our past . . ."

Alik's expression registered surprise that bordered on skepticism. "You mean they flew off into space, and returned to Earth at another time . . . millions of years in the future. Is that *possible*?"

"Einstein thought it was," Savina said. "If someone could find the right portal, there would be a way to traverse the folds of space time."

"And you think the Imazes or Cosegans may have found that way?"

"There are many who believe that Earth was visited by aliens from other worlds in ancient times," Gale said. "Perhaps they helped build the pyramids at Giza, or the Nasca lines in Peru, take your pick of any number of ancient wonders. If it happened—"

"Crying Man claimed it wasn't aliens from a distant planet," Rip interrupted. "Instead, it was visitors from a distant past, from Earth's distant past." Blood was starting to leak through his shirt.

"Cosegans?" Alik asked.

"They've been trying to save us since before we existed."

TWENTY-SIX

Trynn stood up and looked around the seedy joint, as if conspirators wishing to manipulate the origins of Cosegan society might be lurking in the shadows. "They want to use Globotite to change the past?" Trynn repeated, still trying to absorb the shocking news.

"That's what I hear," Mudd said, his smile fading to match Trynn's upset.

"Who?"

"That's not a simple answer."

"A person is trying to acquire Globotite," Mairis said. "Why would their identity be complicated?"

"These are complex times, love," Mudd responded to Mairis in a soothing voice that annoyed Trynn. "The world's on fire. There are those playing wicked games . . . doing wicked things."

"Do the names Markol or Shank mean anything to you?" Trynn asked as a group of Enforcers walked in. The men were the Havlos equivalent of Guardians.

"They do now that you uttered them," he said. "Prior to this moment, I had never heard those names." Mudd's eyes followed the Enforcers moving through the large space. He looked as if he'd seen a ghost.

"Is there a problem?" Mairis asked.

"Not if they don't recognize us," Mudd replied.

"*Us*?" Trynn echoed, confused.

"You're at the center of this, Cosegan," he said, looking over his shoulder.

"Center of what?" Trynn asked, he could imagine a hundred answers to that question, and was curious to know which one Mudd was alluding to.

As it turned out, there wasn't a chance to continue the conversation. The shooting started the instant Trynn said the word "what."

Mudd was moving before Trynn dove for Mairis. As the smuggler slipped between two columns thirty feet away, he shouted back, "Not for you, not for the cause, but for the girl, I'll get you another delivery!" Then he was gone.

Mairis and Trynn crawled along the sticky floor as a firefight of lasers and more traditional projectiles hailed above them. They wove in and out of hundreds of other patrons looking for cover, a way out, or some kind of advantage. Cutthroats, derelicts, bums, rogues, and other unsavory characters Trynn was not used to being around were now caught in the same crossfire.

"Who's fighting the Enforcers?" Mairis yelled as they slithered through the mob.

"Lasers," he replied, desperately looking for an exit, trying to figure out how Mudd had escaped.

Mairis understood. Lasers could only mean Cosegans, and the presence of Cosegans at such a remote and shady location in Havlos lands could only mean they were there for Trynn. "How did they find you?"

"Ask Mudd."

A large, grungy looking fellow with an eyepatch pressed a knee into Trynn's back in an effort to get off the floor. Trynn reeled from the assault, but did not engage in retribution. Instead, he pushed Mairis in between the columns where he'd last seen Mudd. A second later, the grungy-eyepatch man was sliced down by a laser.

"There!" Trynn said, pointing to a half-sized door in one of the columns.

Mairis missed it at first glance, but quickly found a recessed latch and pulled open the door.

"It's a pole."

"Pole?" he echoed, looking into the column.

"To slide down."

Trynn checked behind them. The entire place was quickly cascading into worsening violence. "Go!"

Mairis climbed in, and seconds later, barely got out of the way before Trynn crashed down on top of her. Total darkness and a cold dirt floor greeted them. They both lit their strand-bands at the same time.

"This may be worse than up there," Mairis said.

"This way." Trynn followed a primitive tunnel that looked more like an old mine shaft from the Far Future than anything from Cosegan time.

After navigating the narrow space and stale air for a few minutes, they reached a heavy wooden door. Trynn lifted the thick board that barred it, and pulled the door back into the tunnel. He scoured the area for Guardians before stepping out into the sunlight.

"Where's Mudd?" Mairis asked.

"Long gone."

"Then who barred the door?" she asked. "It had to be done from the inside."

Trynn, accustomed to doors made of light, didn't know the answer. Nor did he care. "Globotite. Do you think he can get more?"

"He will," she said. They dashed across to a back alley that wound between two giant warehouses, which appeared to have fallen into disrepair centuries earlier. "It may cost more than you can pay, but he'll get it."

"We can pay with the future . . . if that's enough."

"Maybe not for a man like Mudd."

"It will have to be."

TWENTY-SEVEN

STANDING in front of a nearly invisible photon window, on the upper most floor of the Reach, a three-thousand-foot tall building constructed of light and sound, Shank admired the view. The top of the highest inhabitable structure in Solas had long housed the residence and private offices of the Arc. Shank gazed across the spectacular skyline and could not help but think how nice it would be to wake up to the incredible scenery every morning, to see Solas from such a vantage point in all phases of time.

The Arc scowled at him. "You will *never* occupy this space!" Her sharp tone, a cross between anger and annoyance, was both cutting and firm.

Shank's face registered surprise. He had not believed the rumors that she possessed mind reading abilities since, until that moment, he had never seen her display them. He'd assumed it was just part of her legend, owed to the careful aura she'd crafted for herself. However, Shank recovered quickly. "It is not about you or luxuries. What we need to focus on is saving our society."

"We are trying to save *all* of humanity," she corrected sternly.

"The same thing," he said, forcing a smile. "This is why you need to step down immediately."

The Arc looked at him as if he'd just told her to jump from the balcony of the Reach. She had been expecting him to make an offer of joint rule, as he had yet to find the support to build a broad enough coalition to remove her. *This is either an act of desperation,* she thought, *or something worse. Boldness.* "How dare you."

"I'm giving you a chance to leave with your dignity."

"You are such a fool, Shank."

"And now you question my intelligence." He shook his head.

"No, I'm not questioning your intelligence. The most brilliant people can do foolish things when their judgment is clouded."

"What clouds my judgment, then?"

"Fear. Mistakes are almost always made from a place of fear."

"Well, then you must be afraid to leave." He looked at her as if she were a child. "Don't you realize that your time is over? It has passed!"

She glared at him with furious eyes.

He smiled conciliatorily. "Don't make mistakes now that will overwrite what is a reasonably decent legacy."

She continued to stare at him incredulously.

"If you don't leave by the end of the day tomorrow, you will be forced out."

"I should have you arrested right now for such a threat."

"There can't be more than a handful of Guardians who would dare attempt to arrest me." Shank lifted a shoulder. "And even if they tried, I would be released immediately."

"You don't have the support to remove me."

"Don't I?"

"I don't think so."

"Then arrest me and make my job much easier."

She knew he was right, but her expression revealed nothing. "Tell me, Shank, if you had what you most covet and were in charge, leading The Circle, guiding the Cosegans, what would you *do*? What is it you are so desperate to do that I am not doing, or that I have not done?"

"The list is long, and it is never wise to reveal too much to an enemy."

"Am I your enemy?" she asked.

He tipped his head. "Don't you consider me yours?"

"Rivals, perhaps, but not enemies."

Shank laughed, as if this amused him very much. "You ask what I would do. I'd unite the planet."

The Arc narrowed her eyes at him. "By unite, you mean stop the Havloses. How?"

"By whatever means necessary."

"You would go to war to dominate Havloses?"

"War will come whether I choose it or not," he said, gazing out beyond the city. "We might as well be the ones to direct its course."

"You'll accelerate the Doom."

"Ha! Funny coming from someone who tried to stop the Doom through Trynn's follies. Surely you can now clearly see that was a horrible mistake."

"No."

"No? Then you are even more delusional than I thought. Trynn demonstrated his flaws and lack of understanding. How many errors can he be allowed when playing with the fate of the world? But you always misunderstood the solution . . . " He looked back at her. "It isn't in the Far Future. The solution is within our own time. That's why the Havloses must be conquered, and the Imaze missions into the Far Future should be halted and redirected."

"You would waste the Imaze advantage?"

He shook his head. "There should be many, *many* more Imaze missions."

"But you just said it wasn't about the Far Future?"

"The Imazes should continue to monitor the Far Future, but the new missions I propose would go into the Far Past."

She gasped. "For what purpose?"

"There is only one purpose," he said in a slick, disrespectful tone. "To stop the Doom."

"You called *me* reckless. If you do something like that, the potential dire consequences are impossible to calculate. A million things could go wrong . . . you could erase our very existence."

"The Terminus Clock has shown the Doom can occur at any time, even once tamed."

"That's why we—"

"Need to be rid of you," Shank interrupted. "It's the main reason you are ill-equipped to deal with this crisis, because you still think it is solvable. As if a one-time solution answers it forever."

"That's not true," she said, squinting at him, amazed by his audacity, his callowness. "The Terminus Doom crisis must be managed by someone competent."

"Exactly."

She looked toward the entrance, deciding again whether to summon a Guardian to arrest him for his brash threats to the Cosegan establishment. "Have you considered, for even a moment, that you misjudged the situation . . . and me?"

"No." He laughed, as if that were a silly notion. "Only once did I ever think I was wrong, but I was mistaken."

TWENTY-EIGHT

Mairis and Trynn made their way back to the vehicle and managed to escape the area undetected through a combination of luck, and Mairis's instincts for survival. It also helped that the Enforcers kept the Cosegan agents busy for quite a while.

That night, Trynn reached Shanoah for what would be one of their final conversations before her departure.

Trynn shivered, the cool air as much responsible as the looming end of the world. *How has it fallen to me? Who would imagine I am worthy of this challenge?* He peered into the holographic eyes of Shanoah's projection and silently relayed the questions from his thoughts.

She smiled, seeing the self-doubt in him. He was the smartest man she'd ever met, the smartest man she'd ever heard of. "You can do it," she whispered.

He nodded, wanting to believe her, but so overwhelmed by the Terminus Doom that sometimes he could hardly breathe.

"And don't worry," she said, winking. "I might just save the world before you."

"Remember, your mission is to protect our descendants."

Her expression changed to concern. "And to stop the Doom."

"That's the best way to stop it."

Trynn gazed out at the stars, imagining for a moment that Shanoah was standing next to him instead of halfway around the world, preparing for the most dangerous mission ever untaken by the Imazes.

"You need to look at the mission differently," he said after a long silence.

It was still light where Shanoah was. She stared through his connection and also gazed into the heavens, albeit with different eyes than his. She saw the places she'd visited, areas of celestial wonder where people close to her had been lost. "My mission is the same as yours," she repeated. "To stop the Doom."

"We can't."

"You're saying the Doom is inevitable?"

Trynn had memorized every expression of her face, and knew she was fighting panic. "There are many more complications now with the looming conflict."

"Surely, we'll find a way to avoid war."

He shook his head. "Preventing war between the Havloses and Cosegans is no longer something we can count on."

"Then the Far Future is more important than ever. Now that I can get through, we have the ability to go to wherever the most difference can be made." His silence alarmed her. "There *is* going to be a Far Future, isn't there? Or does the escalation with the Havloses—"

"It's not the war that I'm most concerned about," Trynn's soft, sanguine voice cut through the thickness. "Although that can certainly stop us, and then nothing else will matter." He smiled defeatedly and paused again, as if letting that play out in his mind for the thousandth time. "What I'm most interested in is our descendants."

"Why?"

"You need to save them."

"From what?"

"From so many things . . . the ripples of the Doom, the limitations of their understanding of health, from each other—but most of all, you need them to save themselves."

"And that's possible?"

"It has to be. The only way to stop the Doom is to save our descendants," he continued to hammer on this point because he knew ultimately it would come down to which descendants survived.

"At what time?" she asked. "Where do we go in? Eleven million years . . . the calculations must be . . . I can't even *begin* to fathom the ramifications of cause and effect across such a chasm."

"Unfortunately, it has to be across multiple periods," he said, as if this were even more terrible than it sounded. "I have chosen the ones with the best chances of affecting the other periods in the hopes of limiting the number of trips."

"The number of trips," she repeated. "How many?"

"Again, I don't know . . . More than three, less than one hundred. It all depends on the success of each mission, what the Havloses do, if the Arc can hold onto power—a thousand, million things. But that's what I'll be doing so long as the Globotite supplies hold. Either way, it's more dangerous because . . . " He hesitated.

"Why?" she asked, imagining all the dangers she'd already faced, wondering if they would make it back.

"Because this time there is another Eysen."

"You did another insertion?" She was not shocked he'd done it again, only surprised he was telling her now.

He shook his head. "Not me. Markol."

"Oh no," she breathed. She looked back through the connection and into the stars of Trynn's sky. "Is there any hope?"

"Too soon to tell. Shank has finally—"

"Shank?"

"Markol would never do this on his own."

"But The Arc is the one. She has control of your old lab. She secured the prisoners, including Markol—at least that's the rumor . . . I thought you knew."

"If that's true, if it was her instead of Shank, then there might still be hope after all."

TWENTY-NINE

Rip wished Booker had stayed longer. He felt safer when the world's richest person was around, but he understood. Booker was busy, and not in the ways popular perceptions made it seem. Many people believed Booker Lipton was a greedy man intent on controlling the world.

If they only knew the truth, Rip thought. *That Booker's actually trying to* save *the world. That would probably terrify them even more.*

Standing alone between the four Eysens, Rip stopped thinking about Booker. Instead, he turned his attention to another individual also trying to save humanity, Crying Man. It had been so long since they'd had any contact from him that it was difficult not to imagine he was dead. It was Savina who insisted Crying Man still survived, but she had left an hour earlier to pursue leads in Egypt for another sphere. With Gale and Cira in another part of the building, researching Nostradamus and Leonardo Da Vinci, he was alone with the four Eysens for the first time, and nothing mattered more than contacting the man who had built them all.

KALOR LOCKE READ THE REPORTS. He wasn't surprised Rip and Savina had escaped. He'd seen it in his Eysen, watched it happen a thousand different ways, days earlier.

Amazing device, he thought. *If only I could figure out how to use it.*

Locke did know how to use it, at least partially, more than Rip and Savina. He had advantages, other technologies to help crack the Sequence, and he'd gotten lucky since his had not been created with the care and precautions that Trynn normally took. Locke's sphere was not created by the master Eysen Maker, but rather by his apprentice, Markol, and it was very different; simpler, less powerful.

Locke understood this, connoted that if his was the only Eysen, it would be more powerful than all the combined human and computer intelligence could comprehend times a trillion, and yet it was not as powerful as any of the Eysens that Booker, via Ripley Gaines, possessed.

Imagine four at once. The power would be . . . would be something like holding all the universe in your hands.

"Bring them to me," Locke whispered into his sphere, practically drooling as he watched the projections—an abstract series of beams circling the earth, each gold band of incredible light representing an Eysen operating. "Soon I will know where you are. And I will have all the Eysens."

TOGETHER, the Eysens created an energy that Rip could feel as a vibration that seemed to make his spine an electrical conduit. The sensation did not reach an uncomfortable level, but it certainly unnerved him that these objects could physically affect him so dramatically. *The power to create and sustain the mass knowledge contained in the Eysens must require a source capable of an equally potent destructive force,* he thought. Yet, as the pulsing in his spine quickened, he recalled a conversation he'd had with Gale about Kundalini, a Sanskrit term used to describe a vital source-energy that Hindus believe lies within each person. Sometimes referred to as the "sleeping goddess", and often depicted as a coiled snake at the base of the spine, Kundalini's presence was said to be centered at the "root chakra." Such spirituality and new age thoughts didn't sit well with Rip's scientific mind, but there was clearly more to the Eysens than simple science, and he could not deny what he was experiencing.

He had researched chakras, the so-called focal energy points of the physical body directly connecting to the ethereal body. It actually wasn't so new a belief, as references to chakras existed for more than three thousand years. He found it interesting in the sense that some depictions of the seven Chakras could be seen as Eysens, representing a connection to the universe.

The reading he'd done on Kundalini had described it as a cosmic energy accumulating within each of us, a vital force that could help lead one to spiritual liberation. He felt it happening, felt all the history of the Universe pulsating through him.

Addictive, he thought. *The Eysens are a drug.* Booker had warned him and Savina numerous times, but Rip didn't care about that. In the emergence of "the everything", as he called it, the Eysens showing him the eternal light, the god energy, making him a god, all he could think of was going further, to find out what was next and to make the ultimate discovery.

In the glowing light, the spiritual stew, and the ghosting

energy of every star, he searched for Crying Man, knowing that was where he needed to go. A quest, a purpose that otherwise would have left him floating in the glow, surrounded by endless darkness. Like a heroin addict coming up for air, he threw himself in.

THIRTY

THE SEAS WERE CHOPPY, but that didn't concern Trynn. What did was the possibility that the vessel could be boarded, which meant the insertion would be interrupted. Even though he'd received asylum from the Havloses, planting an Eysen in territory they controlled was still something that never would've been approved, so he hadn't bothered seeking permission.

He triple checked the holographic images showing the surface of the water for hundreds of miles in all directions. Nothing was there, or at least not yet. Still, he knew at any minute, a Cosegan craft could materialize or Havlos fighter jets could burst onto the scene. Just as concerning were the images coming from the insertion site, a place that one day would be called Egypt.

"People are there who shouldn't be," Trynn said. "As if they're expecting the Eysen."

"It's the 'ancient' world to the Far Future," Nassar said as the images floated around them. "How could they know?"

"Someone has interfered," Trynn responded, moving thousands of scenes with a single movement of his arm and landing precisely on the day and moment he was searching for, as if he'd created it all in some biblical explosion and divine plan—a plan which was in danger of slipping from his control.

"Then we must abort the insertion," Nassar said, a little too loud.

"We cannot stop it," Trynn replied. "We *must* counter Markol's sphere."

"It's too risky to do another one now. If they know, and . . . "

Ovan's thick mane of silver hair emerged from a dark corner devoid of images, where he had been studying other aspects, ramifications, simulations—Eysen data upon Eysens and interpretations of predictive models that rooted the cradle to the grave analysis of humanity. "Push, Trynn, push!"

"But—" Nassar pleaded.

"Do not forget your place, Nassar!" Ovan barked. His silver beard and mustache made him appear ancient in Cosegan terms, yet the strength of his presence, the endlessly determined eyes, could turn the studious scientist into a fiery warrior in an instant.

Nassar backed down.

"The ramifications of someone in that time knowing," Trynn said, in a partial pick up of Nassar's argument. "If the wrong person obtains it at the wrong time, we'll need to do another—"

"You forget," Ovan broke in fiercely. "We needed Egypt *before* Markol's insertion. Now there will have to be another."

"I know," Trynn said, dreading a *sixth* insertion. His Revon induced mind raced. *Globotite. Can Mudd deliver enough? Will he ask too much? How can we trust it all to a smuggler?*

"The archaeologist is attempting contact again," Nassar said, looking sheepishly at Ovan, wondering if mentioning Rip was going to subject him to another tongue lashing. "Can't we enlist his help?"

"If we had more Globotite!" Trynn yelled. His misdirected anger seemed to soften Ovan for a moment.

"The archaeologist will manage," Ovan said. "Our interference will only distort the already numerous mistakes."

"Without our help," Nassar began, "he won't survive much longer."

"Likely not," Ovan conceded. "Markol's insertion all but ensures the archaeologist's premature end."

Nassar looked back into the Far Future and isolated the time when the Sphere they were inserting in Egypt would be discovered. The periods around uncovering an Eysen in the Far Future were typically murky, but this one was considerably worse. Still, he could see enough to know what was going to occur. "They will die."

"Maybe not all of them," Trynn said defensively. "We're doing what we can, but the cause is not to save a few. This is about humanity itself, and to protect the existence of our species, the cost is high. We'd have to be numb to paying that price with one life at a time, or millions, even billions, before we stop the Terminus Doom!"

"I know," Nassar said quietly, watching the death and mourning a person he knew so intimately, even though they had never met.

"Let them go," Ovan said, then reminded Nassar of what Trynn had learned from Mudd. "Markol and Shank want to go into the past. If we don't stop them from doing a reverse insertion, we'll be dead before we even have a chance to save ourselves, let alone a few nobodies from the Far Future."

"But who is in the Far-Past trying to save *us*?" Nassar asked. "Are we the nobodies to them?"

"Of course we are!" Trynn blasted.

"It's ready," a woman said, interrupting the debate.

Trynn, Ovan, and Nassar all looked to the images coming from the insertion site. Nassar checked the time. They had made it. Six seconds remained. A miracle.

"Do we insert?" the woman asked.

Trynn took a deep breath, knowing the death and destruction he was about to unleash, the impossible to contain chaos and ripples that would bleed for millions of years in all directions. He silently cursed Markol and Shank, wondering if there would be enough Globotite to fix it, enough Revon to understand it.

Is it chance? Is it surrender? Trynn thought. Is *it survival? Is it the web that connects it all? And what* is *it all?*

"Trynn?" she asked, an instant before the window would close.

"Do it."

THIRTY-ONE

Gale discovered Rip on the floor, unconscious. "What happened?" she cried. "Cira, get Rone!"

By the time Rone, the closest Blaxer who had medical training, and Cira arrived, Rip was coming to.

"What happened?" Gale repeated, seeing that blood was seeping through his pant leg again.

"I . . . I don't . . . know," Rip said through the fog. He shook his head, trying to focus on the now dark Eysens. "It was so much power . . . nothing like I've ever . . . experienced."

"Did you reach Crying Man?" she asked while Rone checked Rip's vitals and quickly changed the dressings on the deep wound.

"No."

"He's okay," Rone said to Gale, finishing up.

"Thank you."

"Daddy, what happened?" Cira asked, hugging him.

"Whatever powers the Eysens," he said. "It's . . . it's . . . somehow it connects, as if it went through me. Like it's in the air."

Cira looked at her mother for clarification. Gale shook her head.

"Kalor Locke can never be allowed to get another Eysen," Rip said. "The power isn't just about knowledge or the ability to see into other times, the power is *real*."

LATER, after Rip had time to recover, they sat on a covered balcony and overlooked hills that rolled toward the Mediterranean. The island, off the coast of Turkey, was ancient; an undulating painting of craggy rock and gnarled trees accentuated by dusky layers of mountain ranges, draped in a smoky golden sun. Rip wasn't sure if Booker owned the whole thing, or maybe just the land they were on, but it felt secure, even though they had nearly died on another of his islands the night before. There was something about this one that felt strong, sure, incisive.

Rip handed Gale the tablet Barbeau had given him on the yacht. As soon as she digested the text and images on the screen, she knew why he'd waited. "The Divinations," she said, speaking of Clastier's predictions. Clastier, a nineteenth century priest in New Mexico, had spent years studying an Eysen—although they were not certain if he'd been the original recipient, or if he'd acquired it from another source. Either way, he'd written extensively on what he'd learned, and then had hidden the manuscript, which later wound up with Rip's possession and was now held by Booker.

Clastier's papers were divided into three sections: the Attestations, the Divinations, and the Inspirations. All were remarkable and profound, yet it was the second section, the Divinations, and specifically the final four, that haunted and tormented all who had read them.

---

1. *Global pandemics and super-viruses wipe out vast numbers of the world's population.*

2. *A utopian period, after a great plague.*

3. *Climate destabilization, resulting in uncertain levels of mass destruction.*

4. *World War III, a conflict of such proportion that humanity might not survive.*

CLASTIER, like Nostradamus three centuries before him, had accurately foretold many modern happenings. However, Clastier had been more focused and specific. He wrote of the rise of the United States, Hitler's atrocities during World War II, the development and dropping of the atomic bomb, the moon landing, the fall of religions, viral pandemics, and many other significant world events, long before they'd happened. Booker, Gale, and Rip had exhaustively debated on the order of the Divinations—specifically *when* the predicted events were expected to occur, and the actual impact of each. The three of them were determined to somehow stop them from happening.

"Yes," Rip said, "it's coming sooner than we thought. The first of the four Final Divinations. Barbeau has uncovered evidence of a virus being manipulated and weaponized in several labs around the world."

"Then it's not even an accident or a natural occurrence . . . we're doing it to ourselves."

Rip looked at her as if punched. "It's all in our hands. Since the time of the Cosegans, humans have had the ability to save our species or destroy it, and we always seem to head down the path of our own annihilation."

"Why?" Cira asked, overhearing their conversation.

"Fear," Rip said. "Fear there will not be enough, fear someone else will get more, so humans turn to hatred and greed, which are both parts of fear."

"We can still win," Cira said. "Tell him, Mom."

"What?" Rip asked, hopeful for good news.

"What if Leonardo was trying to tell us something more in the Salvador Mundi?" Gale asked, referring to the controversial painting of Christ by Leonardo Da Vinci, which had sold for $450 million, and then disappeared. "He's known for hiding messages in his work."

"Yes, I know, I've read Dan Brown's book. And what clue have *you* discovered?" he asked, winking at Cira.

Cira produced a tablet with a photo of the extraordinary painting. "It's the Eysen," she said, pointing to the orb held by Jesus. "The way Leonardo chose to depict it. He's representing the orb as a Chintamani!"

Rip looked anew at the painting, which seemed to reveal a fresh mystery with each viewing. "It does look familiar."

Cira flipped to another slide, which showed the 14th century Goryeo painting of Ksitigarbha holding a Chintamani. Rip knew that to the Hindu and Buddhist, the Chintamani was a wish-fulfilling jewel that was said to open the doors to higher knowledge and the secrets of the universe.

"Ksitigarbha was a revered bodhisattva," Gale said. "He's the monk who took a vow not to achieve Buddhahood until all hells are emptied, as if to save humanity."

Years ago, if a student had made this point, Rip might have seen it as too big a leap. However, with all that had happened, he jumped on board. "Like the Cosegans are trying to do."

"And us," Cira added.

"Yes," Rip agreed, smiling.

"The best part," Cira continued, "are the three dots." She

pointed back to the Salvador Mundi. "They represent the constellation of Orion."

"The belt?" he asked, confused, looking at the dots that formed a triangle.

"No," she tapped the screen and an overlay of three bright stars from Orion appeared and lined up perfectly on the three dots from the painting. "Betelgeuse, Bellatrix, and Mintaka."

He looked at her.

"The names of the stars," Cira clarified.

"It's interesting," Gale said. "People have long thought the alignment of the three pyramids at Giza and the three in Mexico at Teotihuacán matches the three stars in Orion's belt."

"So what is this telling us? Why are they in the painting?"

"Because the Cosegans came from there," Cira responded before Gale could.

"The Cosegans are humans, from *Earth*," Rip stressed. "We *know* this."

"But how did they get here?" Gale asked. "Maybe Leonardo is telling us Cosegans, their Imazes, came via the Orion star systems."

"Impossible."

"Really?" Gale waved her arm towards the four Eysens. "You must know by now that nothing is impossible."

THIRTY-TWO

WEALS ENTERED the Arc's Reach office not long after Shank left.

"You wanted to see me?" Weals asked tightly. He did not like being this high, thought the sky belonged to the birds.

"Yes," she said, pausing for a moment, considering how things had gotten to the point where one of her most trusted aides was a shifty character such as him.

Weals, a former Guardian, had once been stationed undercover in the Havlos territories. The Arc had handpicked him years earlier for her private use. Back when news of the Terminus Doom first broke, she'd needed "unofficial intelligence," and perhaps, "things done that The Circle would never approve of." If the truth be known, the indeterminant ogre of a man was at least one-quarter Havlos, and perfect for the job. He wasn't in it for the money, or his belief in the Arc, or even to save the world. Weals simply *liked* to spy, to cheat, to steal.

"You need to find Shank."

He scratched a large scar on his forehead. "And?"

"Be ready to detain him."

"Shouldn't the Guardians be the ones . . . ?"

She shook her head.

He knew that wasn't really an option, but he wanted to make sure his own importance to the situation, to the Arc, was evident. "Okay, anything else?"

She nodded and stared past him with a serious expression that made him nervous. "I need you to recruit and oversee a mission and operation into Havlos lands."

"No doubt this involves the Eysen Maker."

"It does. I need you to bring him back here."

He frowned. "That's not such an easy task."

"Precisely why I have given it to you."

He looked at her, unsure whether to be flattered or insulted, then shifted his gaze to his hands, then back to her.

She, of course, understood his meaning. "You will be compensated additionally."

"Number four?"

"Yes, and upon successful completion, the balance."

Weals had already been using trackers and other unsavory Havloses in an attempt to keep tabs on Trynn's progress, so he had a general idea of where to find him. However, there were many complications.

"An operation such as this during these times presents serious difficulties," he said.

"Yes."

Weals thought for a moment. "I'm assuming you want him alive?"

"*Yes*, I want him alive!" the Arc snapped.

"He's not going to come willingly, which means it's very risky, and obviously you'll want us to be acting covertly, since if the Havloses catch wind, we'll have a potential war incident."

The Arc rubbed the back of her neck. "You're good at what you do, Weals. I'm sure you'll find a way."

He nodded. He wanted to bring up the fact that he would be working counter to the Guardians and had to steer clear of other official directives issued by The Circle, but she was just going to say the same thing. Instead, he bid her farewell. He would demand a higher payment *after* he had the Eysen Maker.

Once back on the ground, he stared up at the Reach. It had been the source of much good fortune to him, and yet this job, although very lucrative, scared him. If he could have said no to the Arc, he would have, but it was not an option. She would not tolerate it.

He thought of waiting it out, knowing her days in power were numbered, but it was in his best interest to keep her in charge as long as possible. And there was still a chance he would not have to go to the Havlos lands himself.

JENSO DID NOT ENJOY the intrigue as much as Shank, although she believed the Arc should step down and that Trynn's Eysen approach was not going to stop the Doom. She hoped for a more orderly transition.

"What did she say?" Jenso asked. Her dark, perfectly smooth skin and long, snow-white hair appeared mystical, and always seemed to give her words more importance, as if they penetrated another level of meaning.

"It was just as you expected," Shank said, still irritated by the audacity of the Arc's insistence on clinging to power. "She refuses to leave."

Jenso frowned, not surprised at the news, but part of her hoped that the Arc's wisdom would tell her it was time to go. Instead, they would have to continue playing politics and trying to build a coalition to push her out legitimately. "What is she doing now, I wonder . . . "

"I'm more interested in her next move. What do you think it will be?"

"It works in our favor that her motives are pure." Jenso's brilliance and wisdom were almost intoxicating. People had the impression she was gorgeous. She was not. It was mostly her intelligence that made her appear so. "The crisis is too great She cannot afford the distraction of trying to thwart our efforts. The Arc must be solely focused on attempting to prevent the Doom."

"Ironic that her commitment to the Cosegans will be her undoing."

"Let us hope."

"In the meantime, Trynn is once again becoming a hazard. Now that he's cozying up to Havloses, not only is his existence risking great peril for us in the Far Future, but he's endangering the present even more."

"His great mind, combined with his knowledge of Cosegan technology, makes him an incredible asset to the Havloses," Jenso acknowledged. "How do we stop him?"

"We send a team of the Red Guardians."

Jenso nodded, knowing the Red Guardians were the best of the best, and would be able to find him. "And when they bring him back, then what?"

"They don't bring him back."

The two stared at each other.

"You mean . . . "

"Yes," Shank said, suppressing a smile since he knew she'd view it as inappropriate. Yet he felt joy at the thought of Trynn dead nonetheless .

"Surely there's another way," Jenso implored. "What happens when people find out?"

"No one will ever find out. He is in exile, in enemy territory. Even when news of his death eventually filters back, we will be in the midst of war—and assuming anybody even cares, it will be blamed on the Havloses."

She said nothing for a few moments.

"There is no other way," Shank reiterated.

"What if we try to have him brought back here?"

"Then The Arc or other loyalists will rescue him or protect him." He stared into her mystic eyes. "Trynn must *never* be allowed to return."

THIRTY-THREE

Markol couldn't decide whether he should alert the Arc about the latest information he had gleaned from the Far Future. His botched insertion had set an incalculable number of catastrophes into motion, but it had also given him a window into the Far Future that allowed him much clearer views of that turbulent time.

His original target recipient, a brilliant young man who would be instrumental in the early days of the personal computer, had failed to arrive in Florida in time to find the Sphere. Instead, an unqualified family discovered it and badly fumbled the "strange object."

They actually took it to the media! To the government! Markol shivered.

"Things are not going well," an engineer said as he looked over Markol's shoulder.

Markol, glad he had closed another view that looked ahead fifty years after the family lost the Eysen, mumbled a response.

The window he'd just closed showed things going substantially worse. Markol didn't want anyone to know how horrendously bad his mistake would make things. Fifty years in the Far Future was a mere blink in Markol's lab.

Maybe I can fix it, he thought, riffling through the vast images projecting in the air of High-peak's Room of a Million Futures. *The dynamic in play between then and now, and perhaps I can correct aspects within minutes . . . And what if I could bend the parameters in the Missing-Time . . .*

The other engineer knew how easily it would be to run out the scenarios. "Did you extend and test?" he asked.

"Not yet," Markol lied. "I'm still working on reverses." But, in fact, along with checking out the increasing damage done to the fifty years from the family finding the sphere, all the way up to Rip's time, Markol had also already followed the possession chain of the Eysen and traced it to a man in the Far Future called Kalor Locke, who was, by far, the most dangerous human Markol had ever seen.

"And checking on Trynn, I see," the engineer said, pointing to the floating images of ancient and modern Egypt. "Looks like Trynn is having trouble with his latest insert as well."

"Tricky science, inserting."

"It is," the engineer agreed.

Something in the way he replied told Markol that the man was not to be trusted. Markol had only one question: if the engineer was working for the Arc, or Shank . . . possibly even Trynn. Then a more disturbing idea entered his head.

What if the man is working for Kalor Locke?

GRAYSWA, the great Etheren shaman, strolled among large ponds filled with lotus flowers and concentrated his considerable meditative powers on one person. The distance between them was so vast that the average human could not fully grasp it. "The definition of a million, the picture of it, the understanding of such a sum, the weight of it," Grayswa had once told a student, "is enormous and more complex than one might imagine, and yet it can be touched anywhere in nature. It is but a breath."

The student did not get the concept, and if he were there with Grayswa on that day when the ancient shaman was traveling across eleven million years with thoughts and purpose, the student probably would have given up on the whole idea of ever knowing the meaning of a number so large.

The exercise required all of Grayswa's mental capacity, or he might have recalled that student and smiled, realizing that the way to make him understand was to show him a lotus flower, for as Grayswa often said, "The Lotus contains the sacred patterns of the universe."

He continued sending the images to the man in the Far Future who unknowingly held the fate of humanity in his hands. "There are many who weave this web," Grayswa had once explained to Adjoa, another shaman, the woman who would one day replace him. "However, one man connects them all."

"Does he know?" she had asked.

"He has received many messages to this, yet he does not accept it fully. Still, he works on leaving the clues for others who will come after him."

"Will his work endure?"

"For centuries."

Even then, during that conversation, Grayswa had been concerned. *Will there be enough time to relay the messages? Will Trynn be able to hold the Far Future before the Terminus*

Doom ends humanity? Will the war between the Havloses and Cosegans steal any chance we have?

He moved all those questions from his mind, with the efficiency of someone who had practiced high level meditation for hundreds of years, as if turning off a switch, and returned the entirety of his focus to sending the sacred geometry of the lotus flower to the man who could save it all: Leonardo da Vinci.

THIRTY-FOUR

Jarvo moved through the holographic images like a pedestrian navigating a crowded city sidewalk. "The Cosegans are not as smart as they think they are," he said, sliding a thin monitor around to allow a full view of another screen.

"The Arc believes Naperton was our first strike," Cass said.

"The Cosegans are confused about a great many things. However, they will not miss *the* strike."

"Do you really believe it will get to that point?" she asked, knowing the weapon he planned on using. "Surely they can be convinced long before that."

For a moment, his expression turned into something that Cass would later describe as sadness. Even his eyes seemed mournful, but he quickly shifted back into the more typical arrogance and determination she was used to seeing.

"They underestimate us," he growled.

"There are many things they do not know," Cass reminded him.

"Stun gun." Jarvo was proud of the high-voltage tasers that

fired darts on wires. The weapons delivered electrical pulses that immediately disrupted a person's voluntary muscle control. Havlos stun guns were no match for Cosegan Infer-guns, but they were still more advanced than anything the Guardians believed they possessed.

"The DREAD Silent Weapon System," Cass said, adding to his list, hoping to lead him into another debate about the final strike, knowing he loved to discuss their secret weapon capabilities.

He smiled. "Yes, the DREAD. It can shoot two-thousand rounds per second."

Cass knew the system well. It had been developed under her father's watch. A massive gun that ran on electrical energy —no gunpowder. The alternative charge meant no recoil, which added to its accuracy ratings. It was cold, silent, and deadly. "And HI-MEMS."

Jarvo was particularly obsessed with the insect-machine hybrids, an impressive achievement by the Havloses. A micro-mechanical system inserted into an insect at initial metamorphosis meant the bugs could be controlled remotely. They were equipped with deadly electro-dart stingers infused with poison, cameras, and tracking devices. "HI-MEMS are perhaps our military's second greatest achievement," he marveled, like a kid with a fancy new toy.

"Of course, the strike weapon is the greatest," she said.

"Yes, but let us not forget EXACTOs." Extreme Accuracy Tasked Ordnance system was another amazing advancement in warfare. The maneuverable bullets meant almost anyone could hit a target, just point and shoot. "And Killtrons."

She shuddered at the mention of the killer robots. Killtronics, or Killtrons, for short, were lethal, highly-acrobatic killing machines with AI-assisted operating systems which meant in addition to being controlled from a faraway base, they also could act autonomously. Cass had long feared they could be used against Havloses. "If they don't turn on us first."

"Will never happen," he said with bravado and acuity that she saw right through. Jarvo was too smart not to have concerns about the Killtrons as well.

"With all that, and our brilliant military strategies, we can win without the strike weapon," she said, baiting him.

"This again?"

"You know that—"

"I know that you are too soft, risk adverse, and—"

"Weak?"

He squinted obsidian eyes. "I did not say weak."

"You didn't have to." She glared at him, daring him to bring up her father. He did not. "The Terminus Doom is not good for Havloses."

He said nothing verbally, but the look of disdain he shot her way cautioned her.

"Havloses are human," she ventured. "We'll die, too . . . all of us will."

"You don't know that."

"And you don't know that there are survivors."

"You believe the Eysen Maker?"

"Don't you?"

Jarvo scoffed. "I believe he can predict a great many things, but things change. The variables cannot all be known, because a decision made differently by the Arc, by Shank, by the Imazes—"

"By you."

"—by *any* of us, can change things, and ripple into the future, and into the Far Future, and all will be different."

"Can't you win with HI-MEMS, DREADS, EXACTOs,

and all your brilliant strategy?" Cass asked. "The Cosegans know nothing of war. Surely we can surprise them like we did at Naperton, launch offenses—"

"That is the plan."

"But you still ready the strike weapon . . . "

"Nothing can be left to chance."

"But the strike leaves *everything* to chance," she insisted, frustration bleeding through her. "You are risking all of existence on *what*? An opportunity to beat the Cosegans, to dominate Earth?"

"To dominate the future."

"What future will be left?"

"You assume the strike will fail?"

"No, I fear it will succeed."

He stared at her bitterly. "Careful, Cass. Emotions are leading you down a treasonous path. I may forget that I am fond of you."

"Don't question my loyalty," she snapped. "Ever."

His eyes never left hers. Their conversation continued for several moments in silence.

"The strike will unleash the Doom!" she blurted.

"The strike will alter reality."

"Whose? The Cosegans, or ours?"

He scratched his beard as if thinking, eliciting another smile. "We shall find out soon enough."

ONCE ALONE AGAIN, Jarvo checked the progress of his secret project, the one Trynn was unwittingly helping him with. *The weapon is almost ready,* he thought, reviewing every piece of data coming from Trynn's work, amused that he now had blanket monitoring of their facilities. *Once we strike—thanks to the information from the Eysen Maker—and secure the Globotite, the Havlos military's might will be unchallenged for the next million years.*

THIRTY-FIVE

IMAGES of the Far Future swirled around Trynn, Ovan, and Nassar on board the main research vessel, docked at the Havlos port city of Qwaterrun.

"Markol may have ruined us," Trynn said.

"Because each Eysen insertion complicates things by multiplying the possible scenarios exponentially, and Markol's insertion magnifies the complexities by an as yet unknown factor of thousands, since his inserted-sphere is not linked to the network of Eysens we already have planted in the Far Future?" Nassar asked.

"Yes," Trynn said, unimpressed. "For all those reasons. However, there is another, more dire consideration."

"What?" Nassar asked, genuinely terrified of the answer. The conditions outlined in his prior response had already seemed insurmountable.

Trynn brushed through moving images as if he were actually walking through the battles of World War II and Vietnam, tourists visiting Paris and the Pyramids in Egypt, Houston during the 1969 Moon landing, the World Trade Center on

9/11, financial meltdowns, global pandemics, and other achievements both great and small by the inhabitants of the Far Future. "Markol's Eysen has missed his target."

"Oh no," Nassar breathed, his voice filled with despair in the knowledge that the greatest risk on any insertion was the Eysen falling into the wrong hands. Recipients were vetted through an exhaustive process overseen by Ovan.

"It's worse than a simple 'oh no,' it's beyond anything we feared. A man with sinister ambitions has obtained Markol's sphere and he's looking for more."

Nassar stared, speechless for a moment. "Does he . . . has this man gained access to the core?"

"Not yet," Trynn said, visibly ill. "But he's used it to develop weapons, to see into the future, and it won't be long before he unlocks the core."

"How can that be?" Nassar asked. "The archaeologist has had years, they have multiple Eysens, Booker Lipton has assembled the best scientific minds of their time . . . All that and *they* still haven't broken through to the core."

"This man is different. He has accumulated other technology, he has a different understanding . . . he—"

Ovan held up a hand. "Please don't tell me he is connected."

"To our time?" Nassar asked, the color draining from his face.

"He is connected," Trynn said, waving his hand to bring up an image. "Meet Kalor Locke, the face of the Terminus Doom."

ON THE TURKISH ISLAND, Rip, Gale, and Cira continued to dig deeper into what other clues Da Vinci might have left behind. "We've followed everything Leonardo did since the cave," Gale said. "He was the most documented figure from the Renaissance, and yet in the years between 1476 and 1478, he was basically unaccounted for."

"It's during that time that Leonardo went to the cave where he found the Eysen?" Rip asked, still haunted by what Da Vinci might have seen in the cave, instinctively knowing it must be a key to what had destroyed the Cosegans.

"Yes," Gale replied. "And that event, that entire period, seems to have been a catalyst for everything he did for the rest of his life."

"Another forty years," Cira added. "The four decades when he achieved almost everything he's known for."

"Including The Last Supper," Gale said, as if discussing something magical.

"Is there another clue in The Last Supper?" Rip asked. Cira brought up a photo of the iconic 15th century painting, which depicts the last meal of Jesus with the twelve Apostles before his arrest and crucifixion.

"Possibly."

"I know there have been numerous studies of the masterpiece. It's been subjected to every kind of visual test and procedure the art world could throw at it," Rip said. "What could they have all missed?"

"As you said, they focused too much on the visual," Gale said.

"And they missed the music," Cira added.

"Music?" Rip asked.

"There's music hidden in The Last Supper!"

"And you found it?"

"Well, not really us," Cira said. "An Italian musician and computer technician named Giovanni Maria Pala discovered it."

Gale tapped the tablet's screen, and they heard the translated voice of Pala saying, "Leonardo Da Vinci left clues to a forty-second musical composition in his painting. Each loaf of bread in the picture represents a note."

"It's all laid out perfectly," Cira said excitedly. "Among his other many talents, Leonardo was also a skilled musician."

"But Pala doesn't believe the music hides any secrets. He thinks it's more of a devotion to God."

Cira started a recording of the forty-second hymn, which had been played on the pipe organ.

"It sounds like a requiem," Rip said. "Beautiful, but what does it tell us?"

"We don't know yet," Cira said. "But it can't be an accident."

"Leonardo da Vinci never did anything by accident," Rip said, looking at the Eysens, expecting they might react to the music. "Let's give it to Alik and let him feed it into Booker's super computers with everything we have on Leonardo, the Eysens, and the Cosegans."

They were silent for a couple minutes as the music looped and repeated. They all stared, anticipating something exciting. Nothing happened.

THIRTY-SIX

Kalor Locke walked across the ceramic tiled floor, its geometric pattern created to enhance subtle energy channels in the room.

"They know about you?" Lorne said.

"Yes, apparently," Kalor replied, looking up at her image on the giant screen. The only person Kalor Locke trusted more than Lorne was his brother, Parson Locke, who was currently hunting Savina and Rip.

"How does it feel to be known to people who lived eleven million years ago?" she asked, goading him.

He shook his head, as if he had not thought about it.

"More than known," she continued. "You are feared by them."

"It is not my intent to frighten people."

"Isn't it?"

He stared at her. "You know it isn't."

"Semantics," she said. Her dark hair was pulled back in a tight, severe bun, displaying an angular face and knowing eyes of a wonderful shade of brown, like caramel. An expression of constantly being almost amused softened her features.

"Where are you?" he asked, wanting to change the subject.

"Turkey."

"Why Turkey?"

"Because Ripley Gaines is in Turkey."

"Do you know where?"

"I'm still working on it."

"What's the problem?"

"Booker Lipton."

The name immediately raised his blood pressure. Booker was the one and only person who stood between him and world domination. Sure, there were others—a few Remies, certain members of the Aylantik Foundation, Omnia, a handful of people who caused him aggravation—but most of them would soon fall by the wayside.

Booker, however, was far more dangerous. The man already possessed four Eysens, many key manuscripts, and more money than anyone's god. But there was hope Booker had not yet acquired the one thing that Locke was counting on to win this war: a Cosegan. Booker thought "Crying Man" was on his team, but quite the contrary. In many ways, Trynn was working against him.

Kalor Locke, however, *did* have a Cosegan on his side. A Cosegan actively manipulating events that would allow Locke to achieve his vision of a new society where freedom was more of a quaint theory than something actually practiced, and where the idea of freedom would certainly never be openly discussed.

But the Cosegans would have to wait. Locke pushed a button that opened a video feed to his brother.

"Turkey," Locke said. "Gaines is there, with the Eysens. Get a team going immediately."

ALIK LISTENED PATIENTLY as Rip and Gale outlined all their discoveries before speaking. At the end of her dissertation, Gale played the music from Da Vinci's Last Supper. Once it was completed, Alik looked at them in amazement. "Damn, you have outdone Dan Brown!"

Rip shot him a blank stare.

"You know, Dan Brown? The Da Vinci Code?"

"Yeah, we know who Dan Brown is," Gale said. "But his book is fiction. We're talking about real life here."

"I know, I know," Alik said defensively. "I just meant Da Vinci, secret clues, conspiracy, cover ups, people after you . . . You gotta admit, your life is a little like a thriller novel, right?"

Rip's blank stare had turned into something more incredulous.

"Never mind," Alik said, smiling timidly. "I'll process it and see if the big brain comes up with anything."

"Thanks," Gale said. "I guess I see what you mean about us living in a novel, but the Cosegans seem to be the ones writing this story."

"Yeah," Alik said, looking over the notes. *Whoa,* he thought, *no comic relief here.* "Leonardo's Salvador Mundi has three lights in the orb, which is a representation of the Eysen, symbolizing the three stars of Orion, which is the place the Ancient Egyptians believed was the birthplace of the gods, that they came from Orion."

"Right," Rip confirmed.

"And the stars in Orion's belt also match the alignment of the Egyptian pyramids at Giza and the Mexican pyramids at Teotihuacan."

"You got it."

Alik shook his head. "But what is the Chintamani stone?"

"Leonardo seems to have posed Christ as a Bodhisattvas," Rip explained, "holding the sacred wish-fulfilling jewel of Buddhist tradition."

"Bodhisattvas are people on the path to enlightenment, to Buddhahood," Gale added. "And in this case, a high-level being of great wisdom."

"Why would Leonardo, in the shadow of the Catholic church, do such an important painting in this manner?" Alik asked.

"Because he knew," Rip said. "He had an Eysen, and Jesus had an Eysen. He saw the past, the truth, and the future."

Alik stared blankly.

"He knew we would be here today, on this dusty island, off the coast of Turkey, discussing the Eysens and him," Rip said. "He saw it."

"He participated in the making of this moment," Gale said, realizing the profound nature of her words only after she'd said them.

"But why?" Alik asked.

"He was trying to save us," Rip said. "Not the us in this room, the us as in *all* of us. As in humanity."

"From what?"

"From the Doom. The Terminus Doom."

THIRTY-SEVEN

OVAN WADED through the endless images floating about the vast space. The rapidly changing views of the Far Future did not ease his mind. Instead, he found it all very disturbing. "The race is on," Ovan said. "If the archaeologist finds the sphere before the Pharaoh discovers it . . . our long experiment fails in a fiery disaster."

"I leave this to you," Trynn said, peering deeply into the wise eyes of the old scientist.

"You're going back?"

Trynn watched a view into the Spanish Inquisition, which moved past a scene of the Senator McCarthy hearings, another blurred view showing a world divided over vaccines. "I have to."

"She wouldn't want you to."

"Of course not, but I'd have to go anyway, even if it wasn't personal. In light of Markol's insertion, of Kalor Locke, of the Egypt insertion slipping toward becoming our first lost Eysen . . . Shanoah and the Imazes may be the *only* way we can save us. And we are the only chance the Imazes have to survive."

"It's all a circle," Ovan said.

Trynn looked across at the Far Future, its moving images soaring, crashing, and swirling through themselves, changing infinitely and, as a result, creating new realities which transformed all over again.

"Yes. We're each other's best hope."

IN NYSTALS, a Havlos naval base hundreds of miles away from the port city Qwaterrun, where Trynn had set up the new Eysen facilities, Jarvo inspected the Havloses largest fleets of warships. Until now they had been used against other Havlos groups. The Havlos lands had long been split into seven sections of rival populations. However, times were changing. The world hung on the edge of war.

"Would you have ever guessed that these ships would be turned against the Cosegans?" a subordinate asked Jarvo.

"Yes, I did," he said in a firm tone that invited no further discussion.

The man nodded.

"The tactic is not without risk and controversy," Jarvo said, thinking of Cass.

"Yes," the man said, surprised the supreme commander was continuing.

"The Cosegans seem to have the advantage, as their technologically advanced weapons would suggest—at least to the common conventional wisdom—that they would be able to annihilate Havlos ships."

"Many would think that," the man agreed, silently counting himself among those skeptics who thought a Havlos move against the Cosegans was suicide.

Jarvo glanced at him, quickly reading his face, and smiled slightly. "Don't worry, we have other plans for them."

"It's quite an impressive navy," the man said, as if this is what Jarvo meant.

Jarvo ignored him and turned to greet a guest with a title borrowed from the Far Future. "General."

His newly arrived visitor laughed. "I'm no general. Maybe a general mess, but no military man."

"I knew you would get the reference," Jarvo said, deciding he already liked Jaxx, an arms dealer that Cass had recommended he speak with. "I understand you're a man of history."

"It's always good to know as much as one can about war if that's the business we're in," Jaxx said. "And who knows more about war than those that populate the Far Future."

Jaxx was taller than Jarvo by a few inches, and both would've been considered quite tall by Far Future standards, being 6'3' and 6'5" respectively. Jaxx also sported a mustache and goatee, unusual for Cosegans or Havloses, but Jaxx was an unusual man. Cass called him a rogue, who knew everything about everyone; a profiteer who had valuable contacts on both sides.

"But do you know anything about Jaxx?" Jarvo had asked her.

"Only that he can't be trusted, and it will be hard to win a war without his help."

Jarvo had found out a little more since setting up this meeting. Jaxx was a half-breed, his mother a Havlos, his father a Cosegan. He'd been selling weapons, tech, and secrets to all sides. And he was a very charismatic person, genuinely liked by all who knew him; a man who might betray you by dealing with your enemy, who had somehow managed to not have any enemies of his own. The Havlos leader was fascinated. But more than that, Jarvo needed just such an agent for a grand scheme to bring down the Cosegans.

Cass thought it was in the hopes Jarvo could win *without* the strike, but Jarvo really wanted Jaxx to help ensure the strike would happen.

"I have a little proposition for you, Jaxx," Jarvo said, putting his arm around him.

"Tell me about it," Jaxx said as they walked along the rail overlooking the fleet, leaving the other man behind.

"It's dangerous," Jarvo said, "but it pays well."

"Dangerous is such an expensive word," Jaxx said. "It's hard not to like it."

"I need you to make a sale—some information, critical details about these ships," Jarvo said.

"Who's the buyer?" Jaxx asked.

"The Arc."

Jaxx nodded, happy he would be heading back to Solas.

"Can you get in to see her?"

"Of course," Jaxx said. "She's expecting me."

THIRTY-EIGHT

Shank studied the mind-crystal before him and mumbled. "What dropped the Terminus-Clock?" The horrifying development had shaken everyone. "It's destabilized the Arc even further, and the Circle as well."

He knew they were running out of time to make the move. His office was filled with light filters, falling from the ceiling like hippy beads. The colors and frequencies elevated his mood, also heightening his intelligence and perceptions. Even by light-obsessed Cosegan standards, Shank was an extremist. "I must find Trynn."

"It wasn't Trynn this time," a researcher said, walking into Shank's office.

"How do we know?"

"It was Markol."

The pit of Shank's stomach tightened. He had feared that might be the case, even suspected it, but could not let himself believe it.

"At whose behest?"

The researcher looked at him, not responding, as if to say, "*Do you really need me to answer such a stupid question?*"

"The Arc . . . " He stopped himself from finishing the statement in his head, which went on to say she must die. The fury of his emotions was muted by the light therapy, yet Shank had other reasons for the near outburst. The Arc had allowed Trynn to become a force, and then when his Far Future Eysen adventures had come close to destroying everything, she'd still hedged, letting him slip away. Now she had stolen Shank's protege, and was dabbling with reality yet again. "She must be stopped."

The researcher nodded. Her actions worried him as well. "But how?"

Shank did not answer the underling, as he did not have his confidence, but he knew the answer.

War.

"WHY DID THE ARC SWITCH STRATEGIES?" Ovan said absently while he and Nassar watched results of the latest changes in the Hall of a Million Futures.

"What do you mean?" Nassar asked, unsure if the question had been directed at him or if the old man was just thinking out loud.

"She appeared to be protecting Trynn at the end," Ovan said. "He escaped when he should not have been able to."

"The Arc is careful. It was a prudent calculation. If the Imaze mission fails, Trynn could be the only hope."

"I wonder . . . " Ovan said. "Now she protects Markol. What does she know?"

Nassar frowned. "What *could* she know?"

"The Arc is sometimes underestimated because she is a

political leader, and they are usually made up of ambitions and egos, but she is different."

"Why?"

"The Arc is not here by accident," Ovan replied. "Manipulations into time may appear new to us because we are new to them, but we cannot know how many attempts there have been. The very nature of the Terminus Doom tells us that maneuverings to avoid and transfer cataclysmic events have been going on longer than memory, and now we have reached a finality."

"Finality?"

Ovan gave a single nod. "All debts are due."

MARKOL OPENED the new sphere slowly. The dangerous process could level ten square miles, leaving nothing but a blinding vapor of light. His hand trembled, not from the fear of making a mistake and killing thousands, not because Shank and his faction of Guardians would be coming for him soon, nor was it the realization that Trynn would seek him through the connection of spheres in the Far Future and ignite an Eysen war. All of those things weighed on him, yes, but he had some advantage in them. His ability to navigate across time, to see into the Eysens and anticipate happenings, gave him a certain confidence—or at least a way to cope with the fear.

What he did *not* know how to deal with was the guilt. Killing Huang, his Far Future counterpart, had proven to be a brutal cross to bear.

An assistant looked at Markol's unsteady hand, then to his face. "Are you okay?" he asked his superior nervously, afraid the explorations into the center of the newest Eysen would kill them in the next instant.

"I'm fine," Markol snapped. "It's fine," he added, softening his tone. In truth, his condition had been worsening, and Markol had been questioning his own physical and mental state for days. *How does Trynn do it?*

The misplaced Sphere in Florida had not only been a disaster for the Far Future, but its rippling effects had rocketed back through the Missing-Time, their current world, and even long before his birth. But perhaps even more frightening was it meant that another Sphere needed to go into the Far Future, and it needed to go in fast. This time, it would have to be without the Arc's knowledge or approval, and it had to be done before Shank found him. Another insertion was beyond reckless, yet it might be the only hope of cleaning up the mess he'd made.

Even then, he pegged the odds of success at under thirty-two percent. *A one-in-three chance to save the world,* he thought as the exposed core of the Eysen glowed in front of him.

THIRTY-NINE

THE ARC STOOD before an angry Circle. Even her supporters among the group of elders were beginning to question her leadership.

"Friends, Circle Members, please do not fall victim to the sway of those who would lose sight of our strengths to address these many issues."

Welhey, perhaps her last steadfast ally, nodded at her.

"The Havloses have attacked us," one of the Members said, a woman who, for more than one hundred years, had sided with the Arc.

"Yes, there was an event at the border," the Arc confirmed.

"*Event at the border,*" Jenso mocked. "Ten Guardians were executed in seconds. Play the feed."

Before the Arc could respond, life-size three-dimensional moving images replayed the incident at Naperton.

It looped and repeated six times before the Arc shouted, "Enough!"

As the images faded, the members sat in stunned silence for several moments.

"How did they get past the grid?" a Member shouted, breaking the silence.

"Where were the Havloses?" another called out.

"What weapons were they using?"

"We are at war!"

"This is leading us straight to the Doom."

"Where does the Clock stand?"

Shank suppressed a smile as the entire Circle broke into verbal chaos. In all his time with the governing body, he had never seen it this fractured, an Arc ready to crumble.

The Arc hit the table with an unseen object, producing a thunderous noise. In the echo of it she spoke, "This. Is. Not. War." Her firm, defiant tone quickly regained control of the room. "This was a test, an attempt to divide us. The Havloses are no match for us, so they resort to these guerrilla tactics."

"But they worked. Ten of our finest are dead."

"And we do not grieve them or honor them by marching into a war," the Arc shot back.

"A war we can win in seconds."

The Arc glared at the Member who'd voiced the insult. "Are you so sure? What do you know of war? For that matter, what do *any* of us Cosegans know of war?"

"We are far superior to the Havloses."

"In many areas, that is true, but in war . . . " The Arc waved her hand and the center of the great hall filled with pictures and data once again. This time it showed lists with rotating images that began to move. As the display changed, the Arc described what they were seeing.

"Before you so willingly jump into war, let me outline the Havlos advantages," she said above the murmurs. "The Havloses are considerably more experienced with war. This is their way."

"But our technological superiority!" one of them retorted.

"I'll get to that, but consider that Havloses outnumber Cosegans, particularly Enforcers to Guardians. Their battle-hardened units have a nearly six hundred-to-one advantage over us."

"They are unsophisticated."

"Not in war, they aren't, and it isn't just personnel. Havloses have armies of small weaponized robotic tanks. Recent reports show they also have smart bullets."

"Smart bullets?" someone asked, as if the words were an oxymoron.

"That is to say, the bullets do not follow a given trajectory. They change direction and speed, collect and transmit information, and are apparently extremely accurate and almost always lethal." The Arc slowly met each face around the room while Havlos battle footage continued to float around them.

"You act as if we've already lost," Shank snarled.

"You act as if a war has already begun," the Arc shot back.

"Hasn't it?" Shank rose from his seat, in attack mode.

"Now for our advantages," she said, ignoring Shank. "We have three, and they are considerable." This was the part of the presentation she enjoyed the most, but she needed to be careful not to make them overconfident. An invitation to war was not the objective. "Space: we dominate there, and we are capable of destroying what little off-planet presence they have in a matter of minutes. Our strength there can also be used to hit them from above. We could do serious damage."

The Members nodded—confident, satisfied.

"Perhaps our absolute greatest asset in any conflict is our mastery of light. It is what defines the Cosegan civilization." She paused and made eye contact with Jenso. "We own the light."

"That means lasers," someone said.

"Lasers, grids, baffles, pulses, domes, focused photons," the

Arc continued. "There are endless applications where light can be used to bury any attempt by the Havloses to gain against us."

"We can destroy them," another Member called out.

"In war, things are never quite as easy as they seem," she replied to the man, but met Shank's eyes.

"The third thing?" someone else asked.

"Technology, of all sorts, where we are far ahead of our angry neighbors—but specifically, the Eysen. They have nothing close."

"But how will we use it?" a Member, who she knew was opposed to Trynn's operations, asked.

"The Eysen is the ultimate weapon," she said. "The Eysen sees everything."

"We cannot lose!" several shouted.

The Arc shook her head, and in a soft but stern voice said, "The Eysen is why I know we *cannot* allow this war to occur."

FORTY

The elite team of Blaxers were among the best in Booker's impressive army. Twenty-six of them surrounded Savina, and two members of her team, in a protective web befitting a head of state. Yet they worked hard to blend in, not wanting to call attention to her.

After the massacre on the island when the Blaxers lost the Eysens and dozens of agents, Booker ordered their tactics changed. "We have a new enemy," he told the head of the elite team. "It is the Cosegan technology. Kalor Locke has somehow accessed detailed plans of their weaponry that we have not yet been able to tap. We are now in a war with the future that began in the past."

The Blaxers certainly possessed advanced weapons, and were busy reverse-engineering specific items recovered from the island massacre, but Kalor Locke was leaps ahead, and Booker was worried.

"It feels as if we're fighting the armies of hell," he confided to Rip.

"You don't believe in hell," Rip replied, shocked to see Booker so troubled.

"I didn't until Kalor Locke showed up. The man is evil, he could be the devil incarnate."

Rip thought of Da Vinci's words: *It is the universe that controls humanity and this magical sphere must be from the hand of god, though it obviously depicts the evil work of the devil.* "What does Locke want?"

Booker shook his head, his distraught expression surprising Rip again. "A man like Kalor Locke does not understand reason. He is obsessed with power, focused on a purpose, one we don't yet understand. And Kalor Locke is looking to settle old scores."

"Old scores?" Rip stared at Booker, but Booker looked off into the distance, as if a battle was being waged somewhere out there over things too difficult to explain, impossible to understand.

"You have more money than him," Rip finally said. "We have more Eysens . . . "

"For now," Booker whispered, then added more urgently, "He cannot be allowed to get one more Eysen . . . *ever*!"

Rip had told Savina of the conversation as she was leaving for Egypt. "We have to recover the Pharaoh's Eysen before Kalor Locke."

"We will," she replied, a seething fire in her eyes that at once relaxed and concerned Rip. He had long known that Savina maintained a single-minded preoccupation with the Cosegans, as if she were living in the current world only in an attempt to reach theirs. "Kalor Locke merely thinks he understands the forces with which he is dealing," she added. "In reality, he is lost."

Rip wanted to go to Egypt with her, but understanding the connection between the Jesus, Leonardo, and Nostradamus

Eysens was critical, and might even help them find the Pharaoh's Eysen.

SAVINA KEPT AN ENCRYPTED digital journal where she expressed her theories, doubts, and aspirations for the Eysens, the Cosegans, Booker, and Rip.

Shortly after Huang was killed through the Eysen, she confided her thoughts to the locked diary file.

I feel betrayed by the Cosegans, and yet I still cannot completely believe it. For some time I have suspected a rival faction to Trynn and the Imazes who were attempting another solution to the Doom, and now I wonder if this group might have resorted to sabotage. But why Huang? Perhaps they were trying to kill Rip . . . or me. Could there be dangerous Cosegans coming for me?

Savina revisited those earlier entries and only now discovered some of the answers. Since the massacre on the island, a new idea had emerged in her brilliant mind.

The Cosegans' end, the Doom, the current state of the world, Kalor Locke, the number of Eysens—these things were all connected.

Like a detective unraveling the greatest mystery in human history, Savina pieced together the cosmic puzzle that the Eysens and events surrounding them had presented. She didn't know the name of the Havloses, but she had guessed at their existence, and was beginning to understand their importance in all that had happened.

Where does Kalor Locke get his power? was her final entry when they arrived at The Dazzling Aten, a recently uncovered thirty-four hundred year old "lost city" on the west bank of the Nile, in the southern Egyptian province of Luxor; a place she had reason to believe was the final location of the Pharaoh's Eysen.

Speaking of power, Savina wondered, *how did The Pharaoh Hatshepsut get so much of it?*

They had learned the identity of the Pharaoh and several clues as to its whereabouts through the original Virginia Eysen. Savina had no way of knowing that Parson Locke, Kalor's brother, had also discovered much of this information, and was already in Egypt with a team of Varangians.

But they weren't just looking for the Pharaoh's Eysen. They were hunting Savina.

FORTY-ONE

THE ARC WATCHED Jaxx as he stood in the light lift, which was almost instantly taking him from ground level to the top of the Reach. He didn't know she could see him, but it was obvious he considered it a possibility that someone was watching. A man like Jaxx was always on guard, always wary that others might be doing what he would do if he were them, and he would be watching.

They had met twice before, and she still didn't like the idea of being involved with such a seedy character. Weals was bad enough.

Studying Jaxx, her initial opinions had not changed. *He's a rogue, she thought, handsome in that dangerous way, the slick black hair, a goatee, who wears those? Dark eyes that know a little too much, that keep too many secrets, that look too deceive. He dresses like someone from the Far Future, I think they call that denim. How has it gotten to the point where I place the fate of my people in this arms-dealing criminal half-breed?*

His face went from manipulative contemplation to a broad salesman's smile as he stepped off the lift. "Arc," he said, as if it were more a greeting than her name, holding out both his arms, implying they were old friends. "The day is the same as you," he said to her puzzled face. "Beautiful," he finished.

"Jaxx," she said, forcing a smile, but not taking his arms. *A ladies man? Really?* she thought. *I don't think so. Even worse than I thought.* "Thank you for coming."

"Of course, of course." He moved toward the view. "Breath-taking . . . I don't know how you can get anything done. I would just sit and stare at this all day, all night. I bet it's more amazing at night."

"Yes," she said, as if not buying an ounce of his sincerity. "To business."

"Of course, of course."

"What do the Havloses have that I am not aware of?"

"Me, for one," he said, his smile vanishing. "Jarvo sent me to trick you."

"Really?" she asked, hardly fazed. "How so?"

"I'm to sell you false information on their weapons and capabilities."

"How do I know you are not being honest in an effort to win my confidence so you actually can trick me?" she asked.

"You don't."

"No, I don't."

His face wore an inviting expression, his best "*I'm hiding something, but I'll tell you because you're my favorite*," kind of smile.

"I don't trust you, Jaxx."

"Let's not let petty things like war and the end of humanity get in the way of our friendship."

"We are not friends," the Arc said, but she couldn't help liking him, in spite of herself.

"Then why would I give you such valuable information?"

"I pay you."

"Oh, yeah, there is that. Money makes a good friend, especially in these crazy times."

"I am *busy,*" she prompted him, wishing to move this along.

"Yes, of course, of course." He pulled out a tiny device about the size of his middle finger. It illuminated a field of data and images similar to the format she had used in her briefing to the Circle. "It's called MAARS," he said, pointing to the 3-D moving views of mini robotic tanks. "Stands for Modular Advanced Armed Robotic System. These things can be armed with a four hundred round machine gun, or grenade launchers, and—"

"These are physical ordinances?" she asked, as if this was a defective platform.

"Don't be such a light snob," he said, touching her shoulder in a little too-familiar gesture. "Physical ordinances will penetrate human flesh and kill the same as light. It's just a little messier."

She nodded.

"They can be utilized to evacuate injured soldiers off the battlefield, and behind lines recon, or any number of other operations."

"How fast?"

"They are capable of speeds four times faster than a human."

"Not a match for a goeze," she said, unimpressed.

"They have their place."

"Do you have anything important to tell me?" she asked dismissively.

He leaned close to her, glanced slightly over his shoulder, and whispered, "Don't let this war happen."

She stared at him a moment, attempting to reconcile his words with the fact that nothing could benefit his business more than war. "Do the Havloses believe they can win?"

He shook his head. "They know they can."

She stepped back, the statement an assault. "Where is their confidence coming from?"

"I don't know," he said.

She believed him. "Can you find out?"

"I will try." He looked away, out across Solas. "Perhaps only Jarvo knows."

"It will be profitable for you, if you can provide this answer to me."

"Profitable, but it may cost my life."

"It may cost your life if you don't. It may cost all our lives."

He nodded, and met her eyes again. "Jarvo wants this war."

"Why?"

"Because he is *so* certain he can win."

FORTY-TWO

TRYNN HAD RISKED RETURNING to the Cosegan capital for many reasons. He was looking for Globotite, desperately needed more Revon, and he came for Shanoah, to make sure she knew what had to be done. The Imazes were now their last best hope. But, mostly, he came to say goodbye, knowing it was likely they'd never see each other again.

Trynn looked up at the artificial stars and thought of Rip. "I suppose this is the closest thing we Cosegans have to a church."

"The Far Future does get tangled up with their religious ideas, don't they," Shanoah said, also gazing upward as they sat in moving reclining chairs made of muted blue and purple halos of light. The Imaze planetarium building was massive in its proportions, roughly the size of modern Los Angeles; a kind of gigantic simulator used for training Imazes. Trynn loved it there.

"They confuse themselves with their religions, and they are missing so much."

They were silent for a while, both thinking about the

future, one where they might not be together, one that might not be at all.

"That's the Spectrum Belt," she said, pointing up to a section of space he recognized.

"From there, you can go into the Far Future," he said, still amazed that such a thing was possible, even with all his knowledge of science and technology.

"We have to first go through the Sagan portal."

"Right, but that's the easy part," he said.

She laughed, because she knew he was joking. Then she went silent, thinking of the Spectrum Belt, a place where dreams and nightmares collided in a horrifically beautiful kaleidoscope of physics-bending insanity. Beyond that was the Epic Seam. None of the transitions should be survivable, but there was a way. It was a million to one odds against making it, but she would have to sail through the one and only way.

"I wish you could come," she finally said, still lost in the overwhelming thought of the mission.

"I do, too. Maybe someday, but we both know we have a better chance of stopping the Doom if I stay and you go."

"Work together," she said, touching his hand. "It's so big . . . it's hard to figure out how we can do it . . . can we *really* do it?"

"We have to," he said. "I like to think of it like this. You have all the expertise and confidence that the Imazes can succeed in your mission. And I, in the expectation of your success, and my own confidence that I can accomplish everything I need to do . . . it will happen."

"You're able to grasp it better than I can," she said.

"We can't think of the enormity of it all, just our part."

"Will that be enough?"

"I don't know. We have to count on some help from our descendants. That's why you've got to save them."

She held his hand as they sat absorbing the "stars." Finally, she leaned over and kissed him. "You shouldn't have come."

"I had to," he whispered, disclosing an urgent secret.

"If they catch you . . . you won't be able to do your part."

"I know," he said. "In the overall scheme of things, whether we live or die may not matter as long as we, or someone, accomplish what we need to do."

"Forgive me, but it feels like none of it matters without you."

"I had to say goodbye," he told her. "I couldn't live with myself if I didn't."

"You sound as though we'll never see each other again."

"I pray that is not true."

"Now you sound like those in the Far Future," she said quietly. "Who do you pray to?"

"The stars," he said, motioning up to the artificial sky, which looked more real than the real thing. "Especially when you are among them."

Silence ensued once again as they contemplated the possibility that this was going to be their final night together.

"We are both risking so much," she said. "Let's not talk of the Doom or science or the challenges we face. Let's only talk of love, hope, and future success together."

Soon, they fell into each other's arms, and adjusted the recliners so they could make love as they sought the unity of space and time . . . one last time.

FORTY-THREE

After the meeting with Jaxx, the Arc knew she had to do the thing she least wanted. It was time to contact Jarvo.

"Hello, Arc," Jarvo said as the 3-D holographic image walked into her office. "Lovely, lovely. I must admit, I admire what you people have done with light. Impressive."

"Thank you."

"Yes, and quite a view. I could do some important reconnaissance from here. You don't mind if I take some recordings, do you? It might help us capture and occupy this city faster."

"That will never happen," she said, brushing her arms, shooing him away from the edge.

"We shall see."

"No." She moved toward him threateningly. "This is why we have to talk. A war, whatever the outcome, would solidify the Doom and bring about an instant end to humanity."

"I don't think so."

She stood aghast. "You don't *think* so? How? But, you're *wrong*."

"Why? Because you say so."

"No, we have *seen* it!"

"Eysens? I grow so tired of hearing about Eysens." He tiptoed back to the edge mockingly, as if she might not notice, and pretended to take pictures. "Those same Eysens show a Far Future where humanity is still very much alive and thriving."

"Thriving?"

"Do you have a hearing issue, Arc? Why is it you repeat everything I say?"

"Because you utter such unbelievable garbage," she said tightly. "I understood you were intelligent, but in a matter of minutes you have dispelled that rumor several times."

"It really is a beautiful city, I must say. It will be a shame when it is lost."

"You are wrong to be emboldened by your little raid at Naperton." She paced, as if a school teacher berating an errant student. "Closing trade routes. Picking fights, a few skirmishes on the outer areas and oceans—"

He laughed again. "Do you really think that was anything at all? It was nothing, not even the blink of a beginning of war."

"You bluff a good game, Jarvo, but—"

"Silly woman," he interrupted, his voice rising to anger for the first time. "When I strike, you will know it, because you and all that you hold dear will crumble into the dust of lost existence."

The force of his words, the fury in his eyes, chilled her, but did not dissuade her. "Don't you see that the future is at stake for *all* of us? We cannot allow war."

"No. I see a Far Future much to my liking." Civility returned to his voice. "However, I can understand that you want—"

"What do you hope to achieve by war?" she interrupted.

"The end."

"The end of what?"

"Of Cosegans. I am seeking nothing short of the total extermination of all Cosegans."

FOR WEEKS, Grayswa had been overwhelmed with energetic disturbances. "It is close to the end," he whispered to a confidant. "We must not let a second waste."

"How can we stop it?"

"Only long away in the Far Future can our efforts become strong enough that we may succeed. When we send an instant of love, and maintain that for minutes, hours, days . . . over and across eleven million years, those instants will grow into a much longer reality. That new response will reverberate back out into the universe and time will be transformed."

"Can it work?"

"It is the only hope."

Grayswa assembled teams of Etherens who bombarded the Far Future with love, harmonic sounds, astronomical alignments, and mathematical equations. He held in mind certain individuals, as well as important groups, to be targeted. One of the most crucial people to reach was Leonardo da Vinci. Grayswa sent him specific messages in music, mathematics, and astronomy.

When Adjoa helped convey the agenda across the eons, she realized what Grayswa was doing.

"These are keys," she said to him quietly.

"Yes," he said, his eyes sparkling as he nodded, pleased she had noticed and understood the complex meaning.

"Is that wise?" she asked. "Entrusting so much to a man from that time?"

"He will know."

She studied the old shaman, grasping the consequences of his response. "Are you sure?"

His eyes sparkled again, happy she'd so easily figured it out. "Yes."

"Then these notes, the alignments, he will know from where they came?"

He nodded. His grin made him look decades younger.

"And . . . when he deciphers the music, he will be able to contact us?"

"Yes, yes!"

"So will anyone he plays the music for . . . " She paused and thought for a moment. "But only if they have the rest of the equations, and if . . . " She looked at him again. "And only if they have the same knowledge as he has."

OVAN CHECKED THE VIEWS. The Egyptian insertion was a disaster. "It's not there!" he shouted to Nassar. "Not even close to the Pharaoh!"

Nassar pulled up another view. "It's worse than that. The archaeologist's people are near to finding it."

Ovan, not good at making this type of decision, wondered where Trynn was. He looked at the Terminus Clock. "We have to act or we'll lose it."

"What do we do? The woman will recover the Pharaoh's Eysen in a matter of hours."

"Stop her!" Ovan said, sliding views of Savina to the front.

"You mean . . . ?" Nassar asked.

"There's no choice."

"Won't that give the advantage to Kalor Locke?"

"That will be our next crisis. If *she* gets to that Eysen, Kalor Locke won't matter because the Clock will have already run out!"

FORTY-FOUR

Shanoah, surrounded by the images of all the members of the mission, prepared to lift off in the lead ship. In the final darkness before sunrise, she could still taste Trynn's lips, see his face, and recall each breath they'd shared. But now was the time to look to the future—the Far Future.

"I love you," she whispered silently as she flicked her fingers and initiated the launch, making a conscious decision to leave Trynn in the past, knowing she could not worry about him. *There can be no distractions in the Spectrum Belt.*

The three Imaze ships lifted off simultaneously from the ISS on a mission they hoped would change the future, challenge the Doom, and save the Cosegans.

Shanoah thought of the first challenge, the Epic Seam, though there were so many ahead. Her training and experience told her to take them one at a time, but it required all her concentration not to think about what they would find if they were successful and arrived back on Earth so far from now.

THE ARC GLANCED at the report disbelievingly. "Why would he risk coming back?" she asked the Guardian.

"Love," the man said.

"Yes, I know he loves Shanoah, but these are not foolish youngsters. Trynn and Shanoah are two of our top minds." She paused to stare at the replay of the Imaze launch and check the mission's progress. "Would they really risk the future of all humanity for a final farewell, one last kiss?"

"Apparently," the man said. "As you see, there are credible sightings of him."

"Too risky."

"Then if he didn't sneak back to see her, why is he here?"

The Arc looked at the Terminus-Clock. "To get to Markol."

The man, one of her most trusted Guardians, knew about High-peak and the secret work Markol was undertaking there. "I'll put more people in the area."

She nodded. "Trynn may have any number of routes to High-peak, but there is only one entrance. Unless . . . unless he comes from underwater."

"We have submersibles patrolling."

"Good." She dismissed the Guardian and was left with the nagging suspicion that Trynn had another reason for making such a daring move.

A troubling message arrived from Weals, taking her attention from Trynn and giving it to the more pressing matter—the Havloses.

"Jarvo has a secret," Weals said in a 3-D message.

"No doubt he has many," the Arc responded to the interactive avatar.

"This one he believes could win him the war."

The Arc involuntarily coughed, wishing she could speak to Weals himself instead of this facsimile. "A weapon?"

"It seems the most likely answer. I'm still pursuing leads,

but be warned this is something he believes with certainty will bring the Cosegan people to their knees."

The Arc took a deep breath and said something she was coming to believe with increasing certainty. "The Havloses *are* the Terminus Doom."

SHANK RECEIVED a similar report about Trynn being spotted in Cosegan territory. His first inclination was to have him killed on sight, but he calmed down and allotted resources to capturing his old foe.

"Have you heard Trynn is back?" Jenso asked, walking into Shank's office, a palatial ring of colored lights that she was always annoyed hadn't been designed by her team. If asked, she would have said that it was too big, too bright, and the frequencies were wrong. But no one asked.

"Yes, I saw something on that."

"Aren't you worried?"

"Worried? About Trynn?" He laughed. "The fact that he's back—*if* it's true—simply shows he is powerless. We have stripped him of all resources. The Eysen Maker had no power."

"You underestimate him."

"No, I don't."

"Have you sent a unit to apprehend him?"

"I wouldn't waste my time," he lied.

"If he comes to Solas, I will see him," she said, in a subtle reference to the surveillance she had built into the city of her design. "But he won't be that crazy."

"Trynn is a disaster, but he's not stupid," Shank agreed. "We won't see him in Solas."

She pulled her long white hair behind her, revealing the fullness of her dark face. The action gave Shank a rare glimpse of the power in her eyes. He felt the force of her stare physically weaken him for an instant, but quickly convinced himself he'd had too much Spressen at breakfast, a warm herbal energy drink favored by Cosegans.

"He may have returned because of Shanoah," she said, letting her hair fall loose again. "The Imazes took off this morning."

"Of course," Shank snapped. It infuriated him that Trynn had a personal relationship with the highest ranking Imaze, due to all the potential complications that held for preventing the Doom. But it was the fact that Trynn might be *happy* that angered him more. "Don't worry too much about Trynn. He no longer matters."

She smiled at his hypocrisy, and would have been worried if she thought he believed his words, because as long as Trynn lived, he would *always* be a problem. However, she also knew, better than most, that Shank could be as dangerous as Trynn, the Arc, or even the Havloses, and that worried her. But Jenso had reasons for her alliance with Shank, reasons that would test the limits of the Cosegans' greatest technological advances over light, and the existence of the future.

FORTY-FIVE

Rip knew the risks of being in France were extreme. Kalor Locke had proven he could track them, and would undoubtedly be looking for the Nostradamus Eysen. Had they realized how close they'd come to being captured in Turkey, Rip certainly would not have gone to France.

Booker had obtained Lost Quatrains, and other personal papers of the great seer, and the translations were proving to be helpful in picking up the long trail of the whereabouts of what Trynn sometimes called the "catastro-sphere", since it brought the Doom closer and caused the Circle to lose confidence in him and his Eysen strategies.

"Nostradamus knew where Da Vinci's Eysen was hidden," Gale announced, looking up from her laptop after reading a newly discovered part of Nostradamus's secret journal. "He saw it in his Eysen."

"That's the first absolute confirmation that Nostradamus and Leonardo didn't share the same sphere," Rip said, not taking his eyes from his own screen, which was running a program Alik had developed that sifted and sorted the mountains of data they had accumulated through Eysens, antique papers, and other historical artifacts and actual events, to predict where the Cosegan spheres might have wound up. The Machine Learning program incorporated all available information from prior Eysen finds to increase its accuracy.

"Nostradamus went looking for an Eysen," Gale said. "He wrote that he thought there might be hundreds of them, that they might be as plentiful as veins of gold."

"He went looking for a second one, or did he somehow hear about them before he found his?" Rip asked for clarification.

"It's unclear, but we have information from the Jesus Eysen that said Nostradamus was not supposed to find his until 1550, but he found it early, partially because he was looking, and partially because of the ripple effects of Da Vinci's sphere, which was inserted after."

"It's so complicated," Cira said.

Gale nodded.

"That means Nostradamus found the Eysen during his missing years," Cira said. "Like Da Vinci, he had a period where little is known about what he did or where he was."

"When?" Gale asked.

"From 1535 to 1544."

"What did he do in his missing years?" Rip asked. "Do we get any clues in his journals?"

"Not much, but Booker said there's another document. We should have it soon."

"Good," Rip said. "In the meantime, there's an old church a couple hours south of Paris. It's one of the hotspots on Alik's program."

"When do we leave?" Cira asked.

"Now," Rip replied, knowing every second was needed to beat Locke.

SAVINA DICTATED into her digital journal as she wandered the ruined walls of the Rise of Aten, a city built during the reign of King Tutankhamun's grandfather, Amehotep III, who was the 9th king during the 18th dynasty. However, it wasn't King Tut she was interested in, it was Hatshepsut, the female pharaoh who was the fifth ruler of the 18th dynasty. Her reign ended more than fifty years before Amehotep III's began.

"Hatshepsut, why did you get an Eysen? Why did Trynn choose you? Did it have anything to do with your rise to power?" she asked, as if speaking to the Pharaoh herself. "What did you do with it?"

Savina clicked off the recorder as she moved around a stone corner where a group of archaeologists were working. *Maybe Rip should have come here instead of me,* she mused. But she knew that was out of the question.

Booker had spent a considerable sum of money and favors in order to obtain full access for Savina at the important site. Rip might have been better suited for this part of the search, but he would have been recognized, being a legend among archeologists. His work was still studied in courses around the world, and the controversy that surrounded his exit from the profession was still the subject of many conspiracy theories. Most thought he was dead, others considered him a criminal, the minority saw him as a cult figure and believed he might still be out there somewhere, searching for the elusive proof of his Cosega theory.

"Can I help you?" a man asked in accented English.

Savina showed him her credentials. He smiled suspiciously, but let her pass.

She walked beside a rare zig-zag mud brick wall that continued for hundreds of feet.

A message from Alik came in. **There is a cemetery north of the city. They're still excavating tombs there. It is highly probable that would be the hiding place.**

Okay, she texted back, but Savina still questioned the information. Speaking to Hatshepsut through her digital journal again, she asked the Pharaoh, "What did you do with the Eysen? Whom did you trust? You must have arranged for its safe keeping in the event of your death. All of your decisions in life appear to have been calculated with a high degree of ideology and idealism. Historians all agree you were a clever and cunning woman. You made sure the public and hierarchy believed your ascension to power was in their best interest. You made it a divine message. 'The gods want me. They want me to do this or that.' How impressive that you rose and ruled successfully even before the Eysen. But was it before?" Savina asked rhetorically, realizing that dates and facts in ancient Egypt shifted as easily as the blowing desert sand.

Three dozen men entered the ancient city from the west. Another twenty came in from the south, Parson Locke among them. Suddenly, the elite Blaxers were outnumbered by thirty futuristically armed Varangians.

FORTY-SIX

THE GOEZE CARRIED Trynn rapidly through a beautiful remote countryside, lush with gorgeous vegetation that would long be extinct in the Far Future. This was his favorite section of the trip because of its undisturbed nature and abundant animals, but he always questioned why so many of the species he loved would face extinction in the Missing-Time.

On previous trips, Trynn had been obsessed with finding a way to prevent humanity's own extinction during the Missing-Time, the dark curtain that came down between the Cosegans' grandeur and the rise of the modern humans. But today he was occupied with something more important: Shanoah. Her caress, the tenderness in her voice, those eyes he could never forget, all held firm in his mind, allowing few other thoughts to enter.

Yet, as he grew closer to Sinwind, the outlying settlement where he was to meet Dreemelle, her image and the prospect of a fresh supply of Revon crept into his psyche. Just as quickly, desperate thoughts invaded. *Maybe Dreemelle will think I've reached my limit. And what* of *that limit? Am I jeopardizing my intelligence and creating a mental vulnerability, risking my sanity?* Dreemelle had warned many times that Revon could do irreparable damage to his mind. *And yet what choice do I have? Shanoah is gone. There are only fourteen days remaining on the Terminus Clock, another Eysen Far Future insertion looms . . . how much am I really gambling when everything is already at stake?*

"Other vehicles in the area," the automated voice announced, ripping him back to the dangerous needle he was threading. "Approaching at speed level nine."

The warning startled him, even though before starting out, Trynn had entered a command to be alerted to any nearby people or vehicles. He checked the screen, which showed the road behind, and saw two Guardian goezes. *How did they find me?*

Trynn thought about how in Rip's time the skill of the individual drivers might have made a difference in the outcome of a car chase, when a person took the wheel and had to make decisions based upon their biological and neurological capacity. However, goezes had machine intelligence that would complete those tasks automatically. *And the Guardians' vehicles have the same capacity,* he thought.

The Guardians closed in on his goeze. Already cruising at high speed, he gave the command to go faster, thankful that before he'd left, he had overridden the maximum limits on propulsion. *But I have no idea what restrictive governors are on the Guardians' vehicles.* The increased speed widened the distance between him and the pursuers. "Not today," he muttered hopefully.

The Guardians fired warning lasers past Trynn's goeze, letting him know they were intent on stopping him. He instructed the AI pilot to get as close to the trees as possible and to travel as high as they could without leaving the canopy. The goeze jolted upward, weaving in and out of the tall Finebeale and Nogoff trees at incredible speeds, mere inches from heavy branches and thick trunks. The vehicle's guidance system was so effective that several times the goeze burst through great gatherings of leaves and thin branches.

The Guardian's lasers struck the trees rather than Trynn's goeze. A twistle tree caught fire after the beams of concentrated heat made contact with its thick bark.

It wasn't only the AI's impressive maneuverings that kept the goeze ahead of the Guardians, Trynn also utilized his vast engineering knowledge to create six ghost images of his vehicle. As soon as the Guardians were detected, he initiated a scrambling sequence that would rapidly project what were essentially cloned impressions of his vehicle above, below, in front, behind, or to either side of his goeze. However, the tactic drained substantial amounts of energy, which slowed the goeze.

Banking through the trees, Trynn kept an eye on the rapidly decreasing energy level. The goeze could recharge in flight, but not under these maximum conditions. Trynn knew he was running out of time.

Another round of laser blaster strikes sliced through the clones. *Too close.* He ordered the goeze back up to the top of the canopy.

"I have one final trick for you!" Trynn yelled, hoping the technique would help him avoid capture. The only reason it had a chance of working was, because there was so little crime and few criminals in Cosegan society, the Guardians had no experience with such pursuits, and especially technological countermeasures.

Out in the open now, he knew they would fire again. He used the on-board mind-crystal to calculate when the next shots would come, and a moment prior, he deployed flash boards, which were essentially beams tuned to a frequency so precise that they rendered a reflective surface of photons which, like a mirror, sent the laser back into the pursuing crafts.

He closed his eyes, and gave the command to dive down into the forest, knowing now he had just destroyed two Guardian goezes and killed an unknown number of his fellow Cosegans.

Now they'll hunt me as a murderer.

FORTY-SEVEN

ALIK SENT AN ALARM. Savina looked into her tablet. A map of the city appeared not as it was in its current ruinous state, but how it must have looked thousands of years before. The amazing transformation, its detail and accuracy so complete, could only have come from one source—an Eysen.

She looked at the closest Blaxer. They had all received the same alert, and most were moving away from her, toward the threat. Six more were heading in her direction. They would be the last defense. They might die to protect her.

Booker appeared on her screen. "I've got a helicopter inbound. Three minutes, we'll have you out of there."

"These are Kalor Locke's people?"

"Yes, Varangians," Booker said, knowing she was smart enough to work through the odds.

"They have Cosegan weaponry."

"Yes."

"They aren't here for me. I have no Eysen."

"I know where you're going with this, but I need you alive."

"Oh, I plan to live, but they're here because they *know*

there is an Eysen here."

"The Blaxers won't let them have it." Booker knew this was false confidence. Alik was tapped into the Eysens, and had found the attack just before it happened. It wasn't good.

"We don't even know where the Eysen is yet, and you don't have enough Blaxers to withstand Cosegan weapons," she said, recalling the island massacre.

"There are more on the way." This was true, and in spite of what Alik had seen, Booker knew it could all change in an instant not just based on what his army did, but what happened millions of years earlier between the Cosegans and the Havloses. Even a breath by some unknown person in the Missing-Time could affect everything.

Booker also knew that the same things, or something far more minor during the past eleven million years, could make it so he was never born. The realization that he could vanish from existence at any moment had directed everything he'd done since he'd first read the Clastier papers. Every breath he took was precious, because each could be the one that negated his entire life, or the one to save the future for him and everyone else.

"It won't be soon enough," Savina said, looking around urgently. "I'm going to find the Pharaoh's Eysen before they do."

"And then what?"

"I will use it to stop them."

"How?"

"The same way Hatshepsut did."

PARSON LOCKE, a former Navy SEAL, was versed in all areas of commando raiding techniques and weapons. However, demolition and explosives were his specialty. Not an average officer, Parson had been one of the most decorated in history before the CIA recruited him to be part of the elite Special Operations Group. Yet after only four years with SOG, he had abruptly resigned and gone to work for his brother. Parson was a fair and friendly man who believed in honor and loyalty. However, more than anything else, he believed in his brother.

Even before Kalor had shown Parson the Eysen and explained all that they could do with it, Parson would have died for him. Now, after seeing inside the Eysen, Parson would kill for Kalor, do whatever it took, because he knew his brother had been touched by destiny to save the human race from its infinite past and its messy present. As Kalor had said many times, "Humanity's survival was never assured. There have been countless threats that could have wiped us out at any time, but no danger to humanity is greater than the one we pose to ourselves."

Parson was hunting Savina and Rip not because of a malicious streak, but because they could prevent his brother's rise to power. The fate of the world was at stake, and Parson was going to make sure no one got in Kalor's way.

Kalor had a team providing real time data on the targets—Rip, Savina, Booker, Alik, any Blaxer, Gale, and even Cira, who was actually number four on the hit list. He didn't like the idea of killing a teenage girl, but he would not hesitate. He did, however, hope to make it quick and painless for her.

Parson washed everything out of his mind as he and his fellow Varangians moved into the dusty Rise of Aten, its vastness surprising. The earth bricks reminded him of buildings he'd seen in Afghanistan, but never on a scale like this. He could almost see the ghosts of the inhabitants of the once great city. But that too was pushed out in lieu of a single focus.

Find the Pharaoh's Eysen, and kill Savina.

FORTY-EIGHT

TRYNN'S GOEZE soared just above the lime green upper leaves. The AI voice once again alerted him that more vehicles were approaching. He immediately shifted off the auto-pilot horizon-level control. An emergency warning buzzer made it clear the AI did not approve of his action. However, the override codes meant that the deep-learning program which controlled the goeze could not argue against the commands of the programmer. Trynn's takeover did not prevent the AI from compensating for the moves of the machines chasing them, which was exactly what Trynn was counting on.

As his goeze violently shifted sideways, a rapid drop in elevation set off yet another warning signal. While the light vehicle careened in a spiral around a large tree, Trynn continued mouthing voice commands, telling the goeze to take bold evasive steps. Responding instantly, the craft zoomed into a steep vertical drop and flew under a fallen tree with almost impossible clearance.

Within seconds, the Guardians were back. Trynn hesitated for only a moment before implementing the final defense.

"Death measures, death measures," he repeated urgently. Although he did not like the idea of killing more Cosegans, who were just doing their jobs, there was little choice if he was to continue his work to save humanity.

Fortunately, the machine had no such emotions or reservations about killing Guardians. The detachment of its photon circuitry made it an efficient killer. This time, the entire goeze transformed into a highly reflective mirrored shield, and the next laser shots were immediately returned to their source. Both pursuing vehicles, like the previous pair, instantly vaporized.

Before Trynn could absorb the relief and consequences of his actions, the sophisticated radar indicated nine more incoming Guardian goezes. "They'll never stop coming," he said out loud, confusing the AI for a moment. Trynn knew he'd been lucky to survive their attacks, but nine ships, with potentially additional assets on the way, was far more than he could handle.

There would be no way to get to Sinwind, the village where he was to meet Dreemelle. *What am I going to do without the Revon*, he thought, holding back an addict's tears of despair.

TRACER, a high ranking Guardian, waited for the Arc's hologram to surface. Although not looking forward to the report he was about to give, Tracer did not shy away from trouble. "Trynn has returned," he said.

Her face brightened, even though it wasn't the first time she'd heard this. "Where is he?"

"Apparently, he came to say goodbye to Shanoah, but they

were able to avoid detection. She manipulated her scheduling so we were watching the wrong place."

"I don't care about that—where is *he*?" she repeated.

"We intercepted his trail outside Sinwind. Unfortunately, we lost eight Guardians and he . . . escaped."

Her expression turned as if she had just eaten a lemon. "Trynn *killed* Guardians?"

"No, they . . . not exactly . . . he used evasive measures. Somehow he modified his goeze. They were killed by their own lasers."

"But he is responsible!"

"Yes, that is a valid interpretation."

She scowled. "Either it is him, or it is you who are responsible . . . or *irresponsible*."

"The blame lies with Trynn," Tracer said with finality. "He was warned. He did not stop. He implemented counter measures."

"No further sightings of him?" she asked.

Tracer did not immediately answer, double checking the latest data. "No. We have agents all over the village. We were there immediately, both in person and through FlyWatchers and visuals, but he never showed up."

"How did he escape? Where did he go?"

"We don't know."

She let out an exasperated breath. "Why was he going to a nothing place like Sinwind?"

"No indication of his purpose. However, I'm convinced whatever his business was there, he canceled and fled back to Havlos lands."

"The borders are fully monitored. How did he get through?"

"He's an Eysen Maker," Tracer reminded her.

The Arc had momentarily forgotten that Trynn would've

had a strong working knowledge of their border security surveillance detection systems. "Then you're telling me he can come and go through our borders at will."

"Perhaps he has traded this information to the Havloses."

The Arc shook her head. "I don't think so. Trynn is a loyal Cosegan."

"Is he?" Tracer asked, somewhat surprised by her assessment. "What price are they charging him to stay there?"

"It is your job to keep the borders secure, and to apprehend fugitives. You have failed both. Do not let it happen again," she said, ending the transmission.

The Arc looked at the report again, more worried than ever. *Why was Trynn really here?* she wondered, knowing that a risk like this meant he was desperate. He could be losing his way. The Arc needed him to succeed. He was the best chance they had, he had *always* been their best hope.

It can't be Globotite, she thought, now pacing. *It's something else. What? What? What?*

RIP STARED out the car window from the backseat as a Blaxer drove them out of Paris. "What's wrong?" Gale asked, Cira napping next to her.

He turned to face her, the strain in his eyes evident. "I keep thinking about Leonardo's face. He was terrified. We need to know exactly what he saw inside that Eysen."

"I know," Gale agreed. "When Leonardo said, 'It is the universe that controls humanity and this magical sphere must be from the hand of god, though it obviously depicts the evil work of the devil,' I thought of Clastier. Several of his papers around the final four Divinations refer to the devil wrestling the sphere from the hand of god, and the final four being the work of the devil. The fact that their phrases match could be coincidental . . . except there's no such thing as coincidence." She listed them as if one of them might fit into the puzzle:

1. Global pandemics and super-viruses wipe out vast numbers of the world's population.

2. A utopian period after a great plague.

3. Climate destabilization (man messing with nature) uncertain levels of mass destruction.

4. World War III, a conflict of such proportion that humanity might not survive.

"Leonardo must have seen one of them," Gale said.

Rip turned back to gaze out the window, saying softly, "Or all of them."

FORTY-NINE

Kavid stood at the front of a crowd of friends, gathered in a clearing deep in the Suislaw woods. A vast canopy of finebeale and nogoff trees provided shade and almost complete concealment. "We must use our advantages to repel our oppressors!" the young Etheren shouted.

Several in the crowd cheered.

"The advantages we possess as Etherens have, until now, all but been ignored in our fight against the Cosegan oppressors."

The Etheren's mental abilities of clairvoyance, mind control, thought-planting, and even telekinesis, were incredibly powerful. All Cosegans were exceptionally healthy, fit, capable of great healing knowledge, and possessed physical abilities far beyond Far Future humans. But Etherens exceeded all that. They possessed an extra sense, a way of becoming in-tune with nature that ordinary Cosegans could not match.

"But we are also Cosegans," an older woman shouted.

"We are Etherens first," Kavid responded.

More cheers.

"They outnumber us," another woman yelled.

"Do not forget the Cosegans have another enemy. The Havloses are on the march to war."

"We should side with the Cosegans," the same woman responded.

"We cannot side with the ones that are imprisoning and controlling our people."

"But the Havloses are more dangerous than the Cosegans."

"How can you say that? Do not believe the Cosegan propaganda. Have the Havloses ever hurt you?" Kavid didn't wait for a response. "Havlos have hurt no one you know, imprisoned you or your neighbors. Havloses have not made you work for less than your worth. They haven't taken your lands, accused you unjustly. Not one of you here can make a claim against the Havloses, yet all of us could say Cosegans have done these things to us."

"How can we win against their technology?"

"Their technology is over elements and physical manifestations. We possess something far more powerful. We understand the technology of the mind. Their use of photons is no match for our use of neurons."

"The Cosegans are not a primitive people like the Havloses," an older man said. "They know how to manipulate their cellular activity for benefit, unlike our neighbors on the other side of the globe. They would not be as simple as you say to defeat."

"What Muutock says is true," Kavid admitted. "This is not an easy fight. Cosegans are a powerful force, and I do not propose trying to conquer them. I am advocating Etheren independence. Much in the same way that Havloses exist on this planet in their own sovereign state, Etherens should be afforded no less."

There were loud murmurings among the gathered.

Kavid looked at a woman standing three or four rows back. He knew she was against the uprising, and he needed her. She was so well-liked and respected, she could bring in hundreds to the cause, who, in turn, would attract thousands more. Each phase of support was critical.

He turned back to the crowd and delivered the words he believed could convince her. "I have a list." He held up a holographic form. Its rotating names looked like the ticker-tape that ran along the bottom of the screens in the Far Future. It floated there, near him, as he continued speaking. "Over two thousand names. These are our friends, our brothers and sisters, sons and daughters, mothers and fathers. These are the names of Etherens being held by the Cosegans that you dare not offend, the Cosegans some of you foolishly defend. What crime have these two thousand seventy-two of our fellow Etherens committed? None! By our standards, it is the Cosegans' ever-changing rules that make our people criminals. The Cosegans have grown beyond afraid of the Terminus Doom and of the Havloses, as well as anything that deviates from the standard line of their mainstream acceptable reality."

There was a smattering of cheers.

"We are different from them," Kavid continued. "We have a deeper connection with nature, to the universe, the collective consciousness, and that's why we can see their flaws. You know in your heart I speak the truth. The Cosegans are spinning toward war with Havloses. We cannot allow them to take us with them down this treacherous path. We must preserve the Etheren way! We must free the two thousand seventy-two, or more will join them!"

"Free them! Free-dom!" chants began, "Free them! Free-dom!"

"The only way to liberate our people is to declare our independence from the Cosegans and use our superior abilities to secure freedom for all Etherens!"

The now raucous crowd applauded and cheered. Kavid looked at the woman in the crowd. She was cheering now as well. He had won her.

Kavid's eyes then found Prayta, who was off to the side. She was smiling. A worried, stern smile, but a smile nonetheless. He was triumphant.

Suddenly, the crowd parted. Grayswa appeared. Everyone hushed.

"Let us not become like them," the old shaman said, his voice sounding like a surging engine. "If we act like them, we are no different. If we are no different, we will lose . . . we *must* be different."

"They are about to extinguish us," Kavid argued.

"The Terminus Doom will swallow us all long before the Cosegans. We must concentrate all our efforts to stop the Doom, or we will vanish with the rest."

FIFTY

Markol heard Trynn had been back and wondered if he was coming for him. "I botched the insertion, I killed a man in the Far Future, someone Trynn may have known, someone he probably needed." He stopped and steadied himself, as if stabbed and bleeding. The murder of Huang had been eating at him even before he'd done it. When Markol had first looked into Huang's eyes, he knew the man would haunt him forever. "My former teacher has many reasons to want to destroy me, but I suspect the most obvious ones are the least likely."

"What does that mean?" an assistant asked, unsure why Markol was discussing such matters with him.

"He is simply disappointed in me. That is why he did not come."

AS SAVINA RAN through the earth brick corridors, she wasn't thinking of the Varangians about to descend on her. Instead, she concentrated on the mystery of the female

Pharaoh, believing that if she could understand Hatshepsut, she might locate the Eysen before Kalor Locke's thugs.

The Eysen will protect us, but I must find it first.

Hatshepsut was the only woman who, during the entirety of antiquity, ruled successfully by improving the lives of Egyptians and presiding over a time of expansion and prosperity for Egypt. Her military campaigns were well executed and much wealth was created in her time. Wars in Nubia and Syria brought gold and other riches, insurrections there were put down and gold mines opened. Far reaching trading expeditions also brought vast riches during her reign.

Parson Locke scanned the ruins, and saw the points of attack, the weakness of the Blaxers trying to defend such an area. His HADs—high altitude drones—were already providing precise coordinates. He touched a section of his wrist tablet and unleashed MAYHEM weapons. At the same time, the Spartan equipped Varangians began to engage.

Savina ignored the lasers in the distance as she continued to lead her close unit of Blaxers toward the tombs. Hatshepsut ordered an enormous memorial temple built at Deir el-Bahri, what is now considered one of the architectural wonders of ancient Egypt. In fact, Hatshepsut built more structures than any previous kings. She had innovated the way temples were built. She'd created jobs, wealth, and titles at a startling yet sustainable pace, and had decentralized her power to make the country stronger.

Why was Hatshepsut deliberately forgotten? Savina wondered for the thousandth time as she moved across a detailed floor that seemed out of place. *Erased from history?*

"Savina, we've got to get you out of here," a Blaxer said.

"Not without the Eysen," she said, believing it was her only protection and knowing nothing mattered more, not even her life. "Kalor Locke cannot get there first."

Savina sprinted, sensing where to go, still trying to understand the Pharaoh's story, looking for clues in her ancient, mysterious life. Hatshepsut, daughter of Thutmose I, came to the throne of Egypt in 1478 BC, initially ruling jointly with her stepson, Thutmose III, who ascended to the throne as a child. Then, when Hatshepsut was just twenty, through a series of shrewd strategies, she supplanted the infant boy-king.

I wish I knew those details, Savina thought, ducking under a fully excavated section of what might have been a bakery.

Hatshepsut likely died in her mid-forties, and was buried in the Valley of the Kings in the hills behind Deir el-Bahri. Her stepson (who was also her nephew) Thutmose III retook the throne at her death and ruled for thirty years. Near the end of his reign, however, most evidence of Hatshepsut's rule was eradicated from official records, including statues and anything that linked her to the many massive building projects completed under her watch.

Why?

It wasn't until 1822, when archaeologists were first able to decode hieroglyphics at Deir el-Bahri, that she was rediscovered.

Why would she have left the Eysen here, instead of at Deir el-Bahri?

The lasers came closer. Savina wondered what information Locke had on the Pharaoh's Eysen. A Blaxer less than fifty yards from her fell, sliced by a Spartan laser. She knew his name, and he had just died to save her. She silently apologized and then said a prayer to Hatshepsut.

"Where is the Eysen?"

PARSON LOCKE, positioned behind a 3,400 year-old wall, gripped the stock of the Spartan laser rifle and locked Savina in his sight. Just before pulling the trigger, he recalled a conversation with his brother.

"These are not normal people," Kalor Locke had said. "You cannot kill them in normal ways."

"You're sounding kind of supernatural," Parson had replied. "Don't tell me they're immortal."

"No, they're something far more dangerous . . . they are in possession of Eysens."

"So are you."

"That is why I know," he snapped. "You must lay a trap so elaborate, so cunning, so *lethal*, that they will never see it, never know they've walked into it, and never be able to escape it."

Instead of firing the Spartan laser, Parson touched another field on his wrist screen. A series of explosives he'd designed, which were planted before Savina even arrived at the ancient city, erupted in a timed sequence. "There is no chance for escape," he whispered against the echoing booms. As disintegrating earth bricks, debris, and sand filled the air, forming a blinding storm cloud, Parson Locke wondered how long it would take the AI cameras on the HADs to decipher the footage of the attack and confirm the kill.

FIFTY-ONE

TRYNN MADE it to the coast, but had no way to signal the vessel offshore without alerting the Guardians to his presence. "They'll be here soon," he muttered, looking over his shoulder as he jogged along the rocky shoreline, wondering what to do.

"Need a lift?" a man asked, slipping out from between a jagged section of cliff.

"Who are you?" Trynn barked, frantically looking for Guardians.

"A friend—at least for the moment. I can get you out to sea."

"Why?"

The man shrugged. "Or we could wait here for the Guardians. According to their communications," he pointed to a small device, "they are four minutes from here. That's not a long time, but it is enough time for the Gable."

"The Gable?"

"My boat."

Trynn, without much choice, was already following the man. "I know your boat's name, but not yours."

"I'm Jaxx."

"And how did you find me, Jaxx?"

"I monitor the Guardians."

"Why?"

"There's money in it."

Trynn narrowed his eyes. "How much do you want?"

"No payment necessary from you, Trynn," Jaxx said, smiling, as they reached his boat, moored in a tight cove. "All I ask is a favor."

"What kind of favor?" Trynn asked, willing to do almost anything to escape.

"I'll tell you when I ask."

Trynn stopped just before boarding and looked into Jaxx's dark eyes. "Is this a trap?"

"All of life is a trap," Jaxx said. "Let's make sure it gets set correctly." He motioned for Trynn to board.

Trynn looked at the boat. It was not made of light. "This is a Havlos boat."

"What better way to escape the Cosegans?"

THE ARC LISTENED to simultaneous reports on Havloses hitting several more towns on the outskirts of bigger coastal cities, and another of Trynn somehow slipping away.

"War is coming," she whispered to herself, frustrated by the day's events. "Why are the Havloses so confident? What do they have?"

She contacted Cosegan security engineers and ordered them to totally revamp the border's surveillance system. "The Havloses are preparing for war," the Arc said impatiently. "We cannot let them just walk in."

"It seems extremely unlikely they would dare a full invasion," the director said. "However, sending spies is exactly the kind of scheme these people would do."

She did not agree with the director's assessment, but there was no point in a debate.

Staring at the areas of Trynn's recent sightings, she harbored a secret wish that Trynn was still in Cosegan territory and that he was going to operate from yet another secret location within their borders.

That hope would soon be dashed.

TRACER ENTERED SHANK'S OFFICE, wishing he could have held this meeting via hologram technique transmission as he had done with the Arc, but Shank had insisted he appear in person. Tracer knew he was walking a fine line reporting to Shank without disclosing that information to the Arc, but he was a savvy man, and could see the writing on the wall. There were too many people and challenges pushing the Arc. The odds were high she would soon be out of power and the ambitious Guardian wanted to keep his position. Working with Shank now was the best way to do that.

However, it was more than job security and the chance to rise further in power. Tracer believed Shank had a more forceful initiative, and would handle a potential war with the Havloses better than the Arc—a war where the Guardians would be on the front lines.

AS PROMISED, Jaxx got Trynn back to his vessel and took nothing in return except for the promise of a future favor.

Trynn was suspicious. He knew a man like Jaxx could not be trusted, yet he had passed up the chance of a hefty pay day by not turning Trynn over to the Cosegans, and risked even more by helping him escape.

Trynn did his best to operate on his dwindling supply of Revon, but it wasn't enough and he could see the potential for disastrous mistakes. *I'll have to go back,* he thought, wishing he had someone like Jaxx to escort him through the borderlands again .

"It's more dangerous every hour," Ovan said after Trynn told him he would be leaving again soon. "You just got back!"

"I know, but there are needs . . . "

"What about the skirmishes, rumors of Havlos atrocities against Cosegan coastal towns? How long do you think it'll be until an all-out war?"

"There's a rising on the street tonight," Trynn said, adjusting the Infinity Switch, the mechanism by which he would lock all Eysens at the precise moment the Doom was defeated. Even making the minute changes to its setting now, he worried that on his rationed dose of Revon, he might be missing something. There would only be one chance, one exact instant in time, to press the Infinity Switch and set the Far Future and Cosegan time in stone.

"What's that mean, 'a rising on the street?'"

"In the Far Future . . . what happens here reflects there."

"And the reverse is equally true."

Trynn nodded. "I have to go."

"You're the smartest man I know," Ovan said. "A gifted engineer, the greatest Eysen Maker . . . you don't need the Revon."

"You know?" Trynn asked, shocked.

"Of course."

"Then you know it can't be done without it."

Ovan was silent for a long time. He did know. "It can destroy you."

Trynn knew that, and he knew Ovan knew this because he answered with his eyes. *So can the Terminus Doom.*

FIFTY-TWO

MARKOL, still unsure where to insert his second Eysen, closed his eyes and saw the familiar face of Huang. "Cosegans don't kill," he whispered in a voice he didn't recognize as his own. It was that dynamic, absolute foreign concept of killing another person that had been consuming him like a slow horde of insects eating him alive from the inside. He had taken to searching for the times in the Far Future before he killed Huang, torturing himself by viewing the man while still among the living. Markol had gotten to know Huang very well, but it wasn't helping. "I feel as if I'm living in a graveyard," he muttered, almost amused by the analogy since cemeteries did not exist in Cosegan time. The practice of burying bodies of the dead seemed so primitive, so pointless . . . It fascinated him.

An assistant interrupted, wondering if they were going to try to get the new sphere to the original recipient. Markol checked the images from the original recipient's life. "Born in 1955, the personal computer pioneer had previously lived until 2041, but now his death showed as occurring in 2011. Markol shook his head. "I've killed him, too."

"What?" the assistant asked.

"Nothing. No, we'll be going with a new recipient. When will we be ready?"

"Tomorrow?" the man responded hesitantly, still believing they should have approval from the Arc, or Shank, or *someone*. "It's dangerous not coordinating with Trynn." The assistant had also studied with the great Eysen Master.

"Trynn will know soon enough."

"Too late, though. I mean to alter . . . if it goes wrong again . . . I mean, if anything unforeseen happens . . . "

"It's *all* unforeseen!" Markol snapped as Huang flashed in his mind. The ramifications of every thought seemed to alter reality a billion ways, and each of those ways likewise changed a billion more, and so on. *It's maddening! How did you do it, Trynn? How did you keep it together?*

"Look at this," the assistant said, pointing to an event in Hollywood.

"What year?"

"Let me see . . . 1974. It's a burglary of Howard Hughes's Romaine Street headquarters in Los Angeles."

Markol knew who Hughes was. They had looked at him for the first insertion, but decided against it when simulations showed the billionaire would misuse the power, become an unwitting mover toward the Terminus Doom. "Is there a connection?" Markol asked.

The assistant slid dozens of views around the vast room until he came upon what he was looking for. "Yes."

Markol crouched on the floor. "It keeps getting worse."

"It sure does. We shouldn't do another insert without talking to Trynn."

"Trynn?" Markol yelled, standing up again. "It's impossible."

"Why?"

"Don't you *understand*?" Markol pointed back to the Hughes break-in. "This means the Far Future is tearing apart! The Eysen war has already begun."

THE ARC WATCHED the events from High-peak and read the distress on Markol's face. "He's losing it," she said to Weals.

"Should I have him removed?" Weals asked.

"I'm not sure we have a good replacement." She sighed. "I'll keep an eye on him. He might get it together." The Arc didn't think Markol knew how closely she was watching him, but the Arc didn't know that Markol did know, and had taken steps to conceal his planned second insertion from her.

Weals stared at the images skeptically. He didn't trust Markol, but his opinion meant nothing to the Arc, because Weals trusted no one.

"The war is coming," she said, shifting crisis subjects as easily as if she were changing clothes.

"I've coordinated with the lead engineers," Weals said. "We can access and cripple Havlos technology through secret back doors."

She had used Weals to establish that operation to avoid Shank discovering it. "Of course, that only applies to the tech they obtain from us."

"That is considerable."

"But not enough," she said. "They have more, something big. Jarvo is too confident."

"Perhaps Trynn has provided something."

She shook her head. "What of the assassins?" the Arc asked, changing subjects again. Weals had updated her yesterday on Shank's assassins searching for Trynn. It was of critical interest to her.

"Imagine their surprise when Trynn showed up back here," he said, allowing a rare smile. "Trynn is proving elusive to everyone."

"Shank is growing frustrated."

"I assume with regards to war, Shank is focused on our supremacy in space."

"As is the entire Circle," she replied. "It will allow us to take the initial lead."

"And possibly maintain it."

"No."

"You are convinced of this mysterious Havlos super-weapon."

"Yes."

Weals nodded. "I'll keep our people searching."

"I need some help with the uprisings," she said, moving on to a new and dangerous topic.

"I thought the Guardians were keeping them in check?"

"The Guardians may be inciting some of them."

"Part of Shank's plan?"

"Apparently," she said, looking at a new report on the latest internal troubles. "The Etherens is likely an authentic issue. They certainly have enough to be furious about, but their peaceful and contemplative nature will keep them from becoming too much of an issue. However, there are all these pockets of ordinary Cosegans forming, and our Mind Crystal analysis believes it is organized."

"That doesn't mean it's Shank."

"I know," she agreed, "but it might be, and I hope it is."

"Right," he said. "Because if it's not, we have a real problem."

She looked at him, annoyed that he didn't understand the scores of the "real problems" they already had.

"Figure of speech," he said.

She squinted, still annoyed, but it was misplaced anger. *Where are all the heroes?* she wondered. *Why am I forced into these arrangements with Weals and Jaxx, the likes of Shank and Jenso, Tracer and Markol? The quality of these people is not equal to the moment. Perhaps that alone speaks to the inevitability of the Doom.*

FIFTY-THREE

SAVINA, running hard, felt the earth beneath her give way and suddenly slipped through the loose sand as if being swallowed whole by a grainy monster. In her initial flailing panic, she thought she was about to die—buried alive in Egypt, absent a tomb, lost to Hatshepsut or any other Pharaohs, without ceremony or splendor.

She didn't realize that misstep had saved her life. Even before she landed at the end of a sloping chute, she heard a muffled explosion above her. Immediately, the black crowded space felt like a car crashing into a wall, everything vibrating, moving, closing in. Although the worst of it was partially absorbed by the shifting sands, a newly exposed stone support crumbled next to her, and Savina found herself in some sort of darkened chamber, the only light filtering in from a collapsing ceiling.

Still partially buried, she pushed herself forward and dove into the only opening. A secondary blast demolished it behind her. *I must be in the tombs,* she thought. *A section not yet excavated.*

In her confusion, for an instant, she wondered what had exploded, before realizing it was an attack from the Varangians.

They're still up there, but I am dead. She took a deep breath. The air was stale, heavy with dust, sand, and a millennia's worth of stillness. Now, finally able to shift, Savina knew she was very much alive.

"But they don't know that I'm alive," she whispered, suddenly liberated in her "death" and the freedom it brought.

SHANOAH SPOKE into the communicator just prior to entering the Spectrum Belt. "Everyone ready?"

"Set," Maicks said. "We're looking good."

"Set," Sweed replied. "Clear ahead."

"Excellent," Shanoah said. "All indicators are green. This appears to be a perfect alignment. I'm not seeing any signs of trouble." Her words were true. Every reading was positive. There were no reasons for anything but optimism.

Except, she was worried. Shanoah had a bad feeling they were about to be walloped. She just couldn't figure out where the nightmare was going to come from. They'd had warning on her previous trips, but this time it was eerily quiet. Conditions seemed too good.

I'm just being paranoid, Shanoah told herself. *I'm still suffering from the other catastrophic crossing attempts.* She shivered.

"Perfect tracking," Drifson, the historian, said.

"Any trace of pulsers?" Shanoah asked the science officer.

Lusa checked again. "Nothing."

"Good," Shanoah said.

Trynn entered her mind. She wondered how he was faring with the insertions. Could he see her? Did he know whether they'd made it? Maybe she should try contacting him. It was against all regulations, it probably wouldn't even get through, but she decided to try it anyway.

"Give me a forty-direct," she told the communications officer.

"*Now?*" the man asked for clarification.

"Yes." Shanoah knew it would be difficult to justify with the readings all clear, but something felt very *off* to her, and if Trynn had any information as to the fate of the mission . . .

She looked back at the screens. Empty, open, smooth. No danger anywhere.

"Do it."

"It's a violation," Lusa warned. "On several levels."

"I'm aware."

"Is there something we're missing?" Lusa asked.

"That's what I'm trying to find out."

Lusa nodded.

"Information can be helpful," Drifson said. "It can also be harmful."

"Connecting now," the communications office said.

"Thank you," Shanoah said, relieved. "Trynn?"

"Pull out! *Pull out*!" Trynn yelled as soon as the connection went through. "Make . . . not . . . through."

"What?" she shouted, alarmed. The transmission was breaking up badly.

"Wrong time . . . Pull . . . Pull out! Now!"

Shanoah turned to the screens. She could just make out the faintest outlines of pulsers, and knew it was already too late. "Brace! Brace!"

"What's happening?" the communications officer yelled as the ship suddenly tumbled into a series of forward rolls.

"Phantom pulsers!" Shanoah yelled. The bridge became immersed in long, muted colors. The shades of red and magenta were almost choking, the oxygen seeming to be stolen by the hues.

"The equipment is gone." Lusa coughed. "It's not," she gasped, "giving accurate . . . readings."

In the nightmare of colors and their increasing dominance over every aspect of existence, Shanoah struggled against the flashbacks, the current reality, and her dread of the next few minutes, which she knew could take years to occur.

"We're completely engulfed!" a crew member screamed.

"Wavelength synch is out!" the historian reported, as if his lungs were filled with water.

"More pulsers approaching!" Shanoah yelled. The colors were total, insane, and brighter than she remembered from her last encounter, but what she did recall was the Time hit they were about to take. "Hold on for the Time sweeping!"

"Seismic-seven!" the co-pilot yelled. "We have to do a seismic-seven!"

"No, we'll never get through if we do!" Shanoah yelled.

"Getting through won't matter!" the co-pilot screamed. "We'll die if we don't do the seismic-seven!"

"No!"

"The pulses are going to break us apart!" Lusa yelled. Her voice sounded as if she were yelling through the blades of a fan.

"Do a proton wash," Shanoah ordered. "Now! Now!"

The ship tumbled end-over-end so many times, Shanoah almost passed out, and then the spinning began. By the sixth rotation, she lost consciousness. The colors went insanely saturated and vibrant, then, in an echo of silence, went completely black.

FIFTY-FOUR

GRAYSWA CARESSED a handful of leaves as if he were kneading dough.

Adjoa watched him carefully. His technique for coaxing energy from plants was unlike any other Etheren. "Your expedition into the Far Future went well?" she asked.

"To convince a man to risk his life for a stranger is no simple thing."

"But it is possible, because inside each person is the seed of a hero," she said, brushing flower petals out of her long, gray, braided hair, which reached her waist.

Grayswa nodded. "A hero who would never understand, but had been made to do heroic deeds nonetheless."

"To save three strangers."

"More than that," Grayswa said. "To save us all."

"Let us hope . . . I am glad you returned safely." Her warm green eyes always soothed him. They had been friends for longer than Trynn had been alive. Grayswa relied on her companionship and counsel more than any other.

"The journey is far from over."

"Can we stop the war?" she asked.

His eyes filled with tears, but they did not fall.

She had her answer. "Then why do you still try?" Adjoa asked, always seeking to understand his wisdom.

"If we stop trying to prevent war, we become part of its creation."

RIP, Gale, and Cira arrived at the old church and found it open, but empty.

"We spend a lot of time in churches," Cira said.

"We go where the secrets are, and many of the secrets of the ancient world were held by the church," Rip replied.

"May I help you?" a priest, appearing from the transept, asked in French.

"We'd like to look around," Gale answered in English.

"I'm sorry, but that is not possible," he said, switching to English.

"We must insist," Rip said. Several Blaxers stepped up behind him to make the priest understand it was not a request.

"What is the meaning of this? Who are you?"

"Please take him to a car," Rip asked one of the Blaxers.

After the priest had been removed, Cira asked why they didn't let him stay. "He could have been helpful."

"If he'd planned on being helpful, he would have asked us *why* we wanted to look around before refusing us," Rip explained.

"I've got Alik," Gale said, holding up a tablet, showing the smiling face of the Russian hacker.

"Hey everyone, I see you made it to the church," Alik said. "But now what, right?"

"We could start taking it apart, brick by brick," Rip said, already scanning for an area that might conceal an Eysen.

"Not very practical." Alik laughed, not realizing Rip was serious. "I have some ideas, but first a quick review."

Rip rolled his eyes. He believed he knew more about Nostradamus than Alik ever could, and didn't have time for a history lesson. "Brief," Rip said. "Locke's men are probably close by."

"We're monitoring that," a Blaxer said, staring into a tablet. "We're good.

"That's what they told us on the island, just before the massacre," Rip muttered.

Gale gave him a *you're-being-rude* look.

"Please just keep it brief," Rip said again.

"Okay, first, it's important to know that Leonardo and Nostradamus were near contemporaries. Their lives overlapped sixteen years."

"There is no evidence they ever encountered each other," Rip said, checking the knave.

"Not directly," Alik said. "But there were people who intersected both the lives of Nostradamus and Leonardo."

"Okay," Rip said impatiently, now on his knees inspecting a section of the floor.

"After Nostradamus loses his wife and children to the plague, he decides to leave whatever town he was in and go looking for answers. He had been inspired by the work of Leonardo da Vinci, and he sought out followers of the great master." Alik, seeing Rip kneeling in a church, was about to jokingly ask Rip if he was praying, but decided to let the humor pass. "After a year or two, Nostradamus befriends people who eventually tell him of Leonardo's Eysen. He is, of course, fascinated, but questions the truth of their claim. Somehow, they end up convincing him with explanations of technology, and by other methods that are unclear."

"Where are you getting this information?" Rip asked, annoyed he hadn't been given it to review first, even though he hadn't exactly had the time to do so.

"It's a composite. Data obtained from Booker's Eysen archives," he said, speaking of the years of accumulated data retrieved and recorded from the Eysens. "The Eysen links, and papers Booker has acquired, which includes the secret journals of Nostradamus, and the lost quatrains, etcetera."

"The Eysen links are slowing the connections to the Cosegans," Rip said, as if it were a fact, although they all knew it was simply a theory. Rip and Savina both believed that part of the reason they had not heard from Crying Man, or one of his successors, was that Rip, Savina, and the rest of Booker's researchers were using too much of the Eysens "bandwidth."

"An argument for another day," Alik said. "You asked me to be brief, remember?"

"Go on then," Rip said, moving to the back of the church, where he whispered to a Blaxer to please check the outside.

"Nostradamus asked his new friends what had happened to the Eysen after Leonardo's death. Among the few who knew about it, there were mostly just rumors and hardly any clues. So, Nostradamus decided to go look for himself—and don't forget, this is *before* he becomes a famous seer. He begins his search based on the scraps of information he has picked up from them. For the next couple of years, he stays on the quest that will change history—not just ours, but that of the Cosegans."

"What did he find?" Cira asked excitedly.

Alik's face turned gravely serious. "The end times."

FIFTY-FIVE

JAXX LAUGHED.

"What's so funny?" Jarvo asked.

"The Arc thinks she can win."

"Of course she does," Jarvo said from where he stood before a map of the Cosegan borders. "Cosegans are the most arrogant people in history."

"Which history?" Jaxx asked.

Jarvo eyed him suspiciously. "All of them!"

"Thanks for the payment," Jaxx said. "I think there is little doubt her reign is about to end."

"One way or another," Jarvo said. "Are you trading in Far Future information?" Jarvo's main interest in the Far Future was his understanding on how it reflected and rippled back to the current time. For all his confidence in beating the Cosegans, there were certain things that worried him.

"What makes you ask something like that?" Jaxx asked, grinning as if the question amused him, maybe even flattered him.

"Just answer."

"I dabble in many things."

"Does your information come from the Eysen Maker?"

"Which one?"

"Don't trifle with me," Jarvo said, his expression turning sour. "There is only one Eysen Maker who matters."

"You mean Trynn," Jaxx said, unfazed by Jarvo's anger, but concerned with his interest in the Far Future. There were fortunes to be made in that area of trade and secrets, but it was an extremely dangerous situation to wade into, particularly with Jarvo, although Jaxx still wasn't sure if the Havlos leader understood just how the war would affect the Far Future and vice versa. "No, Trynn is too preoccupied to sell information, and how good can it be, anyway?"

"Why do you say that?"

"Trynn is actively trying to save the world, stopping the Doom and whatever else he thinks is for the betterment of humanity, by manipulating his many Far Future assets. There is no objectivity in him. He's also . . . well, suffice it to say that Trynn is a mess."

Jarvo nodded. "Yeah, that's for sure."

"So you have other sources?"

"I hear things."

"What of the Arc?"

"I told you, her time is short."

"And her successor?"

"His time is also short."

Jarvo's pinched expression turned to one of satisfaction. "Shank falls fast."

"He dies."

This surprised Jarvo.

"Does that upset you?" Jaxx asked.

"Hardly," Jarvo sneered. "I do not celebrate anyone's death, but there are those for whom I cannot weep."

SHANOAH HEARD A PULSING TONE, almost musical in its rhythm, and also like a heartbeat; a chiming bell, drumming, she couldn't tell *what* it was, but it brought her back to the ship. "What?" she yelled, trying to grasp where she was. For a moment, she was convinced it was a simulator and this was a drill. Then she realized the awful truth . . .

We're flinging through space, the Spectrum Belt, the Epic Seam . . . where are we?

Lusa was screaming, a loud moaning, panicked sound. When did that begin?

Shanoah got to her feet. The ship was still spinning, but much slower now. The colors were gone. Oxygen had been restored. Then she saw what Lusa saw and swallowed her own scream.

The ship was plummeting toward earth at a furious speed, nothing controllable, and soon it would be too late to stop the fiery descent.

Shanoah's mind flooded with questions, the most urgent being what time they were about to enter? Would it be the right day, hour, minute, second? She needed the answer, but the controls and readouts were all still distorted. None of it mattered anyway, not if they crashed, and they were about to.

"Flux generators," she yelled, but no one responded. Lusa had taken over for the co-pilot, still slumped in his seat. Shanoah ran to the controls and did the manual override herself.

"It's not working!" Lusa yelled.

"Too much velocity," Shanoah replied. "We're going too fast—it won't take the command because there won't be enough time."

"What about the draft-callers?"

Shanoah had forgotten that. "I'll try it." The craft was shaking. The internal systems were holding things together, but soon they would force a self-destruct to avoid a catastrophic landing that could change a Far Future outcome.

Two more crew members woke up and returned to their posts. "Forty-two seconds!" one of them yelled.

Shanoah knew that's how long they had before the self-destruct command would take full control.

"It'll be irreversible," he added in a pleading tone. They all knew the order would only come when there was not enough time to do anything else.

Forty-two seconds left to live, Shanoah repeated in her mind, but it was already down to thirty-four.

Thirty-two.

Drifson recovered and got to his mind crystals. "We're on target, correct trajectory!" It was exciting news, but only if they didn't die.

Twenty-seven.

"Can you twist the moments?" Shanoah asked, remembering a theory Stave had once put forward that in-between the time they came from and before actually involving in the Far Future, there was a chance to split time between the two "places."

Twenty-three.

"It's never been done," Drifson yelled.

Seventeen.

"Do it anyway!"

Fourteen.

Lusa shouted a complex equation to him.

"I've entered it."

Eleven.

Shanoah shifted the direction, hoping to skim the atmosphere to slow the clock.

Ten.

The warning sirens wailed.

Nine.

Eight.

"Come on!" Drifson yelled.

Seven.

Everything began vibrating.

Six.

The ship spun wildly.

Five.

Shanoah lost the controls.

Four.

Shanoah crawled to the screen.

Three.

Two.

One.

FIFTY-SIX

On a crisp afternoon, deep in the vast unnamed forest outside a small Etheren settlement, Grayswa instructed the apprentices in the purpose. "Because it is a crisis of existence, you may feel stress. You might be overtaken by the urgency, but be assured reality is waiting to be bent by the will of your mind, the intention of your heart. Events do not occur on their own. The world is made from neglect more than anything else, but it is designed to be directed by mindfulness."

"So we are meditating against war between Cosegans and Havloses, and monitoring Far Future events?" one of the more than a thousand assembled Etherens asked.

Grayswa's expression radiated patience. "We are creating peace. We are injecting love into the Far Future, a time when fear dominates the populace."

The old shaman left them to their work and walked a narrow trail with Adjoa.

"What about the shadow shifters?" she asked, once they were a sufficient distance from the gathering. Cosegans could hear three times further than modern humans, and Etherens heard considerably more than that.

"In process," Grayswa replied.

The shadow shifter was perhaps the Etherens' greatest power, and the ability was known to but a few. Grayswa, by far the most accomplished at this skill, had previously directed a shadow shifter in the Far Future to save Rip, Gale, and Cira from Varangians in Italy.

Through deep meditation and by gathering minuscule energetic markers across the eons, Etherens could create a person from the ethers—not a true biological human, but a mental projection of one, a shadow shifter. To those around them, it appeared as a real person able to speak and interact with others, even capable of physical activities such as driving vehicles or piloting planes, but the person was only as real as the imagination who'd created it.

Grayswa, or another creator, could see and hear what was happening in the Far Future through the shadow shifter. "Remember, the difficulty is maintaining a clear and pure mental state so as to not lose the shadow shifter," Grayswa told her. "It is increasingly difficult for me."

"Because of the distance in time?" she asked.

His face lit up as if this was a wonderful thought. "No, it is because I tire more easily now than I used to. There is much to consider and focus on around the Terminus Doom, the war cries, the sinking Far Future . . . "

"I understand."

"You must extend the next interlude with them."

"Am I ready?"

"No one is ready for what has become the Far Future."

TRYNN STOOD in the portside Eysen facility at Qwaterrun in Havlos lands, trying to get the misplaced sphere to the Pharaoh. "Because of Markol, everything is off its timeline. He's made a disaster of the Far Future," Trynn said, sifting through the scenes of what in the Far Future was referred to as ancient Egypt. "Who has the Eysen now?"

"It seems to be a group of merchants," Nassar replied. "It's difficult to ascertain their intentions."

"Do they have any idea what they have?"

"They have referred to it as the 'Eye of God.'"

"Sounds like they know," Trynn said. "Their knowledge could be both good and bad news."

"There is the possibility they are taking it to the Pharaoh."

"Could we be that lucky?"

"Not really," Nassar said. "Because even if we are right and they *are* heading toward Hatshepsut, it may not matter, because there's another group trying to stop them."

"Why?" Trynn asked, mind whirling through the tragic possibilities of two competing factions attempting to wrestle control of the Eysen before it got to its intended recipient.

Nassar moved some of the 3-D holographic images filling the room of a Million Futures. "This is two days ago in ancient Egypt," Nassar said, pointing at an image of three men meeting near a river. "They are talking about the Eysen."

Trynn looked confused. "But two days ago, the Eysen had not yet been unearthed in Egypt. How are they talking about it?" The tension in Trynn's voice revealed his panicked realization that they weren't simply dealing with a misplaced Eysen.

"They knew it was coming," Ovan said, appearing from behind an image of the men meeting. "And they knew approximately where it would be found. There's only one way they could've known these things."

"Markol," Trynn said, trying to contain his frustration.

"Worse than that," Ovan said, walking deeper into the room of a Million Futures, shifting scenes as he went, looking for something specific. "Much worse."

"What?" Trynn asked, the taste of one of the last bits of rationed Revon still on his tongue. Even before Ovan answered, he began putting it all together.

"Kalor Locke," Ovan said. "He somehow got the information to them thousands of years before his own birth."

"Kalor Locke is trying to get the Pharaoh's Eysen before the archaeologist, by manipulating its past."

"If he can prevent Hatshepsut from getting it in the first place," Nassar began, "then Locke decides where it will be left, so that he can find it."

"But he must realize that if the Pharaoh does not receive the Eysen, he will be changing all of history from that point. It will affect *both* directions, and the catastrophic consequences will be beyond calculation. We won't be able to fix it." Trynn jogged through the floating scenes of the Far Future, as if his urgency could somehow prevent the crisis from worsening. "This fool will unravel everything . . . is this not the origin of the Terminus Doom?"

"Kalor Locke is not a fool," Ovan said. "If he were, this would be much easier."

"We must get that sphere to the Pharaoh by whatever means available," Trynn said, weaving in and out of Far Future scenes. "If we don't stop Kalor Locke, there will be nothing left to stop."

FIFTY-SEVEN

Mairis knew that being Trynn's daughter meant she was always in danger. However, because of it, she also understood that everyone was in trouble. The Terminus Clock, if it was even reliable anymore, was down to only a few days.

She walked into the shadows of a strangely smoky end of a vast industrial area. *Like a forest of pipes and wires,* she thought. The place looked like a massive refinery from the Far Future, only more high tech, more height, and it didn't seem to stop expanding. The Havloses were particularly proud of their solar power industry. This "refinery" was operated by Enfii, the fourth largest Havlos energy firm.

Mairis was there to meet a guy named Abstract for a large delivery of Globotite, but Mudd was supposed to have been there already. Mairis was alone.

A few weeks ago, she never could have imagined coming to such a secluded edge of a vast, man-made landscape, the whole facility lit eerily by artificial light against the dark, starless night. But now, the world was near ending, and she had to do things—*anything*—to help find a way to reverse the death.

Mairis found it almost debilitating, and at the same time exhilarating, that she was involved in saving the world. *If I make a mistake, it can mean the end of humanity . . . It's like an endless game of survival. Am I ready to play? Who is the hunter? Who is the prey?*

"It's no game," an old, scratchy voice said from the darkness, and then added a long two-syllable, "Ye-ess."

"Yes, what?" Mairis asked, hardly breathing.

The old man stepped forward from behind a large wooden post that smelled of creosote. "Yes, I can read your mind." His voice sounded like metal scraping through the sandy bottom of a creek. "And hunted or prey is not the question."

"What is?" she asked, unaware she was backing up.

"Surrender or escape are the worries of the day."

"How can—"

"I'm not a Havlos," he interrupted "Not all who inhabit these lands are. Are you a Havlos? No you are not, and you are not an Etheren, yet you were raised by them in their villages, their forests."

"Who are . . . " She involuntarily looked behind her only to see shadows layered on blackness.

"The worries of the night are something else altogether, Mairis, daughter of Trynn and Carrin."

"How do—"

"In the space between the sun, we must wonder where are the fires, who are the liars, can the Imazes get any higher, what is it to which you aspire?"

"Are you—"

"Yes, I am Abstract."

"Do you have the delivery?" she asked, trying to sound braver than she felt, braver than she ever could be.

"Do you know the story of Little Red Riding Hood?" he asked in a gravely whisper.

She shook her head.

"This girl, who dressed in red, lived in the Far Future, and she one day visited her grandmother on a night not unlike this one. You do not know of her?" he asked again in a quiet yet excited voice, ready to impart a great secret.

"No."

"Strange, because you remind me of her, this girl wandering through the woods. She had a basket, did you know that? And in this basket was something valuable—not as valuable as we would find an air mineral, forbidden to be traded, but just as meaningful to the girl, and even more so to her grandmother. This rare commodity was . . . do you know, can you guess?"

"I have no idea. I'm not here for stories of the Far Future."

"Oh, yes. You. Are. Here. For. Just. Such. A. Story!" His voice had deepened with anger.

"Do you have the delivery or not?" she asked again, searching for any sign of Mudd in the darkness.

"Little Red Riding Hood carried in her basket the one thing that could protect her from the wolf. Did I mention the wolf?" he sounded calmer now, but her fear was apparent to them both. He paused only a moment before continuing without her answer. "The wolf, you see, was an important part of this event. The wolf was hungry. He wanted the contents of the basket and the only way to escape for the girl—hunted or prey, remember, you asked—was to use what she carried to escape, or would you have her surrender?"

"I'm leaving."

"No. You. Are. Not!" He moved closer, as if he was going to grab her, but he did not. Still, he was only inches from her face. She could smell fish and garlic on his warm breath, and felt the spit of his words on her face as he continued. "You are here for something you must have, Trynn is counting on you, and the only way to get it is to know what the girl was carrying through the woods to her grandmother's house."

"It's the Far Future, how would I know?"

"You do know. The Far Future runs through everything, there is no Far Future, there is no past, there is no now, there is only one thing—this moment. So what was the girl carrying?" His voice grew much louder. "What was the one thing that could save her?"

"I don't know. Time? Was it time?"

"No! It isn't time, why would time save her, we just established that time is only an illusion so we all don't go insane! Weren't you listening, were you even here for that part?"

"What is it then!?"

"*I* know the answer. Why would you ask me when I already know? It is *you* who must answer. The girl is about to die, the wolf will kill her, she will never escape the woods, never see her grandmother again, she will be dead in a moment, unless you save her, Mairis, what is in that basket?"

"I don't know!"

"You do, Mairis, you do," he hissed, as if he might be an evil sorcerer about to inflict a gruesome spell. "What is the one thing you cannot live without? What does the girl carry?"

"Love! She carries love!"

"Yes." Abstract smiled as he stepped back. "The girl carried love."

The air suddenly lit with lasers cutting through the darkness. Abstract fell to the ground.

FIFTY-EIGHT

THE COLORS SWIRLED in an infinite kaleidoscope. As the Imaze ships emerged erratically from the Belt, the crafts vibrated violently. "Horrible! It's horribly wrong!" Shanoah yelled, attempting to get a bearing on the other two ships. "All the meters and gauges are off!" The monitors only showed the insanity of colors. "Maicks, Sweed, are you out?" she shouted, a feeling of loss welling deep within her.

Garbled responses came back. Although indecipherable, it was enough to tell her they had survived, at least thus far.

"Continue on my bearing," she said before issuing a longer string of commands that came right out of the training and simulators they'd practiced and memorized for just such circumstances. Yet, as she completed the protocols, Shanoah knew this was something different; beyond even when she had lost her husband, and even more dangerous than the last seismic-seven, when the airless void took so many Imazes.

They'd avoided the galactic storm, the pulsers, and a range of other hazards in the Epic Seam, but now, approaching the

Oordan-field, she could already feel the electro pressure. "Something else is happening!"

The route had been proven. She checked the course. It all seemed correct, but even her copilot understood they were encountering something completely new.

"It's a vortex!" the co-pilot yelled.

"I see it! I see it!" A funneling black hole appeared, interlaced with the remnant colors of the Spectrum Belt's signal.

"We can't . . . The skim," the co-pilot was fighting the controls. "ACAL needs to be disabled!"

But Shanoah knew that the anti-collision algorithms built into the onboard AI might not come back up if they took it down before the time hop. "The system hasn't completed the pass through time!" She questioned her calculations. What had she led them into?

"Can we reverse?" the co-pilot pressed.

There were countless reasons why they could not. They'd never escape the pull of the vortex before getting crushed. The wrong angle and the ship would be destroyed, obliterated into a vaporized mass of molecules scattered across different eons. Then, of course, the failure would lead to the certainty of the Terminus Doom.

"Maicks! Sweed!"

Only Sweed responded, but it was as if she was talking backwards, a language Shanoah could not decipher.

"We *have* to take ACAL off!" the co-pilot shouted. "A collision in the vortex and the ships following will break apart."

She considered the order. "Not yet."

"We're going to lose our projection into the Far Future," the navigator warned. "Who knows where any of the ships will wind up, with damage that impacts inside the vortex."

It all raced through Shanoah's mind in an instant. "No!"

She tried to raise Sweed and Maicks again. This time there were clear words from Maicks.

"I can see the Stave," Maicks said, referring to Shanoah's ship, named for her late husband, "and the Conners," named for another lost Imaze captain. "Do you have visual on us?"

She looked at the other officers. No one could detect his ship, the Bullington. "We aren't seeing you yet."

"How can I see you and you not see me?"

"It must be a cassiam-bend," she said, but doubted that was it. "This should clear as soon as we get through."

"What is that?" Maicks asked.

She knew he meant the vortex. "The final passage," she answered, wondering if the word 'final' would have a good or bad meaning. She shouted additional commands, changes in their projections. A garbled response seemed like an acknowledgment from Sweed.

Lusa and Drifson were also on the bridge of the Stave, trying to interpret data and reestablishing projected times and crosses into the Far Future. "There's not enough room," Drifson announced. "This vortex has pushed everything."

"Not enough room for what?" Lusa said.

"I don't see how we'll be able to all arrive at the same time," Drifson said.

"How far off will we be?" Shanoah asked. The idea that only some of them would make it had not occurred to her. Until that moment, Shanoah had believed they would all live or die together, but there was a protocol for this as well.

"Seven or eight thousand years, give or take a century." The historian's answer shocked them all. "I could be a thousand years off, I'm still working on precise alignments, but we don't have enough parameters to narrow it." He kept talking, but Shanoah had stopped listening.

Thousands of years apart, she thought. The ramifications were astonishing. *I wish I could talk to Trynn.*

"If we do, in fact, arrive at different times," Lusa said, "that alone could precipitate the Doom."

"It's worse than that," Drifson said.

His voice brought Shanoah back and she wondered, *Worse than what?* Did he know what she was thinking? But, of course they, had to be thinking the same things.

The ship jolted as if they'd crashed into a planet, but nothing was there, nothing but the ever expanding vortex. The Stave shook violently as the vortex pulled them closer.

"What is that?" the co-pilot yelled.

No one heard him. The ship was filled with an overwhelmingly frightening noise—human voices. The reason the sound sickened each of them was the source of the voices. They were the words of the lost Imazes, transmissions of the dead echoing into oblivion.

"Could they still be in the vortex?" Shanoah asked, thinking of her long gone husband. She was glad no one heard her. She'd been there when he died. There were no survivors. The voices began to fade as the spinning around the vortex accelerated. "Worse than what?" Shanoah blurted out, realizing the historian had never finished.

"It doesn't look like we all get out of this," Drifson said, still frantically reviewing Eysen data projections. "And you're going to have to choose between the Bullington and the Conners."

"Choose?"

"Decide which crew lives and which dies in the vortex."

FIFTY-NINE

Blaxers burst into the church. "Varangians are two minutes out. We've got to go, now!"

"I'm not done searching," Rip yelled, frustrated that they were fleeing. "We can't leave this Eysen for Kalor Locke."

"We're *going*," one of the Blaxers said.

"Can't you defend this place, fight them off?" Rip argued, moving to another part of the church, checking the Apse, a semicircular vaulted recess located at the termination of the sanctuary end of the church.

"We're outnumbered."

"Again? Why can't Booker send more? Doesn't he understand what's happening? How close we are to *losing everything*?" He began looking at the base of the ornate altar. "We *have* to find this Eysen!"

"Rip!" Gale yelled. "Let's go!"

Rip glanced around, took a deep breath, made eye contact with Gale and Cira, then headed toward the door.

"Don't worry," Alik said from the tablet as they bolted away from the entrance. "The Eysen isn't in there."

Rip grabbed the tablet as they got into the back of a car. "Then where is it?"

"I don't know," Alik said. "But it's not at that church. I'll send you what I have, and maybe you can figure it out."

AS THEY DROVE through the French countryside, heading toward an airfield, Rip tried to make sense of all the new Nostradamus material while Gale called Savina.

"Nothing," Gale reported. "Straight to voicemail. I left a message and told her we're coming there."

"Okay," Rip said, hardly hearing her. "These pages from Nostradamus's journal are incredible."

"Any mention of the Eysen?"

"Just listen," Rip said, sounding more excited than he had in days. "Eventually Nostradamus winds up at an old monastery in Italy."

"Which one?" Gale asked.

Rip shrugged. "He doesn't say. We'll see if the AI can figure it out. There were tunnels underneath it filled with clay pots containing scrolls. He also describes old books and other writings being stored there. But here's the thing, when Nostradamus first arrived, the monks seemed astounded. They stared at him in reverence and awe, he writes that some were even fearful of him."

"Why?" Cira asked.

"They led him through a maze of tunnels and at the very end there was some sort of configured stone vault that they had made. The monks went through a long ceremonial process to open it, apparently for the first time in decades. And inside, what do you think they had?"

"An Eysen!" Cira yelled.

"That's right," Rip said, smiling at his daughter as if reading her a bedtime story. "They open it up and there's an Eysen. Nostradamus believes it is the legendary Leonardo Eysen."

"But it's not?" Gale asked, checking behind to see they weren't being followed.

"The monks explain to him that if they take it outside, it will light up, but they've never been able to see anything in it other than one image."

"What image?" Cira asked.

"They take the Eysen outside, and after almost a minute in the sunlight, it illuminates an image of a man's face with a long beard and intense eyes. It's Nostradamus."

"They knew," Cira said. "The Eysen knew. It was waiting for him."

"It's incredible," Rip said, always amazed by the Cosegans' ability to thread their way through time eleven million years after their own.

"What did he do?" Gale asked.

"Nostradamus stayed at the monastery for another year or so, studying the Eysen and figuring out how to get deeper and deeper into it, but he is still limited by something. And that's when this part of the journal ends."

"But he obviously figured it out."

"Sometime in the early 1550s, he began publishing and making predictions. He worked as an astrologer for wealthy people, and then in 1555 he published Les Prophéties, cementing his place in history. But there is much more to his story, including the lost quatrains, his secret journals, and private prophecies."

"It brings up a question," Gale interjected. "Since he was the first to share and publish information as predictions, the knowledge he obtained from an Eysen, did he change the outcome of the future?"

Rip nodded. "And did that create problems that plague the Cosegans and us to this day?"

"If you knew the world was going to experience a cataclysmic World War III in two weeks, wouldn't you act differently?" Gale said. "And if everyone did that, it could change the outcome. Maybe instead of a million survivors, there might be only a thousand, a hundred, none . . . "

"His quatrains predict multiple things—Hitler, Kennedy's assassination, 9/11, super volcanos, all kinds of events over the past four centuries—but there's another very troubling aspect to this," Rip said as they pulled up to a waiting corporate jet. "Since Nostradamus had an Eysen, that means his predictions were real."

"Oh no," Gale said, looking at Cira, already figuring out where Rip's thinking was going.

"What?" Cira asked, alarmed.

"Nostradamus could not see to the end of time, but he could see to the end of the world," Rip said quietly. "Nostradamus predicted the end of the world."

SIXTY

It was risky returning to the Cosegan territory, but Trynn needed Revon, and Dreemelle would only give it to him directly.

Need, he thought as he carefully moved through the trees, looking for the cabin where he was to meet her. *Need is too weak a word. If I don't get more Revon, all of it ends. History, the future, the here and now, it all vanishes from existence. What word can convey such drastic need, a word for that cannot be uttered or known, lest it would consume all it meant to define.*

This was the seventh time that Trynn had met Dreemelle. He kept track because each encounter with her was something of a life-altering event. She had a timeless beauty that belied her impossibly advanced age. Cosegans measured time, the length of one's life, and other things, differently than modern humans, who were obsessed with the linear. There was no way to convey her actual age, but she had certainly lived two to three times as long as he had. Yet she looked like a woman from a dream, or a dream herself, with eyes that mesmerized all in her presence.

An iridescent glow surrounded her at all times; an aura of sorts, fluctuating with her energy and mirroring the environment. Dreemelle always appeared calm and exuded a mystical wisdom. Trynn had described her to Shanoah as a woman of light, and that's how he thought of her, as if the radiant being had arrived in a sunbeam that would never diminish its magic.

She smiled when she saw him, the way someone does when being observed in adoration by a loved one. He steadied himself for the embrace, for Dreemelle always graced him with a hug so warm and all-encompassing that, for a moment, he felt as if he were a part of her light himself. This time, though, just before she held out her arms, he noticed the look of concern on her face. His gift of telepathy told him what she would never say—that she was worried about him, that he looked stressed beyond repair, that he was undertaking dangerous things, including the use of the herb that she would provide.

UPON SEEING HER, he thought of the words of the friend who had introduced him to Dreemelle. "There are two kinds of men in the world: those in love with Dreemelle, and those who haven't met her yet."

It was true. He'd fallen under her spell the moment he'd first laid eyes on her. But it wasn't something as primitive as lust for a vision of desire, it was more a longing for connection to the universal energy she seemed to embody.

"I need more," he whispered, suddenly finding it difficult to gather his thoughts.

"You are using too much."

"Do you realize what I am doing?"

"It is affecting you . . . isn't it?"

"I'm fine." He looked back through the trees, wondering how close the Guardians were.

She shook her head. "I told you to be careful, Trynn."

He gazed at her beauty as if seeing his first sunset over the ocean. It was difficult for him, or anyone, not to get lost in the aura of Dreemelle. He recalled all of her warnings, even from the first time they'd met, when she had told him, *"A powerful substance like Revon, as with all things in the universe, has an equally dangerous side. What it can give, it can take away."*

"How can I heed those warnings with so much at stake?" he asked.

"How can you not?"

The urgency he felt melted in the serenity of her presence. "I need more," he said again.

"Any more is suicide," she said. "Revon steals your mind bit by bit."

"That's just the price I have to pay," he said. "What good is my mind if there's no world left to use it in?"

"I don't pretend to know the details of what you do, but I understand what it is you are trying, and there must be a way that you can do it *without* Revon."

"There is no way," he said, sounding desperate and sick. "I'm not even sure I can do it *with* Revon." He looked over his shoulder again.

"There is no one coming," she said. "Not yet at least."

In some ways, Guardians were the smallest part of his worries. "Will you give me some?" He tried not to sound like an addict.

She stared at him, caressing him with her eyes. A look both mournful and hopeful.

"How much more time do I have before . . . " he began.

"Before the Revon turns on you?" she finished.

"Yes."

"It is hard to say. Revon is unpredictable, and it affects everyone differently. There are people whose minds have been erased, those that have gone mad, living in delusions, while others are only slightly crazy. And all of them have used less than you."

His hand trembled as he swallowed hard.

"You have a great mind. Your purpose is true. Perhaps Revon responds to such things and is giving you more time."

"It does that?"

"Yes." She smiled. It was as if the sun suddenly emerged from behind storm clouds.

"You're saying the herb, or whatever it is, has some kind of intelligence of its own?"

She nodded, her expression changing to something more like joy. "All things have an intelligence. Could you imagine it differently . . . how could it give that which it does not possess?"

Trynn had never considered that before. "Where does Revon get its power? How does it bring such clarity?"

"How does Globotite contain near infinite energy?"

He looked back through the trees, this time not in the direction from which he'd come. Instead, his eyes followed the thinning forest to the beyond. He couldn't hear the ocean, but he knew it was there, the vast waters that separated the Cosegans and Havloses.

His mind tried to fathom how it had come to this. Could something in the past have changed all that, the same as he was trying to do in the Far Future?

SIXTY-ONE

SAVINA MOVED FORWARD, imagining what those ancient Egyptians who built this place thousands of years earlier were thinking, intending, attempting to create. *Was it a place to honor their leaders, or was it a place to protect them in the afterlife? Or was it a hiding place? A place for the Eysen?*

"Thirty-five hundred years is a long time to hide something," she whispered as she came across a relief of hieroglyphics showing the female pharaoh holding what appeared to be a glowing beam from the sun. "That looks like an Eysen to me."

Savina studied the section of wall, and for the first time, wished Rip was there to help her interpret it. Archaeology was not her expertise. Then she realized her knowledge of physics could be applied. Several minutes later, with the batteries in her light nearly depleted, she found the connecting point in construction and traced it back to a seam next to the depiction of Hatshepsut and the sun. She counted the spaces representing stars in the constellation of Orion. Her fingers ended at a large eye.

"The eye of Ra," she breathed, what the Egyptians often referred to as the sun. A small circle, or sphere, was located under the eye. "A sun disc or . . . an Eysen."

She pressed it. The panel moved.

Savina gasped. "Incredible," she exclaimed, staring at the most beautiful thing she'd ever seen.

MAIRIS, unsure of where the laser attack was coming from, dove to the ground. *It has to be Cosegan Guardians,* she thought. *Havloses don't have lasers—at least I don't think so.* She also realized that her odds of escape were low.

"Abstract!" she yelled, crawling behind a large pipe elbow about the size of a fully grown oak. "Are you alive?"

"Take a lot more than a Guardian to kill me," he said, but it sounded like one long moan rather than separate words.

"I can't get to you," she said.

"Don't worry about me, Little Red Riding Hood, worry about the wolves."

Lasers zipped in from behind her. *Return fire,* she thought. *Maybe they aren't after me, maybe I'm just caught in the crossfire.*

"Mairis, over here!"

She turned and saw a figure, but couldn't make out who it was.

"Mairis, it's Mudd!" he yelled.

Staying as low as possible, she ran toward him. He'd secured a good strategic location in some sort of large intake vent. They were protected from above and behind. Grates allowed a view of the area while staying concealed. "How did we walk into this mess?" she hissed angrily.

"Nice to see you, too." He shoved her out of the way and fired. "Watch your back."

"Who are they?" she asked.

"Assassins," he said. "Most likely sent to kill you and your father."

"Me?"

"Anyone involved in the Eysen project."

"Why?" she asked, still surprised she had become a target of some sort of Cosegan hit squad.

"The Terminus Doom complicates everything."

"I'll say."

He fired and hit one of them.

"Good shot," she said. "I'm not sure I should be happy you just killed a man, but . . . "

"You want to survive."

"Yeah," she said, suddenly feeling overwhelmed. "What about Abstract?"

"Working on it." Lasers continued to light up the area.

"Where did you get that thing anyway?"

"Borrowed it from a friend."

"Does your friend have an escape plan?"

"The only escape plan is to kill all the rest of those Guardians."

"Are you going to be able to do that?"

"No, but *we* might be able to." He handed her the gun. "Keep shooting."

"Wait, *what*?"

Mudd crawled over to Abstract. Mairis fired off a few beams, her first time ever doing so. It wasn't so hard, there was no recoil or kickback of any kind on the weapon, but she wasn't hitting anyone.

Seconds later, she saw the silhouettes of Mudd helping Abstract over to the vent.

"Are you sure he didn't bring them?"

"Yeah," Mudd said, sticking something in Abstract's mouth. "He's one of the good guys."

"How do I know *you're* one of the good guys?"

Mudd glanced her way. "Because I'm in love with you."

She laughed, not really believing him. "That doesn't mean you're good."

"Doesn't mean I'm bad either." He leaned Abstract up against the metal wall, then ran off again.

"Where are you going?"

"Be right back," he said. "Keep shooting."

"Red Riding Hood," Abstract said, his voice sounding stronger.

"What?" Mairis replied, annoyed she was answering to that name and bothered that Mudd had disappeared.

"He really is a good guy," Abstract said. "And he probably does love you."

"Like I believe anything you say." She fired again.

Abstract smiled, although she couldn't see it. "Easy to be confused when you're young."

"I'm not confused."

"Okay, if you say so."

Mudd returned.

"Where'd you get those?" she asked, looking at two more laser guns in his arms.

"Same friend."

"Great, now all of us can shoot, but we're still wildly outnumbered. How are we supposed to get out of this?"

"We just need to hold them off until Enfii's security people get here," Abstract said. "Enfii is very particular about trespassers, especially the Cosegan kind." Abstract checked his wound, it was already healing.

"But Enfii's security forces probably won't take kindly to us either," Mairis said.

"We'll be gone by then," Abstract said. "Long gone."

An explosion behind the attacking Cosegans shook the area.

SIXTY-TWO

Trynn looked at Dreemelle as a drowned man thrown a life preserver. He was still trying to understand her explanations that Globotite was cosmic debris left over from the most recent big bang and trapped in Earth's atmosphere.

"It's finite," she'd said. "But there is more than we could ever use."

"And Revon?" he asked again.

"Even more complex. It's actually connected to Globotite in that it can't grow without it, but it draws its power from the universal consciousness. That is why the intention of the user is so important."

"So my good intentions may mean I won't suffer the next—"

"No, that is not possible," she said calmly. "If you continue to use, you *will* lose something. The universe will always maintain balance."

"But, I need it."

"Revon is a powerful substance. As you know, there is always a source to the power."

Some purple leaves floated by on the breeze. Others, in shades of blue, swirled, following them. "They are from the indigo tree," he said absently, thinking that it was one of the many trees and animals that would not still grace the earth in Rip's time. It made him sad and always led back to the question of what happens in the Missing-Time. The loss of so many beautiful creatures and plants seemed to have occurred in that period. Why?

"And, of course, all those plants and animals had their own unique intelligence," she said, voicing his thoughts. "If we think of existence as a single human body, you can only lose so much blood, have so many organs fail, not enough oxygen . . . having limbs severed . . . Even with our advanced health abilities, the person will eventually die. It is the same with existence." She looked at him, appearing suddenly like a glowing goddess. "We are all one. We must keep it together. Why do Indigo trees not exist eleven million years from now? When did we lose them, and why? They should be there. The intelligence was also needed. You want to save humanity while maintaining your mind? Use less Revon, and instead look into the Missing-Time and the absence of what we've lost."

He was silent for a long time, trying to absorb her advice and wisdom. But in the end, the need for Revon overwhelmed his mind.

"Please, I need more."

She handed him a bag, seemingly produced from thin air.

"Are you disappointed?" he asked, feeling ashamed.

Dreemelle shook her head. "The stars still shine, so perhaps . . . there is always hope."

Her words gave him more relief than he could believe.

"Now go, the Guardians are close."

He scanned in all directions, but saw nothing.

She motioned toward the sea.

He ran. Halfway to the cliffs, he heard them call his name, with an order to stop.

SAVINA STOOD TRANSFIXED as she beheld a stunning Eysen cradled in an oversized chalice. The gleaming gold reflected the glowing sphere. "How is it illuminating?" she questioned out loud. The muted space was sheltered in an ancient darkness. She quickly shined her light around, looking for another source of energy, even an opening—nothing. "It must be an Odeon chip." She inspected the orb closer. "It could be a different design," she murmured, admiring the fuchsia, amber, and cyan swirls emanating from the Eysen.

Searching her mind, Savina recalled the details of every previous discovery of Cosegan artifacts. None had ever been located that were "on" or "viewable" until they were exposed to a period of sunlight.

Is this different because of something the Pharaoh did, the sun god? Ancient Egypt holds many anomalies and mysteries . . .

A rumbling sound from above brought her attention back to the present. *The Varangians are still up there.* Savina reached out to take the Eysen off its stand. Holding the Eysen in that instant, she decided it was special, more so than the others, and more radiant, too. "You are a stunning one," she said, talking to it as if it were alive.

The glowing sphere suddenly vanished from her hands.

"What!?" she yelled, stunned by its instantaneous disappearance. Savina spun around, frantically searching for intruders who might have somehow taken the Eysen. She stood alone.

The cramped space, now much darker in the failing glow of

her flickering flashlight, was as empty as it had always been, except the golden holder remained.

What happened to it? Savina snatched the empty chalice. The weight of the solid gold artifact convinced her it was real, but there was no trace of the Pharaoh's Eysen. *It's as if it's slipped back in time,* she thought, still frantically searching.

More rumblings above told her it was time to leave. After one last look, she moved through the tiny room, deciding to explore further. Clinging tightly to the chalice, and lured by a desperate hope of finding the Eysen again, she pushed on.

Savina made it to the other wall before the ceiling collapsed on her.

SIXTY-THREE

Across an encrypted video call, Booker sounded more distressed than Rip had ever heard him. He relayed the news that they had lost track of Savina during a Varangian attack in Egypt.

"Why don't we have more Blaxers protecting the Eysens, us, and Savina?" Rip asked. "What could be more important?"

"Protecting the Eysens, and all of you, is far more complicated than you might think," Booker said. He looked off camera for a moment. "Our resources are spread thin all around the globe. We are in a war. Not just with those we've been fighting since the beginning—the elements of the Church, the NSA, the Foundation, and the rest of them—and not just against Kalor Locke and his Varangians."

"Then who?" Rip asked, wondering how it could possibly be worse.

"We are battling time itself," Booker said, now staring straight into the camera.

"Time is a funny thing," Rip said.

"It's not so funny anymore."

"What do you mean 'time itself'?" Gale asked.

"It seems that Crying Man has inserted so many Eysens into what they refer to as the Far Future, but what we call the present and recent history, that there has been a kind of merging."

"Merging?" Rip echoed, dread weighing in his stomach.

"Difficult to explain, but when something happens here, in our day, it also happens to the Cosegans, and vice versa."

Rip and Gale stared at their wealthy benefactor, trying to comprehend the ramifications of his words. "But the Cosegan's world is about to collapse."

Booker nodded. "And the concern before was that if they ceased to be, we might never have been, but that was all theory, and nothing was close to certain. However, now it is different. The Eysens, combined with other steps the Cosegans have taken to save themselves, have created a 'loop', for lack of a better explanation. As before, as again."

"What can we do?" Gale asked.

"I'm not sure, but I do know this. The Cosegans are entering a world war in their time, and that will certainly bring about the same here. The Final Divination—the ultimate and final war. Before that happens, we must obtain all the Eysens they inserted here, and we must stop Kalor Locke."

"What if he's already gotten the Pharaoh's Eysen?"

"I don't know if Savina is dead or alive, but Locke does *not* have that sphere yet. Alik has been monitoring, and we would know."

Gale looked at Rip with a horrified expression. He knew she was concerned about Savina, and appalled by Booker's apparent callousness about her fate.

"We have more information than Locke," Cira, sensing the tension, said. "Leonardo da Vinci left clues about where the Eysens are and about the Cosegans."

"I know, Cira, and I'll bet you can figure it all out." Booker smiled. "Alik is working on it too."

"Leonardo may be the key," Rip said.

Booker looked off camera again. An expression of concern filled his face. "I hope so," he said. "Meantime, get to Egypt and find that Eysen."

TRYNN LOOKED AHEAD to the cliff. He could hear the massive waves crashing on the rocks far below.

Trapped.

The bag of precious Revon safely tucked into a strapped pouch under his clothes, he ran closer to the edge, hoping the Arc wanted him alive. *Maybe there's a cave, a tunnel, a way out.*

"Trynn, this is your final warning," an unnaturally loud voice boomed.

I shouldn't have risked coming back for the Revon, he thought. *Did Dreemelle escape?* The salty wind whipped his cheeks, a slapping reality he didn't want to face. *Of course she did.*

"There is nowhere to go!" the voice said.

He's right, Trynn thought, now running sideways on a rocky outcropping at the end of the continent. The great ocean far below appeared angry, as if a vast cauldron of Doom . . . The Terminus Doom.

"Stop, or we'll shoot!"

For the first time, Trynn glanced back. There were so many Guardians, he couldn't count them all—more than fifty. *Are they just here for me, or are they expecting a Havlos invasion?*

It didn't matter. There were dozens of Guardians with screamer guns, infer-guns, and other Cosegan weapons of light, all aimed at him.

"Lasers are locked on!" the voice shouted. "Target will be obtained instantly."

Trynn, an engineer, knew how the technology worked. He scanned wildly, searching for help, an answer, somewhere to hide.

There was nowhere. The cliffs were too high, the enemy too numerous.

"Surrender now, or you'll be dead in a tenth of a second."

At the cliff's highest point, his back to the ocean, he finally stopped.

The end of the Eysen Maker? he wondered, in a strange moment of calm. *The calm before the fall.*

Then Trynn did the only thing left to do. He jumped.

SIXTY-FOUR

THE EXPLOSION at the Enfii energy facility set off a chain reaction of blasts. The whole area lit up like daylight.

"Did the Enfii security people do that?" Mairis asked, hopefully.

"No, I did that," Mudd said.

"How?"

"I came by earlier, made some preparations." He winked. "I always like to be prepared."

"We should leave," Abstract said. "Before something else explodes."

"If you knew this place was so dangerous, why did we meet here?" Mairis asked.

"Because the Globotite is here."

"Why?" Mairis asked, finding it difficult to believe that something so valuable would be kept somewhere like this.

"Enfii is part of a massive Globotite smuggling ring," Mudd said. "They use Enfii's wind power operations as a source for the rare air mineral."

"They're *mining* Globotite on a commercial scale?" she asked, shocked.

"More than a commercial scale. They're taking it on an industrial scale."

"Why?" Mairis asked, now scared. "Who's using that much Globotite?"

"I don't know," Mudd said, caught up by her concern. "I guess the identity of the user could matter to you and your father."

"Of course it does," she said, looking to Abstract for an answer.

"I have some suspicions," Abstract said, "but you don't want to know."

TRYNN HIT water far faster than he should have, and the rocky bottom greeted him much quicker than it should have in a brutal assault that he wished had killed him. Yet, in spite of the darkness, he knew he was still alive, as the pain was worse than anything he'd ever experienced.

As he surfaced, every part of him seemed either numb, throbbing, or on fire. With grueling effort, he rolled, startled by his own screams, and swam. He realized he wasn't in the ocean, but instead had landed in some kind of tidal pool, caught by a craggy ledge. *If I can get there . . .* he thought, struggling against his agony, trying to reach the underside of an overhang that would hide his presence from anyone looking over the cliff. *Made it!*

But he couldn't stay there. *They'll figure it out. They'll send FlyWatchers and Visuals. They'll be here any second!*

Trynn managed to use some Etheren training to compartmentalize the pain, but there was no time to begin the cellular healing. He dragged himself out of the water and crawled to an opening that led to another gap. He found himself in a small canyon that appeared to have been created by a seasonal waterfall, perhaps dry for at least a century. He climbed further down, suddenly noticing the darkening sky.

Nothing wreaks havoc with laser weapons like lightning, he thought. *Please let that storm come now!*

A few minutes later, Trynn got his wish. *Careful what you wish for.* The sky opened and the echo of thunder off the cliffs created the sounds of a Far Future war machine. The deafening booms were sandwiched by wild lightning, which looked to be splitting the sky open as streaks of electrified energy lit cracks through the air. He slipped and fell closer and closer to the churning ocean. *I've made it this far only to be smashed by the rocks,* he thought as the storm surge battered the cliffs, lapping at his legs.

Then he saw the Havlos boat.

JARVO GLANCED at the plans for a weapon system that he was confident would win him the war. "Everything is in place," he said to his deputy, Cass.

"You don't have to use it," she said, daring to test the limits of their relationship again. "You could inform the Arc, Shank, the whole Circle of what we have, what it will do, and ask them to surrender."

He laughed. "And ruin the surprise?"

"It is not a pleasant thing."

"Depends on your point of view."

"You are a brilliant man, Jarvo," she tried once again to reason. "You do not need to do things out of hatred and vengeance. Do them instead with wisdom and vision."

"There is not as much difference between vengeance and vision as you think," he said in a surprisingly caring tone, as if he wanted her approval. "We *have* to do this. I know you think it is a mistake, but as you said, I am brilliant . . . "

"Think about the warning. It would save a lot of lives."

"Perhaps millions."

"Yes."

"A warning would also give them time to defend," Jarvo replied callously.

"*Is* there a defense?"

"Not against a traitor."

SIXTY-FIVE

Jaxx waved to Trynn from the deck of the Havlos boat, as if he were out for a pleasure cruise.

Trynn didn't know whether to be happy or afraid, but Jaxx had saved him before, and the storm was only going to hold off the Guardians for so long.

Jaxx pointed to an overhang. The rocks and waves meant he couldn't get too close to the shore, and for Trynn to swim trough the treacherous surf would be suicide.

It was a difficult climb. Trynn slipped several times, almost falling into the stew. The rocks were sharp and wet, a horrible combination, but he continued to claw his way out onto the overhang. He clung there while Jaxx positioned the boat below. Trynn could barely handle the aches and strain inflicted from his last jump.

I've got to jump again, he thought, looking down at the hard deck of the boat. *That's not going to be a soft landing. And what if I miss!?* The raging waters and unforgiving rocks would beat him to death instantly.

It didn't matter, his numb fingers lost their grip on the slick surface. He closed his eyes and fell.

Jaxx shoved a cushion out just in time, making Trynn's landing more bearable. The Eysen Maker lay silently on the deck, trying to catch his breath, working on his cells before the damage inflicted by his ordeal overtook his ability to heal.

Rain poured harder, making Trynn feel as if he'd gone in the ocean. Everything was wet and cold. The waves tossed and tumbled the boat as it tried to move away from shore. Eventually, the hydro motors won and they were speeding out to sea.

"The storm may keep the Guardians from pursuing," Jaxx said, seemingly unbothered by the deluge of rain. "You okay?"

Trynn, still being pelted by the water coming from the sky as if being poured by the gods, had made enough healing progress to speak. "Who are you really?"

"I need a favor."

"What?" Trynn asked wearily.

"Jarvo has a weapon. I need to know what it is."

THE IMAZE LANDING, more like a crash, somehow ended with them upright and mostly intact.

"Contact the others," Shanoah ordered, even before checking on the health of her crew or the condition of the Stave.

The co-pilot was already attempting connections.

"Welcome to the Far Future," Drifson said, making it official—they had survived, arrived, and were alive.

"Did the others make it?" Shanoah shouted impatiently.

Lusa swiveled the holograms, searching. "Nothing yet."

"Come on!" Shanoah yelled, as if Sweed and Maicks could hear her.

"No sign of them on the scopes," the co-pilot reported.

"What happened to them?"

"I don't know yet," Lusa responded, sifting through an endless amount of three-dimensional data. "The plasmid interface isn't online."

"Get it up!"

"We're working on it."

"The Conners is safely down," Sweed's voice came across the system moments before her 3-D holographic body entered the bridge.

Shanoah wanted to hug her.

"What about the Bullington?" Sweed asked.

"Nothing yet," Shanoah replied.

The co-pilot shook his head. "They are not here."

"Any sign of where they might be?" Shanoah asked, already feeling guilty.

"They did get through," Drifson said, looking into a series of mind-crystal projected images.

"Where?" Shanoah asked, suddenly hopeful the mission could be saved.

"In a time before us."

"Oh no," she breathed.

"Which means..." Sweed began.

"Which means they could have left an impression, somehow gotten through to us. If that's true, we might find evidence."

"You mean of where they've been?" the copilot asked.

"Yes." She paused, then reasoned, "Well, it's a large planet, but it's definitely possible."

"Large planet," Lusa repeated. "However, we can scan and search for anomalies. I believe the Far Future archeologists call them 'out of place artifacts.'"

"First we have to find out if they're there," Shanoah said.

"Where?" Lusa asked.

"Exactly," Drifson said. "Wherever there is, and when it is."

The co-pilot was still scanning for any entry from Maicks, in case the historian was wrong. "No other entries detected, just the Stave and the Conners."

"How do we know the Bullington survived the vortex at all?" Shanoah asked, knowing it was very possible that Maicks' ship could have been caught in the compression pulse that closed behind them.

"They would've been trying to get in with us," the copilot said.

"Anything is possible out there," Lusa added.

"I don't want to try to guess what could've happened," Shanoah said. "I want to find them."

Drifson showed her images of etched discs.

"When is that?" she asked.

"It's almost ten thousand years prior to now."

"Ten thousand," she said, devastated. "At least they made it."

"And they left us a message," he said, studying the strange discs.

"Why would they do that?" the copilot asked. "They should've initiated the suicide protocol and never left a message that could be found."

"It was found in history instead," he said. "Well into the Far Future from now." He studied mind crystal projections further, then looked at Shanoah. "They appear to have been found around the time of the archaeologist's life."

She knew he meant Ripley Gaines, the man who had found an Eysen and communicated with Trynn. Shanoah closed her eyes and said a silent prayer to Trynn.

"Why didn't Maicks end it?" the co-pilot asked again. "He's

contaminated all of this and made it almost impossible for our mission to end in anything other than catastrophic failure."

Shanoah remembered Trynn's warning before they entered the belt. She thought he'd meant that they weren't going to make it, but he'd been trying to tell her that Maicks went to another time.

"What have we done?" she whispered, more scared than she'd ever been.

SIXTY-SIX

THE FACE of Nostradamus filled the back corner of the room of a Million Futures like a demon holding sway over a kingdom in the final days.

"I wasn't there," Nassar said, motioning to the 3-D apparition of the seer. "What happened? Why did the Nostradamus insertion go so wrong?"

Trynn, who had only just returned from Cosega and was still recovering from another near miss of being captured on the coast, thought of his promise to Jaxx, wondering how the war profiteer always seemed to find him. He fought the feeling that everything was spinning out of control.

Trynn turned and stared at his apprentice for a moment as if he might unleash all his anxiety and frustration by yelling at him. Instead, he took a deep breath, chewed a bit of fresh Revon, and recalled the Nostradamus fiasco. In light of the crisis with the Pharaoh's Eysen, Trynn knew he needed to avoid another calamity like the one that followed the Nostradamus insertion. *The Pharaoh's Eysen could be the final disaster,* Trynn thought, before he began telling Nassar the story. "The day of the Nostradamus insertion, everything went wrong."

"One of the reasons Nostradamus went so badly," Ovan said, joining the conversation, "was because I made a major miscalculation."

"You?" Nassar asked, surprised. "I didn't think you ever made mistakes."

"It is rare," Ovan said, with a hint of shame. "But this one was enough to count as thousands of errors."

"It wasn't all his fault," Trynn said. "Nostradamus was the first Eysen we inserted, but in the Far Future timeline, Leonardo found his Eysen first."

"See, that was my error," Ovan said. "They were too close in time."

"Nostradamus heard about Leonardo's. They knew people in common," Trynn continued. "So there were all kinds of conflicts and issues between the two Eysen effects."

"I remember the day Nostradamus found his Eysen," Ovan said. "We were watching, trying to do everything we could to prevent it."

"Why?" Nassar asked, checking on the Egypt situation.

"As you know with the Pharaoh, all our calculations are done based on the instant of discovery. If a recipient gets there early or late, everything falls apart."

"Because he knew about Leonardo's, Nostradamus went looking for an Eysen. He was early—very, very early. We stood at High-peak watching when a group of Monks first showed Nostradamus the Eysen."

"Trynn was screaming, 'No, no, no!'" Ovan said, recalling the moment. "But there was nothing we could do."

"Nostradamus was not supposed to find the Eysen for two more years," Trynn said, appearing as if he might be sick.

"That set off the beginnings of the calamities of the

Nostradamus insertion. The Circle lost faith in the Eysen project, in Trynn, in anything to do with the Far Future, really."

"Other than the Imazes," Nassar said.

"Yes, because the Imazes are hands-on. They can actually go there—*physically*. The Circle is more comfortable with that approach rather than just manipulating visions and projections across the ethers through the haze of millions of years," Ovan said, waving his arm toward the infinite views of the future.

"Why couldn't you turn it off?" Nassar asked.

"We didn't have the capability yet. It's why, in all the insertions after Nostradamus, we built more control into the Eysens," Trynn said. "As you know, we can now track each one when they are powered on, and we can turn them off. But when they're off, we have no idea where they are."

"But you could not remotely turn off the Nostradamus Eysen?" Nassar asked, trying to clarify the crucial point.

"No," Trynn said. "And that mistake belongs to me."

"Big mistake," Nassar blurted.

Trynn inclined his head a fraction. "One of my biggest."

Nassar wondered what could have been worse, but decided that conversation was better left for another time.

"We can still fix it," Ovan said. "But only if we get the Pharaoh's Eysen into the hands of Hatshepsut before either the archaeologist or Kalor Locke get hold of it."

"What happens if we don't?"

Neither Trynn nor Ovan responded. Both men just stared into the views of the Far Future as if searching for any trace of a remaining Cosegan society. Perhaps they were wondering if they had ever existed at all.

IN ANOTHER AREA of the room, blocked by views of all the Nostradamus drama and hundreds of floating images of Rip and Kalor Locke, was a window into the time of Hatshepsut. Seventeen men were battling to the death, using a newly developed weapon, the Khopesh. The bronze sword was cast in a sickle-like shape. Opposite its handle, the blade had a slight hook.

The skilled warriors fought on the banks of the Nile, the bloody rage occurring among fire, smoke, and a strange aura of energy. Those participating in the reckoning moved with an intensity that seemed to indicate the winners would decide the fate of the world—because they would.

Off to the side, where three men lay bleeding to death, a crate tipped on its side. It looked unimportant, as if it contained a common store of goods to trade. Instead, it housed the most incredible object these men had ever imagined, a magical piece of the stars, a gift from the gods, an Eysen.

SIXTY-SEVEN

The Mortuary Temple of Hatshepsut, a massive structure of limestone, sandstone, and granite, extended from the imposing cliffs of Deir el-Bahari, on the west side of the Nile. Somehow, Booker had gotten the entire site closed for several hours. He never did say how.

Rip, Gale, and Cira moved swiftly through the three grand terraces rising from the desert floor, weaving in and out of the seemingly endless columns that formed imposing lines at the top of a causeway that extended for thousands of feet.

"We should be searching for Savina," Gale said. "She was just a mile and a half from here."

"She'd rather us find the Eysen," Rip said.

"What if she already has it?"

Rip didn't know how to respond, but believed they would know if Savina had found the Pharaoh's Eysen. He continued to read hieroglyphics, looking for clues.

"Look at the Eysens in their art," Cira said, pointing to a statue of the female Pharaoh holding two round objects.

"That's something else," Rip explained. "It's showing Hatshepsut holding two round offering jars."

"Is it?" she asked skeptically, and then motioned to a glowing sphere depicted on the head of another noble person. "Some archeologist decided they were offering jars . . . but archaeologists make mistakes all the time, don't they, dad?"

"Everything in history looks different once you've seen an Eysen," Gale said.

Rip spotted what he'd been looking for, another clue. He suddenly realized Savina was probably already dead, and that soon they all might be joining her.

JAXX READ the projections from his strandband as if eating snacks, some salty, some sweet. Cosegans uprising against the Arc in almost every city, being put down by Guardians. Large Etheren demonstrations. Numerous Havlos incursions into Cosegan territory. Border skirmishes.

"It doesn't look pretty," he told his girlfriend.

"Are you making the mess worse?"

"If it'll help things," he said, grinning. Then a message came in from Trynn, and his smile faded. His expression twisted in full despair.

"What is it?" she asked, touching his face softly, a lover trying to ease his distress.

"If the Cosegans lose this war, the Terminus Doom is assured."

"The world's gone mad," she said.

"You have no idea how badly." He read Trynn's message again. "There is one last chance, but only if Jarvo trusts me."

"But no one trusts you, not even me."

He winked at her. "That's because you're smart enough to know better."

"Jarvo's smart. Much smarter than me."

"True, but he also has a weakness. He wants to win at any cost."

"It's the 'at any cost,' part that you're going to take advantage of, isn't it?"

"See how smart you are?"

ABSTRACT HELD his hands about an inch above a bright silver metallic plate embedded into the motored floor. Minor explosions still jarred the ground in sporadic blasts. Fires provided most of the illumination near them, but in the distance, powerful searchlights were scanning.

"We don't have much time," Mudd said. Laser battles were visible on both sides of them.

Without responding, Abstract continued concentrating on the plate.

"What's he doing?" Mairis asked.

"Globotite is hidden in there," Mudd said. "He's trying to open it."

Mairis watched the old man carefully. "He's an Etheren?" she said, confused.

"Yeah," Mudd said, impressed.

She pulled Mudd out of earshot from Abstract. "He's *Eastwood*!" she whispered through gritted teeth.

"Who?"

"Eastwood." She looked to the sky, suddenly realizing they were in trouble. "I've always heard stories about an Etheren who moved to Havlos lands more than twenty years ago, after he fell in love with a Havlos woman he'd met at the markets."

"So?"

"His name was Eastwood, but everyone calls him 'the man who left'. They say slowly, during all those years, he became corrupt." She looked over her shoulder to make sure he still couldn't hear them.

"So?"

"I mean corrupt like Far Future corrupt," she stressed. "He's dangerous, not to be trusted."

"Why?"

"He uses his Etheren abilities to mine Globotite for the highest bidder."

He looked back at her blankly. "Today that's us."

"It seems like it may cost us more than we bargained for." She looked off to the fires. "We've landed in the middle of a war."

"That's not his fault."

"How do you know?"

"We are in a war. Shank has sent a squad to secure the Globotite, and assassins after Trynn. The Arc has loyalists on the same trail, Jarvo has people following you, teams countering the Cosegan factions are here, and Enfii Security is not a trivial force. It's only been two years since the Havlos corporate wars ended when Jarvo brought together a diverse coalition of players unified against the Cosegans, and Enfii was one of the most powerful. We are in a war," he repeated, taking her hand and looking into her eyes. "But Abstract didn't start the war. He's the best chance we have of ending it. Trynn needs Globotite to do that, and Abstract is, by far, the biggest source I know."

"He's stealing it."

"So?"

"I am not stealing it," Abstract said, now standing behind her.

Mairis whirled around as if about to be attacked. "What's that?" she asked, pointing to two large pouches he was carrying.

"Globotite."

"All that?" she asked, stunned, then looked at the open plate that she knew he'd unlocked with his mind.

"I may have known Eastwood, could even be possible that I was him once, or I might have killed Eastwood a long time ago, but none of that matters now, sweetheart. My Havlos name is Abstract, and I'd consider it a personal gift, a sweet kindness, if that's what you'd call me."

Mairis tried to recall the stories about the man that left, but suddenly all she could think of was the large quantity of Globotite that he held in his hands. "Okay," she said. "Thank you, Abstract."

He met her eyes, smiled, and pushed the pouches to her.

"Thank you," she repeated.

"Now let's see if we can get out of here alive," Mudd said as the fires and lasers grew closer.

SIXTY-EIGHT

After a secondary explosion, an avalanche of desert earth pushed over Savina like a tsunami. The taste of grit and ancient air choked her in a suffocating cascade of terror. Her every focus on the Pharaoh's magical sphere, her every thought on the Cosegans who sent it, Savina had little care about her own safety.

In the turmoil of sand and debris, as she struggled to avoid a living burial, Savina lost the golden chalice. "Sand!" she screamed, as if the word were profanity. "Where is the Eysen!?"

Flailing her arms, digging, scratching, Savina didn't know if she was trying to find the chalice, the Eysen, or fighting to escape.

"I saw it! I *saw* it!" she shouted, trying to convince herself the Eysen had not been a mirage. In her fury and panic, she didn't realize how much earth had shifted. The explosions had caused multiple waves of seismic movement at the surface, opening chambers and making the entire area unstable.

I can't lose it! Unwilling to move, afraid to let go of the orientation of where the Eysen had been, she slipped in a fresh deluge of sand, and was swallowed by the desert. Instead of yelling for help, the last words out of her mouth, before it filled with dirt, were, "It was real!"

OVAN FOUND Trynn watching the scene, a pained expression on his face. "That's the physicist, the one that works with the archaeologist."

"Yes," Trynn said.

"What happened?"

"She found the Pharaoh's Eysen."

"Oh no." He quickly searched another view to see if the Eysen had made it to the Pharaoh yet. Once he confirmed Hatshepsut had still not received it, he checked the Terminus-Clock to see how much damage had been done by Savina reaching it first. "The Clock has hardly moved," he said, confused.

"I know," Trynn said, continuing to watch the sand and chaos around the site, Blaxers and Varangians fighting, Savina buried alive. "I took it from her."

"Took what from whom?"

"I took the Eysen from the physicist."

"You *what*?" Ovan began sifting through prior views. "How?"

"She was close. Too close."

Ovan watched Savina approach the room, the chalice holding the sphere as it had been left thousands of years earlier. The most protected of all Eysen inserts. "She was more than close," Ovan said, watching her every move. "She found it. She *held* it." He looked back at the Terminus Clock again, not believing there was any time left. "And you . . . "

"Took it from her," Trynn finished.

"How did you find it?" Ovan asked, knowing it had not been active for very long, they weren't even sure where it was.

"I noticed Kalor Locke's army engaging her security detail. It was in the general vicinity of where we suspected it had been secured. Locke's people were overly aggressive."

"He knew where it was," Ovan said.

"It appears so."

"We're in trouble, Trynn. Having to fight both now and in the Far Future—"

"I know. And it seems to be bleeding into the Missing-Time."

"It can't . . . "

Now Trynn looked at the Clock. "We'll know soon enough."

"But how did you take the Eysen?" Ovan asked, awed Trynn had achieved such a dramatic physical manipulation in the Far Future.

Trynn still tasted the extra dose of Revon he'd ingested, the most ever at one time. He tried to think of a way to explain it so Ovan's brilliant, but un-enhanced mind could understand it. "I did a series of shifts."

Ovan looked at him skeptically. "A series? How far back did you start?"

"Yesterday."

"You've been working on it since yesterday?"

"No, I mean I did the first shift here yesterday about our work on the placement."

Ovan appeared shocked. "And? How? You kept going into the Far Future? How many manipulations?"

Trynn shook his head.

"Thousands?" Ovan guessed.

"Millions."

Ovan's already aghast expression turned to concern. "How much Revon did you take?"

"Too much."

"You need to be careful."

Trynn let out a strained laugh, thought of Shanoah out in space, the Havlos war, Markol's rogue Eysen, and a hundred other tragic details of the Terminus Doom. "Careful? I don't even know what that means anymore."

SIXTY-NINE

Shanoah's crew and the crew of the Conners had spent hours offloading and concealing the ships. Lusa had used the same time to laser-etch a series of caves where the Imazes could be safe from any hostile "locals" that might be running around that section of ancient China.

Sweed and Shanoah walked alone, trailing a small party of Imaze scouts led by Drifson, as they tried to ascertain the details of their new reality.

"Back in the Belt," Sweed began as they crested a large hill. "Why did you save me?"

"As mission commander, it's my job."

"I know that. But you had a choice."

Shanoah stared into the distance, recalling the beautiful horrors they had come through, and questioning her every decision. *What if there'd been another way out?* Sweed's question confused her. "I did?"

"You had a choice between saving Maicks or me. You chose me. Why?"

"The choice was between the Bullington and the

Conners," she said, trying to make it seem less personal, if only to herself. Shanoah thought back to the terrible moment she'd had to decide the fate of Maicks and Sweed and perhaps all of humanity. The light was lost to the shadow. The scene played over in her mind as if it was happening again . . . They had just discovered that the trajectory and gravitational pulls of the three ships was throwing off the consistency of the time load, which meant they would all be crushed in the void.

"What will happen to the other one?" Shanoah had asked in a frantic voice not her own, while adjusting controls and watching the holographic digital alignment tracker projection gauges. "We must keep focused on the veesep, it's our only entry point! Keep us steady on that line!"

Lusa, struggling with the beams, barely looked up. "Whichever ship you let go will be spun into another time and most likely be trapped there."

Shanoah knew that was a death sentence. All Imazes were trained, and had taken an oath that if they were ever to get stuck in the Far Future, immediate suicide was required to avoid catastrophic damage. They'd been shown simulations, it had been drilled into them that even a few days beyond the mission would wreak havoc—weeks or months would do massive, irrevocable harm.

"You have to make the cut!" the co-pilot yelled.

More garbled communications came in from Sweed.

"Fourteen seconds before the first gap closes," Lusa reported.

"What if it's a set of false gaps?" Shanoah asked.

"Negative, checked."

Everything the Imazes did was precise, worked out to the nano. The location of the landing was exact down to the millimeter. Anything off those standards could trip events that would change forever. Shanoah thought of Trynn. Could he see this? Did he already know whether they lived or died?

All her training told her that pushing this far was irresponsible, yet they had to get through the pulse gap, or they could wind up at an entirely different landing spot—or worse, a different time. And that was *if* they made it through at all.

"Cut the Bullington!"

JARVO PREPARED for the final strike by lecturing his lieutenants, several of whom were once adversaries, about attack plans. His deputy, Cass, looked on, knowing it was too late to stop his horrible plan. She recalled him telling her last time she asked: *"I cannot simply decide to halt the strike because it is destiny."*

Cass listened as he pushed that same theme on his subordinates. "You do not have free will," Jarvo said to those gathered. "If a mind crystal, an Eysen, a rudimentary AI, even a person, knew all the variables that make you, you—the chemical composition of your body, how you were raised, the environment, how you slept, your health, what you ate that morning for breakfast, your education, every interaction you'd ever had with anyone, etcetera, etcetera, etcetera—then they could predict what you will do in any given situation. Therefore, no free will exists because you will do what all those variables together say you will—you must."

Cass inwardly smiled at all the confused expressions in the room. They had no idea that the supreme commander was talking only to her. Then he continued to outline the moments and days after the strike.

"We will own the Cosegans for all eternity."

Cass thought of Trynn and wondered if he could change

that outcome. *He's the only one who has a chance . . . if he survives.*

A FRIEND of Mudd's helped Mairis, Mudd, and Abstract through a maze of tunnels and buildings. When they finally reached safety on the outskirts of the massive facility, Mairis kissed Mudd.

"What's that for?"

"You saved my life."

"What about a kiss for old Abstract?" Abstract asked.

She shook her head, but flashed him a smile.

"I'm off," Mudd's friend said. "You're good from here."

"Yes," Mudd said. "I owe you one."

"More than one," the friend said. He slipped into the darkness and disappeared.

"We should move with haste," Abstract said. "There'll be patrols by soon."

"Why are so many people desperate for Globotite?" Mairis asked.

"There are Cosegans experimenting in the Far Past who need massive quantities of it," Abstract said. "But there are also rumors of a Havlos super weapon."

"A weapon based on Globotite?" Mairis asked, horrified.

"That's what I hear," he said as he, too, moved into the darkness. "Protect what I gave you. There may be no more."

SEVENTY

Markol wandered the corridors of High-peak as if trying to invoke the ghost of Trynn. His eyes were red, mind confused. The young Eysenist had tried everything to fix the Florida insertion.

"We're ready," an engineer said, finding him looking out a large underwater port into the ocean.

Markol had seen Huang floating among the fish, sharks occasionally taking bites from the decaying body of the man he'd killed, but never consuming enough to erase Huang's face from Markol's tired thoughts.

"I'm coming," he said, shaking off the illusion. "Any change on Florida?"

The man silently shook his head.

Markol was not surprised. Each attempt to improve the situation only continued to make things worse. He'd even tried to destroy the Eysen. The exercise had not only failed, it had also consumed a large reserve of Globotite used for relaying data between it and High-Peak. "What about the down-cycle?"

The man looked at him as if he were crazy. "The Globotite burn has left us with almost no control over the sphere."

"It shouldn't require more than an initiating code."

"We tried. It failed." The man pulled up a holographic image of the zone. "The Terminus Clock is plummeting again."

Markol swallowed his fear and hurried back to the Room of a Million Futures, checking his strandband along the way. Reading messages from the Arc, Shank, and a coded reverb from eleven million years in the future, Markol rubbed his stinging eyes. Kalor Locke had found a way to communicate, and he'd been hounding Markol for hours. "We have to stop the Florida Sphere from getting to HITE!" Markol barked.

"I know," the engineer said, surprised by the outburst. "That's what the new insertion is meant to do."

"How are our preparations looking?"

"It all depends on what happens with Trynn and Egypt."

Markol knew that, and he knew a lot more. It also depended on the Havloses, the Arc, Shank, Jarvo, the Imazes, every Eysen ever inserted, plus a few yet to come. *Nostradamus, and at least twenty other residents of the Far Future, will also impact whether or not the new insertion works,* Markol thought. It would be the most complex undertaking ever into the Far Future.

Success relies on so many things, but perhaps most of all, it depends on what I am about to do.

JENSO LOOKED over the defense plans for several of the cities she had designed. "It doesn't matter what kind of weapon these primitives have devised, nothing can penetrate our light and sound barriers."

Shank nodded. "Excellent."

"They are only confident in being able to defeat us because they are ignorant of our greatness."

"Yet they are making progress on our borders."

Jenso scowled, her dark face suddenly appearing aged at such a thought, but the radiance she was known for returned quickly. "They are mosquitoes. A small breeze will dispose of them."

"I'm not so sure." Shank rubbed the stubble on his chin. "What if they get inland?"

She pointed to the diagrams floating before them. "I told you, they cannot."

Shank continued to probe, wanting to be sure he understood how the Havloses could be stopped. "The Arc is not going to be able to handle this," Shank said. "We have to fight back against the Havloses. She refuses."

"We've called for the Circle to consider our resolution."

"But there still aren't enough votes to bring her down."

"As the Havloses make more incursions into the border areas, she will lose support," Jenso said, used to Shank's impatience on the subject of the Arc.

"There isn't enough time," he said, pointing to an image of the Terminus Clock projecting from his strandband.

"The Imazes must already be in the Far Future. Perhaps they will be able—"

"The reports aren't good," he said. "Moments ago, I was informed that the Imazes lost a ship."

"Oh no . . . Shanoah?"

"We don't know yet, but according to ISS, there was a catastrophic failure. One of the ships skipped into another time."

Jenso understood enough about the Far Future dynamic manipulation to know they were now facing an even greater crisis. She stole a glance at the still projecting Terminus

Clock, surprised it had any time left. "We must stop the war."

"I agree," Shank said. "Which is why it might be time to implement the counter-run."

Jenso twirled a finger in her long silver hair, as she always did when nervous. "Too risky."

The counter-run was Shank's plan to kidnap the Arc and blame it on the Etherens. Jenso was sickened by the idea, but even as she resisted again, she knew it was likely to be their final chance now that the Imaze mission was in peril. "Let's give it one more day."

"We don't *have* one more day!"

Jenso's gaze returned to the Clock. "What do you propose?" she asked reluctantly.

"Just before dawn, they'll take her."

Jenso was about to ask another question, but decided it would be better if she didn't know the details. "Leave me out of it."

"Of course," he said, suppressing a smile, knowing he would soon be rid of the Arc, and then the inevitability of him being in charge of the entire planet could no longer be denied.

SEVENTY-ONE

Trynn, immersed in the views of the runners in ancient Egypt trying to get the Eysen to the Pharaoh, searched for a gap, any moment in time where he could correct the spiral. "Egypt was supposed to be easy," he said to Ovan. "Thanks to Markol, it's turned into a nightmare."

"It appears Markol has been trying to make adjustments," Ovan replied. "It has not been going well for him."

"Not for any of us!"

Ovan understood Trynn's frustration as he watched the Eysen Maker flinging scenes of the Far Future into a merging kaleidoscopic flow of tense directions, changing outcomes and creating new beginnings at a pace impossible for anyone to follow.

"What's he doing?" Nassar asked with fearful eyes.

"Either saving the world, or making our humanity's final hours more colorful," Ovan replied.

"We're part of humanity," Nassar said, as if Ovan might not have been aware he was talking about *their* final hours as well.

"Yes, but hopefully not the last part."

Trynn could hear them talking behind him. He could hear everything with his Revon-ratcheted senses, but he ignored their trivial words. He was unwilling to risk even a single precious moment on anything other than his mission, which was ultimately to stop the Terminus Doom, but it all began with making sure the Pharaoh got her Eysen.

Ovan, seeing the patterns changing, told Nassar to recalculate the delivery factors.

After engaging a string of Mind Crystals, he reported that it was still unlikely the Pharaoh would get it in time. "One in three hundred thousand eighty-seven."

"That's within the target range," Ovan said, his optimism surprising Nassar.

"Where is the Pharaoh's Eysen now?" Trynn shouted, his voice amplified as if ten men were speaking in unison.

"The temple," Ovan replied.

Nassar pulled an area of air open, revealing a beautiful ancient city. "Waset," he said. "This is the key area of Hatshepsut's reign." A map, illuminating around them, showed Waset's location along the Nile River, five hundred miles south of the Mediterranean Sea. They had all studied the region and knew where the temple was, but that wasn't what Trynn meant. He didn't care where it was in Rip's time, at least not in that moment, he wanted to know where it was in Hatshepsut's time, where the runners were.

"The insertion!" Trynn's ten voices shouted, as if to clarify.

"Closer," Nassar said, suddenly amazed. "They are closer!" He and Ovan turned into the scene while Trynn kept moving millions of instances like an ocean wave rearranging the sands of an entire coastline in seconds.

"They're on a boat," Ovan said, equally stunned by the dramatic progress Trynn had made.

"Where's that coming from?" Nassar cried out, pointing at the boat carrying the Pharaoh's Eysen. "It's going to sink it!"

Ovan must have blinked, because he had no idea how the boat, seemingly alone on the great river, had suddenly become a raging inferno. "They're being attacked!"

A PATTERN in the hieroglyphics perfectly matched a similar set Rip had seen at the temple, and now he knew what they meant. "You may be right about those vases and the sun sign on their heads," he said to Cira. "They may be Eysens." He traced the images. "Kalor Locke and me, racing for the Eysens. See, one, two, three, four . . . "

"I see it!" she said. "And here, this shows a man stealing the stars."

Rip nodded.

"And this?" She pointed to what he had first seen. "What does . . . " Cira paused. "He's going to . . . " Her eyes filled with panic.

"It's a battle," Rip lied. "It depicts a coming war, an Eysen war." And he believed there was considerable truth to his statement, but glossed over the part of them dying first. There was only so much terror he could allow his daughter to endure.

Cira didn't miss it. "How could they have known?"

"Because the Pharaoh had an Eysen," Rip reminded her. He showed her images on his tablet. "Look at this."

Her confused expression made him smile even though he knew they were in mortal danger. "It looks exactly like a helicopter," Cira said.

"It's called the 'helicopter hieroglyph.' Egyptologists have come up with a variety of theories to try to explain it away, but it isn't an isolated example. There are numerous instances of futuristic depictions in ancient Egyptian art."

"How is that possible?" she asked, her expression now that of great concern.

"It means Kalor Locke is having influence."

"How?"

"He is in contact with someone in the Cosegans' time, and they are directing things in the future, our time, and our recent past, including ancient Egypt."

"A few thousand years ago is recent?" Cira said skeptically.

"Relative to eleven million, yes."

"Then he may know where the Pharaoh's Eysen is, because whoever's helping him knows where it is?"

Rip nodded. "We have to talk to Crying Man."

"What if Crying Man is the one helping Locke? Knowingly or unknowingly?"

"That might explain how and why the Cosegans killed Huang."

"And now maybe Savina?" she asked, sadly.

Rip was always amazed by his daughter's ability to deduce facts from so little information.

Gale suddenly screamed.

Rip and Cira pivoted, searching for her.

"Varangians!" Gale yelled, coming around the corner. "Run!"

SEVENTY-TWO

Shanoah stood on a narrow ridge, staring at the red morning sky. The night had been long, the air difficult. She had studied the phenomena of the time-breathing, but experiencing it was far more challenging than she had thought it would be. The concept would not even occur to Far Future scientists, who still believed time was some kind of linear construct. However, Einstein could have explained it, if he'd spent more time with an Eysen.

She scanned reports and predictive measures about the Bullington. The information, being projected via a 3-D holographic image into the heavy air—air she was having problems with, and caused her to recall one of the many courses she'd taken on the subject of time-breathing.

Each era of time, defined by a Cosegan formula, was obtained by calculating the continuous rotations around the sun, multiplied by the number of human inhabitants on the planet at any given time, overlaid by the occurrence of repeating patterns. Most eras were millions of years long. However, some could be much shorter. Time-breathing meant the air was different in each era. Although the molecular makeup of the oxygen would be little changed, there was something else that affected the lungs' interaction with it. The weight of human existence, their triumphs and tragedies, their love and war, truth and lies, all of it contributed to the quality of the air. Visiting from another time, multiple eras apart, meant that breathing would be challenging, as if they'd come from another planet instead of another time.

As she considered options for aborting the mission, Shanoah wondered if Maicks and the crew of the Bullington were breathing air of a different era, or was it still part of this one.

Would that affect our chances at a rescue?

Shanoah swallowed three air pills, one of the ways Imazes had devised to cope with the differences, another being the air-adjusters—a small, straw-like device placed in the mouth or against the nose that would transform the oxygen into Cosegan era quality.

"The cave is nearly complete," Lusa reported as she joined Shanoah on the ridge. They'd needed it to insulate themselves from the locals, several of whom they'd encountered shortly after landing.

"Good," Shanoah replied. "Any sign of the Bullington?"

"Time is vague," Lusa said. "We still can't pinpoint exactly when we arrived, and, as you know, that helps us determine what place and time they hit."

"We need to start the rounding," she said, as if resigned to maybe never knowing the fate of the Bullington.

Lusa looked at her. "It's too soon."

"We need to finish and get back."

"Back?" she asked, wondering if Shanoah meant to their time, or if she was going to try to get to Maicks.

"Yes," she said, not clarifying.

"The Bullington is lost," she said softy. "All hands should have already completed the suicide protocol. They are gone."

Shanoah shook her head. "They didn't do it."

Lusa grimaced and cursed Maicks.

"He must have had a reason."

"Yes, he's a coward," Lusa bit out.

"He is not."

"Somehow we have to cover their tracks."

Shanoah shook her head. "Too complex. We have to save them."

"Impossible."

"I know," Shanoah said, taking another air pill. "I know."

"Maicks could be what triggered the Terminus Doom . . ."

"I know," she said again. "But it's not his fault . . . it's mine."

GRAYSWA WATCHED through hazy dreams of a million lifetimes as his small army of conjured beings swept through the Egyptian temple, already ancient and not yet constructed. The old shaman steadied his hands against the drain of energy required to create ghost warriors and roam into times unknown. Wading through the quintillion breaths took a level of concentration and focus only obtained after centuries of meditation.

His missions had been successful several times before. He'd rescued Rip, Gale, and Cira from certain death in Italy weeks earlier, and had, since then, navigated them out of several other near misses. But this was, by far, the largest number of surrogates, and the most complex intervention Grayswa had endeavored.

"RIP, LOOK!" Gale yelled.

He followed her line of sight and saw Varangians fighting with what appeared to be monks. The cloaked opponents of Kalor Locke's high-tech bandits seemed able to dodge bullets and bend the light from the Varangians' laser weapons.

"Who are they?" he asked.

"No idea."

"Let's go!" Cira said.

They ran down another corridor. At the end, a single monk held up a hand and spoke in a hoarse whisper that seemed too quiet to hear, and yet it was as if no other sound existed.

"Don't let fear blind you to the answers you seek. Everything you desire is just beyond that fear."

TRYNN HAD, thus far, ignored the news that the Imazes had lost a ship and resisted the temptation to spend time and resources on trying to determine the fate of Maicks and the Bullington. He had seen it all in advance, but everything was in flux. It all could be different a hundred ways by now. Still, it was possible that Shanoah might have died after their landing. The odds were against her, but he couldn't turn away from Egypt to check.

When Ovan asked him about the Imaze mission, Trynn evaded. "My personal feelings cannot be allowed to interfere."

Nassar recalled Trynn had seemed more upset when he had learned that Markol had killed Huang than the news of Imaze's missing a ship. At the time, he'd said, "*The direct interference into the Far Future is too dangerous for a novice to undertake. He has no idea of the consequences.*" Nassar wondered if what Trynn was doing was more dangerous, and what about the Imazes? It all seemed in conflict with stability and continuity, but maybe those were unimportant. He'd also overheard private conversations between Trynn and Ovan about what some of the Etheren shamans might be doing. He figured Trynn was annoyed about Markol because it was another mess to clean up, but he was wrong. Markol was a much bigger problem than Nassar could ever imagine.

SEVENTY-THREE

Trynn wandered alone through the Room of a Million Futures, feeling empty and shaky. Colliding images, flames against rain, tyrants transposed with heroes, crumbling empires, triumphant armies, the Renaissance, space age America, nuclear weapons, the rise of AI, global pandemics, secrets and lies . . . he viewed it all through immortal eyes. At least his window into eternity gave him the sense of immortality.

Unable to find a solution, filled with frustration, Trynn took another Revon. "Why can't I see the connections?" he whispered—or yelled, it was impossible to know the difference amongst the avalanche of outcomes.

Eysen data streamed through faster than ever before, massive tectonic changes occurring each millisecond. Even fully dosed, he could not keep up. "I'm going to lose the Far Future," he said. "Where is the thread?"

The thread was an elusive line through to the Far Future which he theorized would unlock the blockages causing the Terminus Doom. As insurmountable as the Doom seemed, Trynn believed there was a relatively simple solution.

He continually scanned for any recognizable fragment of the Far Future, desperate to latch on to an original piece of history that would allow him to enter and assemble a new "cause point," a singular moment in time he could use to build a thread. Anything to regain control.

Increasingly, he saw only wars fought since the end of the Missing-Time. *Throughout modern human history, there is so much war . . . constant war. How did it get to that?* he wondered. *Don't they realize war is never against "someone else"? It is always against ourselves.* Trynn thought of the Havloses burgeoning conflict with the Cosegans and closed his eyes for a moment, contemplating the ramifications and far-reaching effects of the first war in his own time.

As he opened his eyes, he saw a nuclear explosion. "That's a new one," he said to himself. He had never seen a nuclear explosion in the Far Future before, because it hadn't taken place before.

"This is a result of our war," he said, voice heavy with dread. "The Doom is expanding, and it's my fault." Trynn felt himself melt into the nuclear eruption as if the toxic destruction created him and vice versa.

Shanoah, he thought. *Every breath the Imazes take in the Far Future means more changes, instantaneous, exponential . . .*

It was all swirling now, too much to keep track of. He reached into his pocket for another dose of Revon. He was already beyond the maximum amount, but it wasn't helping. *Too out of control.* He considered taking another half dose and, recalling Dreemelle's warnings, wondered if the effects would permanently damage his mind.

Another nuclear explosion detonated before his eyes, a major city in Europe gone, the fallout adding to the existing nuclear winter. He took another full dose of Revon.

The transformation was immediate. Clarity returned,

insight beyond what he had ever known washing over him. "I am saved," he cried with gratitude. "I can do this! It all is so clear!"

Tasting the answers, evaporating the hunger of despair, Trynn knew what to do, each step perfectly logical and outlined before him. The answers came with such precision, as fully formed concepts.

"There it is!" Even his voice sounded stronger. "The thread. I *see* the thread. It leads to the end of the Terminus Doom. It's so clear!"

Trynn began reaching into the scenes and adjusting them to achieve the exact pattern needed, reorganizing and tweaking his Eysen commands. "We've been so far off," he said, laughing. "And that one was completely backwards." He motioned to another screen. "Nassar, Ovan!" He called them, and the others, forgetting they weren't there. It didn't matter, Trynn knew he could fix it. He could do anything.

Trynn saw the Pharaoh, and the path to make sure she received her Eysen. "There," he said, moving more views of the Far Future, assisting the men moving the Eysen. Something blurred. "Wait." Invisible lines trailed off every movement. He couldn't see them, but he sure could *feel* them.

"Ow!" The force hit him like a hammer blow to his gut. Then another sent him to his knees. Trynn buckled. "I need to get the Pharaoh's Eysen to her!" His voice weakened, suddenly sounding like a man taking bullets. He recovered for a moment, found his feet, and ran to another part of the room. He adjusted more scenes in Egypt. "The clarity is so incredible." Another blow came into his midsection, then another hit his shoulder. He spun and stumbled. The hardest yet pummeled his head. Trynn went down fast, landing in a tangle heap of himself.

And then he saw Shanoah.

SEVENTY-FOUR

MARKOL LISTENED to the man who had opened a 3-D holographic conversation across the millions of years separating them, amazed by his knowledge of the Far Future, suddenly believing he had not erred at all with his insertion.

"You see, I was meant to have it," Kalor Locke told him. "I am the only hope."

Markol found the statement hard to argue with after seeing the results of all that Locke had already done. "Trynn believes it is the Archaeologist."

"Of course he does. His mistake is long and has skewed everything he has done. But *you* can clearly see that he can't find the solution because he is merely attempting to fit everything into his initial failure."

"I see that now," Markol said, the relief in his voice evident even to himself. *So much pressure removed . . .*

"It is my hope that the great Eysen Maker will one day be able to admit his mistakes and join us. We don't *absolutely* need him, but we could definitely *use* him."

"I'll talk to him," Markol said. "And what about Shank?"

Kalor Locke shook his head. "He is misguided."

"He will soon have all the power here."

"Never let yourself get caught up in another man's delusions."

"How do you know he won't succeed?"

Kalor Locke smiled, and then read off a long series of numbers.

"What's that?" Markol asked.

"Coordinates."

"Coordinates?" Markol asked, looking through time with a confused expression.

That made Locke's smile widen. "How do you Cosegans do anything without coordinates?"

Markol shook his head, still not understanding. "We use star lines and universal time parsings."

"I'm sure you do," Locke said. "But navigating the Eysen, using coordinates, is faster."

This time Markol smiled. "Maybe for Far Futurians like you." He let a mind crystal convert the coordinates, and then stopped smiling. "How does this happen?" Markol asked, stunned by the horrific image. "*When* does it happen?"

"That's the work of your friend."

He shook his head. "Shank could not have done this."

"He did. And it will give him short-term power, but obtaining anything by means such as those . . . well, surely you understand enough to know it will not last."

Markol took another look at the images. "We must stop it."

"Not possible." Locke held a finger over his lips. "However, if we can stop the Pharaoh from getting an Eysen, then many more things will be possible. And you can help."

Markol had the sudden realization that he had somehow gotten caught up in some kind of epic battle for the fate of humanity, and that, without understanding how, he'd become a pawn between the three big players.

He thought of Shank, and of Trynn, then he turned to Kalor Locke, the man he believed would prevail, and decided he would do whatever it took to make sure he did not.

OVAN FOUND the great Eysenist collapsed on the floor, a million futures swirling over him. No one knew how long he had been there, or how long he'd been out. It was hours until Trynn regained consciousness, hours more until he was coherent.

Mairis held his hand. She also made sure that all his ramblings were recorded, but little of it made sense. Babbling and outbursts about the Terminus Doom, occasional crying pleas for Shanoah, gibberish views he'd seen in the Eysens, in the million futures. The last thing he shouted before coming out of the Revon overdose coma was, "I know how to stop the Doom!"

But when he recovered, he couldn't remember any details, only that is was possible.

"No more Revon," Ovan said when Trynn returned to work.

"I just need to be more careful," he said, allocating the Globotite Mairis had brought in.

Ovan shook his head. "Next time, you might not wake up."

Trynn didn't respond, but had his own concerns. He could not recall things he knew he'd done prior to the overdose. It was as if holes existed in his memory, and they kept growing. Now, more than ever, Trynn realized there wasn't much time left.

Nassar burst into the room. "The archaeologist is about to find the Pharaoh's Eysen!" he yelled.

"Where is the Pharaoh?" Trynn asked, meaning how close were the runners to reaching her.

"We lost them," Ovan said. "Kalor Locke has found a great advantage. He sees all sides."

"How?"

"It could only be Markol."

"We'll deal with him later," Trynn said. "If Rip gets the Eysen first, Markol won't matter, and neither will Kalor Locke. All that will be left is the echo of humanity diminishing into quarks of space, forgotten before they ever existed."

SEVENTY-FIVE

SHANOAH LOOKED AT THE CALCULATIONS. They had been in Ancient China for more than a year, but only a day had transpired back in their Cosegan time. "I wonder if Trynn has seen this," she said to Sweed.

"I wonder if our people are still there," Sweed said.

"How can you say that? You saw the numbers, it's only been a day."

"We have no idea of the resulting calamity of Maicks not following the suicide protocol."

Shanoah thought about that for a moment. It weighed heavily on her every day. As the mission's commander, she would be blamed for the Maicks disaster when they got back —*if* they got back. "And yet we are still alive."

"Just because we've survived thus far, does not mean our world isn't coming apart. Whenever there's a blinding light, don't close your eyes."

Shanoah knew what she meant. The crisis was real, even if they couldn't see it yet. "We must prepare to leave."

"The journey will be more dangerous now."

"Of course."

"We should take back the glotons," Sweed said, referring to the photon glow light sticks they'd given the people they'd been protecting.

Shanoah shook her head. "They'll need them."

"It's a trace," Sweed said. "A violation."

Shanoah waved her arm dismissively. "They will dissipate long before they are a problem."

Sweed's skeptical expression made her position clear, although she did not argue.

"It is fifteen thousand years until these caves are discovered," Shanoah said. "Don't worry."

Sweed laughed.

"What's so funny?" Lusa said as she walked up.

"Nothing," Shanoah said. "Do you have a total?"

"We have them all," Lusa said. "Five hundred twenty-nine people. We didn't lose a single one. A successful mission."

"Except for losing a ship full of Imazes and contaminating the next fifteen thousand years," Sweed said sarcastically. "Yes, we did a *great* job."

"We were supposed to protect these people. We did," Shanoah said. "Now we must leave."

"What about Maicks?" Lusa asked.

Shanoah knew she meant the briefly debated idea of trying to reach him in the time he'd crashed. "No."

"It's probably the reason they didn't kill themselves," Sweed said. "Maicks is waiting for us to rescue him."

"I can't risk everyone else," Shanoah said, knowing that Maicks was almost certainly expecting a rescue, even though it violated every Imaze regulation. Even though she desperately wanted to save him. "We're going home."

RIP AND GALE EXCHANGED A GLANCE. When they turned back to the monk, he was gone.

"This way," Cira said, as if she'd seen the direction the monk had taken.

They found themselves in a large empty room with more hieroglyphs. "There it is again," Rip said, pointing to an image of Hatshepsut holding spheres. He stopped to study them.

"What about the Varangians?" Gale asked.

"The monk told us not to be afraid," Cira said.

"Where is the monk?" she asked. "Was he even real?"

"The translation of the Pharaoh's royal Horus name, Ma'at-ka-re, is 'the Goddess of Truth is the life force of the Sun God,'" Rip said. "The Eysen is the truth. The Eysen is the sun."

"They knew she had an Eysen," Cira said

Rip nodded. "And I think this indicates she first put the Eysen here at the Djeser-Djeseru. The name of the temple roughly translates to 'the most sacred of sacred.'"

"Then this is where she left the Eysen," Gale said. "So why is Savina at the Dazzling Aten?"

"Maybe someone found it and it was later taken there. It's only a mile and half from here." Rip looked around, as if he might see a secret slot for an Eysen. "It has to be here."

"What did you say?" Gale asked, brows creased thoughtfully.

Rip recalled that even the pyramids' sizes were related to the brightness of the Orion stars. Two of the pyramids were identical, but the third was half as high. The equation correlated to two of the stars being equally bright, and the third shining half as bright. "The Pharaoh's Eysen," he said. "It could have been moved more than once, but this is where it has to be."

"Why are you so sure?"

"The Varangians, the monks, *us* . . . why would we all be here if it wasn't?"

Gale smiled, always amused when Rip, such a staunch scientist, deferred to the mystical. "Destiny," she said.

Rip, still haunted by what Leonardo might have seen, knew there was not much time left to find the other Eysens and discover what had so greatly disturbed the great Renaissance man.

Then he saw the final clue. A shaft of light appeared from the long hall they'd come through. Rip tried, only for a moment, to recall from where it had originated. The temple's design was so precise that this light could only appear in the room once every year, possibly less frequently. Watching it climb the wall, he became oddly fearful.

He scanned the area, searching for Varangians, the Blaxers, or even the monks. They were alone in the most ancient of rooms. Suddenly, it filled with sand, as if a desert storm had found a way to penetrate the depths of the temple.

SEVENTY-SIX

TRYNN EXPENDED a vast amount of Globotite to shift events utilizing all prior Eysen inserts. Ovan continued to provide data on all recipients and those who inherited Eysens. Trynn risked more Revon, but kept under Dreemelle's limits. "Each moment matters," Trynn yelled to Nassar, who was now overseeing dozens of Eysen engineers. They worked to make minute adjustments through the happenings across the ages that the recipients could affect.

"We're close!" Ovan announced well into the night.

Trynn saw horses racing down long roads. Flames were everywhere. So many windows in the Room of a Million Futures were burning that they could almost feel the heat from the Far Future fires. Chariots burst out of the flames, thundering hoofbeats from the galloping beasts pulling them vibrated through the room. Pursued by Kalor Locke's brutes, the Pharaoh's loyalists fought from the rolling platforms, desperate to deliver the futuristic artifact and the future itself.

Trynn kept tweaking things, trying to figure it out, to *save* it. "We're making progress with the delivery," Nassar announced, "but the archaeologist is too far ahead. He's about to see it."

"Can't you move it, like you did with the woman?" Ovan asked.

"I'm *trying*," Trynn said. "Even if we had enough Globotite, I'd need more Revon."

"Someone else is interfering!" Nassar said. "Look!"

As soon as Trynn saw the sandstorm inside the temple, he knew it had to be the work of Grayswa. The power of it stunned him, but there was no time to marvel.

"The Pharaoh's guard has joined the fight!"

Trynn looked back at the temple where Rip was, and then again at the battle raging in the Pharaoh's time. "It will come down to one breath taken in a muted moment, at an unremarkable point somewhere across eleven million years, by an unknown person, who otherwise wouldn't matter . . . and that's the exact instant when the fate of humanity will be decided."

INSIDE THE TEMPLE, the sands subsided as quickly as they'd come. Rip called anxiously to Cira and Gale. Both were fine. *It's here!* he thought, trying to recall where the light had been. Running his hands over the wall, he found evidence of an old inscription, long since removed. "Damnato memoriae," he whispered.

"What?" Cira asked.

"The damnation of memory," Rip translated. "Twenty years after Hatshepsut's death, they chiseled her name away, destroyed statuary and images."

"Why?"

"It is unclear. Perhaps because she was a woman, or because her power and lineage threatened the future, but for whatever reason, they attempted to erase her memory from history."

"But we know about her now," Cira said. "So they failed."

"Yes," he agreed, looking on the wall for a place to press, a hidden lever, a secret button, a latch, *something*. But there was nothing. *Where had the light been?* Rip touched the spot and looked up. And then, slowly, he looked down.

It hadn't finished . . .

He mumbled something.

"What?" Gale asked, searching for the elusive spot that would open the wall as well.

"The light had not finished its movement. The sand obscured it." He pointed to the ceiling, which was decorated with a row of what looked like shiny beads. "It was going to hit there and then reflect back down to here," he said, kneeling quickly on the ground and beginning to rapidly clear sand and dust with his hands.

AT THE SAME MOMENT TRYNN, Ovan, and Nassar watched Rip about to uncover the Pharaoh's Eysen, they saw another event unfolding in ancient Egypt.

After dismissing her advisors and servants, alone in the double walled, open-aired courtyard of her palace, the Pharaoh stared at the wooden box for a long time. She did not know exactly what was contained within the blackened boards, but she knew how many had died to deliver it to her.

Hatshepsut had also had a dream about an ordained gift from Ra, the Egyptian sun god. She believed in dreams. Destiny was not an idea to her, rather it defined her life.

The Pharaoh paced in circles around the dangerous box, savoring the moment, somehow knowing that, in many respects, this was the end of her. That everything in her life would be measured in what had occurred *before* she opened the box and what happened *after*.

She had accomplished much in her years. In that part of the world, in that ancient time, there was no one more important than herself.

Hatshepsut sensed something about the gravity of the situation. She steadied herself, contemplating what she was about to uncover.

The lid, fitted with a series of metal hinges and flat double-clasps, appeared impossible to open. But she had a tool. She'd been given it by her father. He told her it was important, but she never knew why, or even what it did, until she saw the box and realized she had the key—a kind of key anyway. The flat piece of gold and some other metal had slots and a hooked end.

The Pharaoh sighed deeply and slid the tool under the metal straps. Inside, she found a stone sphere with etched rows of circles within circles that were interrupted by lines of two different lengths and columns of dashes. The surface of the "globe" had three evenly spaced gold bands running around the "equator." It seemed magical to her, the most beautiful object she had ever laid eyes on.

And then it fell open. Inside, the glowing orb instantly took her breath away.

RIP DUG and scraped until he was able to loosen the long-covered floor tile.

"Hurry," Cira said. "Someone's coming!"

He pried the tile out. "A handle!"

Gale helped him pull and twist until an ancient seal broke

free. "It feels like the first time!" Rip said as he slid the stone casing of the Pharaoh's Eysen from its hiding place.

"They're almost here!" Cira panicked.

Rip quickly checked to be sure the Eysen was inside the casing, and then, as he had years earlier in Virginia, wrapped it in a shirt and stuffed it in his pack.

"Time to go!"

SEVENTY-SEVEN

Tunssee glowed in the morning sun. The city, the Cosegans' fifth largest, had been designed by Jenso, and some considered it even more glorious than Solas because of its mountainous setting.

The morning was typical for that time of year; brisk, clear, a floral scent in the air, the mixture of hundreds of varieties of blooming plants. Tunssee was known as the "garden of Cosega." The glowing aura that surrounded every Cosegan city seemed slightly less vibrant, but that was hardly noticeable, and otherwise, it seemed typically beautiful.

In a society which had known peace for a hundred thousand years or more, recent skirmishes and hostilities between their neighbors on the other side of the world had unnerved the naturally optimistic energy of most cities. Yet those troubles seemed so far away from Tunssee. The majority of Cosegans still believed they were isolated from such unpleasant activities. The looming idea of an actual war paled against the impending Terminus Doom. Even to those who considered the two catastrophes linked, the prospect of a real war was almost as difficult to fathom as the imminent extinction event. War? Doom? Unlikely, regardless of logic.

In a health lounge, a man readied the morning elixirs. He prided himself on knowing the exact concoctions that his earliest customers preferred, specific to their taste and needs. Next door, one of the many galleries was set for a major opening of new Imaze art to correspond with the exciting mission Shanoah was leading. Even before their Terminus missions, the Imazes had been revered among the Cosegans. The advanced people had no religion, yet worshiped light in a peculiar way, particularly its source emanating from the stars, where the Imazes roamed.

Children worked on their mind crystals, studying hundreds of different subjects. Cosegan students toiled at graduate level, understanding at the same age Far Future children would have been in elementary school. Before they reached their teens, Cosegans could easily surpass knowledge of the brightest physicists and other scientists of Rip's time.

Everything was normal. The intricate, glorious light city was extraordinary to behold. A waterfall of light, its incredible array of colors and universal filters, created a place the stars themselves might have been dreamed into existence.

The idyllic morning was shattered by a flash so intense and violent it could have mimicked a stellar explosion, a supernova. For a terrifyingly long few moments, the luminosity of Tunssee seemed to increase millions of times.

An observer hundreds of miles away declared, "It was as if a runaway nuclear fusion had been triggered by some collapsing neutron star, and then a black hole. Tunssee was completely destroyed. Gone."

More than two million Cosegans died instantly as the city made of light and sound collapsed into itself, sending people plummeting to their ends. Excruciating sound waves did damage for more than a hundred miles, and could be heard nearly a thousand miles away. The catastrophic light explosions and hellish photon vortexes created multi-hued light storms with shards of laser-like lights cutting through anything in their path, igniting fires and blinding anyone who could have seen it too closely.

The average Cosegan felt the event as an internal blow even before they heard the news. The Etherens were more physically affected. "So much loss at once," Grayswa said. "The balance may take eons to regain."

Jarvo watched the event from high altitude cameras located far enough away in low-space orbit, positioned at precise angles in the atmosphere to withstand the event—yet several were still damaged.

"That was absolutely extraordinary and quite exciting," he said to Cass. "Don't you think so?"

Silence was her response.

"No, you wouldn't, would you? Well, *I* certainly do, and the Cosegans now know that the Havloses are not their inferiors."

"Do you really believe they will think that?" she asked.

"Of course," he replied, genuinely surprised. "This shows them."

"They will see it differently. Inflicting this kind of destruction is not the mark of a superior being."

"Oh, you believe they will see us as evil." He laughed. "The Cosegans know much about evil, and I am not it."

"Do you expect them to bow to you?"

"They will."

"They will *not*."

"Then they will know more misery. Tunssee will not be the final blow, but only the first strike."

SEVENTY-EIGHT

The Arc watched the images in absolute horror, feeling as if she were seeing one of Trynn's Far Future views. The scale of destruction was something Cosegans had not seen in thousands of generations, if ever. "It's as if twenty-first century people from the Far Future have come back to attack us," she muttered to herself. "Americans, Russians, Chinese, Germans, and all the other names they call themselves . . . " Her patience for them had long ago vanished.

The Arc checked the Terminus Clock, believing they must be only seconds from the Doom. Twenty-eight minutes. She felt its strangling like a slow brutal murderer in the darkness. The Doom had been closing in for so long that the killer's face now appeared so familiar, it could have been that of a lover.

A chime told her someone was approaching the entrance to her private quarters. She half expected it to be the Terminus Doom in the guise of a giant, grotesque monster. Yet experience told her it was more likely to be a squadron of Guardians sent by Shank, and other disloyal members of the Circle, with orders to arrest her for such outrageous dereliction of duty.

Then she saw the facial ID of a man whose trust she paid handsomely and regularly. The Arc gave the voice command to allow his entry.

"I assume we will be leaving Solas immediately," Weals said without any signs of emotions, worry, or shock that one would expect from a Cosegan, particularly one in the employ of the Arc after experiencing such an apocalyptic event.

"Yes, prepare a route."

"To where?" he asked with an undertone of impatience.

"Teason," she said, as if it should be obvious.

"The Etherens? Do you think that's wise?"

The Arc did not respond, nor did he expect her to. If Weals had stopped to think about it, it was the obvious choice—the *only* choice. The Arc would no longer be safe in any Cosegan cities, and since war would be raging with the Havloses, the neutral lands of the Etherens might be the last chance she had to escape with her life. "But will they have you?" he asked, not loud enough for her to hear.

The Arc brought up direct contact links with her most trusted lieutenant. "I'm relieved you are safe," the woman on the other end said.

"You know what to do," the Arc replied, alluding to a previously cloaked directive that had remained dormant, waiting for such a catastrophe as this.

"Of course," the lieutenant replied. "I will begin to move the mineral immediately."

"Thank you." The Arc wondered if there was still time to preserve the safety of the largest remaining stash of mined Globotite in existence. "I don't have to remind you what is at stake."

The woman also had an open view to the shocking photon void that was once Tunssee and its two million inhabitants. If she'd ever had any doubts as to the importance of the Arc's plans for the precious mineral, they would have been buried along with the Cosegans at Tunssee. "There should be no question as to my loyalty."

The Arc nodded. She believed her, but these were strange times. No one could be entirely trusted. "You know how dangerous your mission is, how careful you must be."

"I will not fail."

The Arc allowed a smile, one that conveyed no joy, merely satisfaction, perhaps a hint of appreciation, then signed off. Preparations had been made. There was nothing more she could do except escape herself.

The Arc had long maintained an emergency goeze on the roof of the Reach, and today, with crowds massing in the streets below, it was her only chance to break free. The Arc suspected Shank had prompted and arranged the rare demonstration of outrage against Cosegan leadership. She gazed out across Solas as she and Weals flew over the city, wondering if it might at any moment disintegrate beneath them. On-board monitors allowed her to watch the growing unrest surrounding the Reach. The Arc had never seen such anger and rage displayed by so many Cosegans, and had certainly never expected it to be directed at her.

"They'll be coming for you," Weals said. "Not just Shank's Guardians, but the mobs. They will blame you for the Doom, for the war, and now for Tunssee."

"I know," she said, looking back at Solas. "I died today."

SEVENTY-NINE

JENSO FOUND Shank in his office at the Great Hall, preparing for an emergency meeting of the Circle.

"How could you?"

"What?" he asked impatiently, wanting to tell her he didn't have time for one of her scenes. *I'm busy, doesn't she know I have a world to save!?*

"You know what!"

"Jenso, I don't read minds."

"But you read mine, didn't you. The Havloses could only have destroyed Tun—ssee," she choked on the word. "*You* fed them that! You gave them two million souls, to the barbarians, to the monster!"

"What are you talking about?" He looked past her to a Guardian, realizing she was going to have to be arrested.

"You got the defense codes from me and gave them to Jarvo! You let them in! You opened the door for them, you let the monster inside!"

"You're talking crazy."

"You're the crazy one! So drunk with power, blinded by

your hatred for the Arc, for Trynn, you have lost all sense—" She ran at him and landed two hard slaps across his face before the Guardians pulled her away. She spat in his face and clawed at the Guardians. "You killed them! You killed them all! How will you live with that—how will you sleep!?"

"I didn't know what would happen," he admitted. "Jarvo assured me they were only going to take the city. I needed that to rid us of the Arc once and for all. I knew we could easily win back Tunssee."

"Win it *back*?" Jenso screamed, still struggling against the Guardians. "There isn't anything *to* win back!"

"I know that now." He stared at her as if she were a child throwing a tantrum. "It was a mistake."

"More than two million Cosegans are dead! The city was *wiped off* the face of the earth! That's more than a mistake, that's an apocalypse!"

THE ARC KNEW there were only minutes remaining in her rule. "There is just time for a few more directives," she said, as she issued a coded command, effective immediately—the cancellation of all strandband monitoring of the "Trynn-five": Cardd, Julae, Prayta, Kavid, and Anjee.

Next, she ordered the immediate release of all Etherens who had been detained in recent months. All along, the Arc had made certain that those being held were treated more as guests than prisoners. She had never been in favor of rounding up Etherens. It had only been done because of political pressures and maneuverings to pacify Shank, Jenso, and their wing of the Circle.

She'd also made certain that there was always adequate

transport and loyal Guardians on stand-by who could evacuate the prisoners if need be.

The Arc may have never imagined a city like Tunssee being evaporated, but she had envisioned numerous other ways in which her power would end. With those final orders given, the Arc placed an encrypted video call to Markol at High-peak.

"We are in the countdown," she announced to the brilliant scientist with whom she had differed so much during their tumultuous forced relationship.

"Tunssee will not be the last city to fall," he said, acknowledging the desperate position they were now in.

The Arc shuddered at the thought. "Shank wants power for power's sake," she blurted out, knowing this was not entirely accurate, yet her statement did contain a certain amount of truth. She didn't like to admit that Shank was taking these dangerous and unprecedented actions because he believed his ideas were more likely to save the Cosegans, and all of humanity, than the course she'd been following. "The Terminus Clock has evaporated along with Tunssee. You can afford no more mistakes."

Markol thought of Huang.

"After Tunssee, he will be looking for you," the Arc added, speaking of Markol's former mentor. "And he will possess far more resources than before."

"He will be looking for *you* as well."

"You must not reveal yourself," she replied, ignoring his comment. "Markol, I'm counting on you to remain at your work and to keep the enders on board." She saw a reluctance on his face, but trusted in his intelligence, in what he had seen of the Far Future, what he had, in fact, contributed to the misery of it all.

"You have my word."

The Arc didn't trust Markol for three reasons–she still

wasn't sure if he held any allegiances to Shank, he had made a catastrophic error with his Eysen insert, but most of all, she had recently learned of his communications with a dangerous man from the Far Future named Kalor Locke. "Don't let me down," she said, knowing her waning power made her statement weaker than it might have been hours before.

He nodded.

That's when she saw the deception in his eyes. Only a flicker, but enough to know she needed to reach the one person who still held enough power to stop the conspiracy building against the Cosegans.

EIGHTY

"The Arc! Where is the Arc?" Shank yelled as he swept into the Great Hall. Nobody seemed to know the whereabouts of the most important Cosegan. There was rising concern that she had been killed by Havloses.

"Should we evacuate Solas?" a Circle member asked. "If they can do that to Tunssee, we may be next."

"The defenses will hold," Shank insisted. "But the Arc has failed us. I am ordering her arrest."

Welhey had not yet arrived, but all knew he would have objected the loudest. Even without him, several questioned Shank's unprecedented order.

Shank scoffed at the objections and launched into a well rehearsed rant. "She has been negligent, incompetent, and possibly even complicit with the enemy. Her desire to avoid war at every turn has cost *millions* of Cosegan lives, and left us dangerously unprepared to defend ourselves. The Arc's failed leadership, *along* with the Havlos aggression, has destroyed one of our great cities. *She* brought us this war!" He briefly surveyed the room, but continued before anyone else could speak. "Make no mistake, we *are* at war, and I am in charge. I am the Arc."

Now flanked by a dark force of Guardians, he silenced the murmurs. "The *former* Arc will be stripped of her title effective immediately, and known only by her given name, Kwana." Shank looked around the Circle and could tell several members were ready to voice their concerns. "In these dire times, emergency measures are needed," Shank said quickly. "Therefore, anyone who objects to my new orders will be considered in league with the traitor Kwana, and charged as an enemy sympathizer."

A man slipped quietly out of the room in hopes of intercepting his superior, Welhey. With Shank's voice still echoing through the vast space, the deputy was stopped in a corridor leading from the Great Hall.

"Where is Welhey?" she asked.

The deputy recognized her as an assistant to one of Welhey's allies on the Circle.

"I'm going to find him."

"Shank has ordered his arrest," she said.

"Then it is worse than I fear."

"You must flee."

"I have to get to Welhey," he said, running toward the exit.

"HOW ARE we going to defend against such a weapon?" one of the Members asked Shank as images of the complete destruction of Tunssee continued playing in the center of the room.

"I have ordered special units of the Guardians to conduct missions inside Havlos lands. Our people will disable their super weapon systems."

"How can we be so sure they will succeed?" another asked.

"In anticipation of the failure of Kwana to prevent such a catastrophic defeat, I have taken many measures. First and foremost is to bring back the Eysen Maker. We have evidence that Trynn has been assisting the Havloses, and certainly is responsible for the success of their super weapon system."

"Is this true?" one of them asked, shocked.

"They could not have made these technological leaps *without* the expertise of Trynn."

The few in the room who still supported or had loyalties to Trynn did not dare to speak, and even after such a horrific display of awesome power from the Havloses, they wondered if, somehow, Trynn had made a kind of horrible bargain with the Havloses.

"I repeat, we are now *at war,* and although war is unknown to Cosegans, I have seen this coming. I have studied and prepared," Shank said, walking through the center of the room. "For months, I've been telling you that Kwana was not competent to lead us in this time. Now you know I was right. She may have been fine during peace and prosperity, but as soon as the Terminus Doom appeared and real leadership was required, she faltered again and again and again, making wrong choices, backing Trynn, trying to placate the Havloses; she led us into the first war in the history of our long memory, and she has brought us to the brink of the Doom."

Some saw Shank's words as an obvious final attempt to justify his takeover. They remained silent as his rant continued for fear of arrest.

"Rather than help us," Shank said in a disgusted tone, "she has made everything *much* worse. We will be lucky to survive." He waved his hands toward the horrors of Tunssee. "Now, I must tend to the war plans and other commitments. I will reconvene with you later today."

Several of the members wanted to question *why* they were

not being consulted with plans or any other decisions, but with the presence of the dark force of Guardians and the arrest order against the former Arc, no one dared.

As he walked out of the room, Shank quietly said to Tracer, "You find me Markol. There is no greater priority."

Tracer looked at him questioningly. "The Arc—I mean Kwana, has also vanished before we were able to detain her."

Shank unleashed a furious expression. He had ordered her house arrest, and was looking forward to interrogating and humiliating her. "Markol is still the priority, but be sure that the former Arc does not get far. Use lethal force if necessary."

Tracer again looked at Shank, unsure, but replied with an affirmative, then asked, "What are you going to do now?"

"Remove every last Havlos from existence."

THE DEPUTY REACHED WELHEY, who was already packing, and warned him of Shank's intentions. "Where will we hide? Danger is everywhere."

However, minutes earlier, Welhey had received a message from the former Arc and already knew of Shank's coup. He looked at his trusted deputy and replied, "At the end of the world, there is no place left to hide."

EIGHTY-ONE

After breaking from Earth's atmosphere, Shanoah reported to ISS, and just prior to entering the Spectrum Belt, she contacted Trynn.

"How much time on the Clock?" she asked instead of saying and asking a million other things.

"Under three minutes," he said.

"How is that possible? We completed our mission. Could Maicks have caused . . . he skipped, landed in another time . . . didn't suicide. Have you seen any trace of him?"

"It's not Maicks. Didn't ISS tell you?"

"Tell me what?"

"The Havloses—"

Dread hit her like a physical blow. "The war really happened then?"

"Yes. It is worse than you can imagine."

She tried to understand what could have pushed the Clock to three minutes. Even after all her studies of the Far Future, war was such a difficult concept for her to understand. "What did it?"

"The Havloses obliterated Tunssee. More than two million dead."

Her eyes filled with tears, but she could find no words to respond to such gruesome news.

"You have to go back," Trynn said.

His strange statement surprised her. "What?"

"You have to go to another site in the Far Future."

"To find Maicks?"

"No," he said, knowing how difficult it would be to hear that. "Maicks is lost to time. You have to go back to save someone else."

"No, we're coming home."

Trynn looked at the Clock again, and then into the Room of a Million Futures. "There won't be anything to come back to. At least if you go, we'll have a chance."

"How good of a chance?"

"Not very, but something."

"Trynn, I want to come back home. I *need* to."

He shook his head sadly. "You can't come back. If you do, they won't let you leave again."

"I might be fine with that," she said, thinking of Maicks, dreading another trip through the Belt.

"Our best chance is in the Far Future, but there are those who want to destroy them. We *have* to protect them."

"Who could be so important?"

"There are millions of ways to destroy the world and end humanity," Trynn said. "Humans are experts at creating and finding those ways. However, there are only a few people who can figure out how to *save* the world. They are Cosegan descendants, and *those* are whom we must protect."

RIP, Gale, and Cira sat in the well-guarded facility, grateful to be alive. Blaxers had overcome the Varangians forces in Egypt, but only with the help of the mysterious monks—the monks who had come and gone without a trace.

During the airlift out of Egypt, they had flown over the area where Savina had been lost. "It looks like the desert has swallowed up the entire Dazzling Aten once again," Rip said as they viewed the destruction from above.

"Did they find her body?" Gale had asked.

"Not yet."

The Blaxers delivered Rip, Gale, Cira, and the Pharaoh's Eysen to a secret location on another island, one of the more than a thousand Booker owned. This one, somewhere off the coast of Indonesia, a country with more than eighteen thousand islands, was one of Booker's most well guarded.

Rip had never been there before, but one of the Blaxers told him its defenses were updated on a daily basis. "It can withstand attacks from air, sea, and space."

Sitting with the five Eysens, including the Pharaoh's, that they had yet to power on, it felt strange not to have Savina there with them.

"She would have wanted us to go on without her," Gale said.

"Savina knows all the answers now," Cira said. "Maybe she's even met Crying Man."

"How's my timing?" Booker said, interrupting the wake.

"Perfect, as always," Rip replied, holding out his hand.

"We've been waiting to start until you got here," Cira said.

Booker smiled. Cira had long been his special "granddaughter." He gave Rip and Gale a nod. "Well then, we better get started."

As the Pharaoh's Eysen began the familiar Sequence, Rip realized he was holding his breath and forced himself to slowly exhale. He looked up at the Tekfabriks above the courtyard. Booker had assured him that while it would allow in the sunlight the Eysens needed to charge, it would make them completely invisible from the air. He thought of the Varangian's attack on the island days earlier and wondered if they really were safer this time. Booker's presence both eased his mind and increased his worry.

"It's talking about the Terminus Doom," Gale said.

"The Cosegan's mastery of light, time, and space allowed them, for the first time, to see everything that existed across eternity."

"That's Savina's voice," Cira said. They all looked around, hoping she might somehow be there with them.

"How is her voice coming from the Eysen?" Gale asked.

"Maybe she really did meet Crying Man," Rip said, wondering if Crying Man was also dead. It had been so long since they'd heard anything from him. "Or, maybe she somehow programmed it in to one of the other Eysens and the Pharaoh's linked to it."

Savina's voice continued. "Eysens made it simple to access any point in time and to understand how each decision, action, or event, across all of history, past present and future, affected everything else."

"We know this already," Cira said.

Gale shushed her.

"The Cosegans discovered that we were heading toward complete destruction, and that the catalyst for this ending would occur sometime between the periods we refer to as 1950 and 2150."

"Why couldn't they pinpoint the exact date?" Rip wondered aloud.

As if she'd heard him, Savina's voice said, "The difficulty of narrowing it down to a singular event, or precise moment in time, is that everything is in constant flux. The challenge proved even more complex once Cosegans began to manipulate our time, which they know as 'the Far Future.'"

Savina's voice paused. Booker looked at Rip questioningly. Rip shrugged, unsure if it was over. A series of views projected from the Eysen, showing mostly world events from 1950 to the early 2020s.

"Demonstrated," Savina's voice began again. "The Cosegans discovered a scale to measure and qualify the end of the world."

Another pause, as if to give them time to grasp such an amazing statement. Then, the voice continued, "They labeled the end the Terminus Doom. Eventually, through complex, yet subtle, manipulations, Cosegans found they could slow or prevent the Doom. Unfortunately, they realized if they made the wrong adjustments, their interference could also hasten the Doom. So, the Terminus Doom isn't one apocalyptic thing, it is the understanding of the end . . . and the end begins now."

EIGHTY-TWO

The Room of a Million Futures lit an electric blue as culminations of times and events collided into a final crushing. The Terminus Clock counted down the final minutes to the Doom. Sounds intensified, making the normally quiet hum of the place more like thousands of distant chainsaws, a windstorm, whirls of ticking, the grinding of gears, moans and cries, all amplified by a pulsing drumming.

"What can we do in three minutes?" Nassar asked above the noise.

"There's only one thing left to do," Trynn said. "Use our remaining Globotite for something else."

"What?" Nassar asked urgently as the views blew and rotated with the wind.

"To contact Rip."

"END OF THE WORLD," Rip whispered, looking at his daughter. He glanced back at the Eysens, as if they must have an answer. One of them, the one they'd found in the wall, began illuminating. It showed the cave where Leonardo discovered his sphere. "It's showing us what Leonard saw in the cave!" Rip yelled, excited to finally be able to view what so disturbed the great master.

A stunningly exquisite Cosegan city of light filled the room: Tunssee. The projection's dimension and advanced technologies allowed them to wander through the magnificent city. They marveled at its glory, unable to fathom how such a place could be real, yet believing it to be.

Then an American city, New York at night, appeared. In a shimmering shift, as if a double exposure overlaid on Tunssee, both were fully visible. New York, dim and unremarkable compared to the great Cosegan metropolis, still held a certain beauty in its familiarity and energy.

"Why are we seeing this?" Cira asked.

Without warning, Tunssee imploded in a spectacular fury. At the same time, New York began to crumble.

"This is what Leonardo saw. Five hundred years ago, he saw the heights of human civilization, what we would achieve, the possibilities of his genius imagination realized. Then he saw it all lost."

"Is this happening *now*?" Cira yelped.

Booker checked his phone for news updates. "Not yet."

"But we don't know what's happening in the Cosega world," Gale said.

"We do, though," Rip said. "It's the same. It always seems like another world, but it's our world. If we are falling apart, so are they, and if they are dying . . ."

"LOOK!" Gale shouted.

They all watched Crying Man's avatar appear from the Pharaoh's Eysen.

Rip stared into Trynn's eyes and had no doubt that Crying Man was alive at that present moment. "We thought you were dead," he admitted quietly, ashamed they had given up on the one person who had never given up, the man who had given them everything. He looked over at Gale and knew what she was thinking. Ever since they'd first seen Crying Man, and came to understand that he was from eleven million years ago, but could still communicate with them, they'd had difficulty grasping the flexibility of time. Yet here he was once again, sharing wisdom from the ages.

"I almost was," Trynn said. "All of us almost were."

"The Terminus Doom?"

"Yes."

"Why didn't you contact us sooner?"

"There is a rare mineral which is the key energy source for the Eysens. It is in short supply here. We did not have enough, and even if I could risk a few grams of Globotite that would be required to have a conversation, there is evidence that any communication would throw off the course of events."

"Bring the Doom faster?"

"Yes. I had to trust that you would figure it out," Trynn said. "And you did."

Rip nodded, but was not sure how much he'd actually figured out yet.

"We heard Savina's voice," Cira said. "Is she still alive?"

Trynn shook his head, the guilt of what happened to her weighed on him. Not as Markol bore Huang's death, but a burden nonetheless. *A price,* he thought, *one of thousands of prices I will pay, the cost to save billions.*

Cira's eyes filled with tears.

"Death," Trynn began. "It is a part of every life, only the timing of it changes how we perceive its meaning. One life, a million lifetimes, understand?"

"Are we all about to die?" Cira asked.

"Everyone is always about to die," Trynn answered.

TRYNN USED the time difference between then and the Far Future to continue his plan. "Get the insertion done! Do it now!" he yelled to his team, making sure his words did not transmit to Rip.

Nassar looked at the Terminus Clock, wondering why they were bothering, but then realized it had not moved.

"The Clock is stopped!" he yelled, as if this was news to Trynn.

"It hasn't stopped, it's just slowed down."

Nassar checked again. It still appeared not to have moved. "Then it's slowed down *a lot*."

"Just finish the insertion!"

As Nassar turned away from the Clock, something caught his eye. He turned back. "It's under two minutes. So it *is* moving."

"Go!"

Ovan was waiting for Nassar.

"How is the Clock moving so slow?" Nassar asked him.

"Trynn found a glitch. A trick, really. The Doom is not just in our time, it's in the Far Future as well. By opening up all the Eysens on both ends, it momentarily halts time by pulling it in both directions at once."

"Incredible, but how long can it work?'

"Until the Globotite runs out and we lose the connection," Ovan explained.

Nassar checked the gauges. "That's only a few more minutes!"

"That's why we have to get this inserted. Saint Malachy is our only hope to get the course righted."

"WE KNOW WHAT'S HAPPENING," Rip said. "The end of everything, us, you—"

"And all that has occurred before and after you," Trynn finished.

"What you call the Terminus Doom."

"Yes, it is upon us."

"How much time do we have left?"

Trynn shook his head. "A few minutes."

Rip looked at Cira and Gale. "There must be a way to—"

"We want to try something, but even if it works, it will only buy us a little more time. Hours at most."

"What do we do?" Rip asked.

"Major earthquakes in Los Angeles and San Francisco!" Booker reported. "New York City is in flames. At least twenty-two plane crashes have occurred in the last few minutes!"

"It has begun there," Trynn said.

"Tell me what to do," Rip repeated.

"How many Odeon chips do you have?"

"Four," Booker replied.

"Good." Trynn looked into the Million Futures as view after view collapsed in a hurricane of destruction. "Take the Chips and instead of putting them under the Eysens, put them *between* each sphere."

"What will that do?" Rip asked as he took the Chips from Booker and began inserting them between the Eysens.

"It will maximize the Globotite and create an infinite loop. The effect will magnify our abilities beyond the force of a hundred suns."

"Then what?"

"Then . . . we look into the Missing-Time."

EIGHTY-THREE

Kwana, the former Arc, slipped into the woods, having walked the last few miles to avoid patrols on the roads. Aware that she might not be able to stay with the Etherens for an extended time, she hoped that her long-guarded secret was safe, that Shank would assume the Etherens would never shelter the woman who had arrested so many of them.

Grayswa emerged from a thick stand of StarWatcher trees, as if he'd been expecting her.

"Are you well?" she asked him.

He nodded.

"The end has come," she said, as if ashamed.

"I know."

"I have nowhere else to go."

"There are many places one can seek safety . . . this is the right place for you at this time."

"It has been such a long time," she said. "I'm sorry about that."

He nodded again.

She felt like she could see the centuries she'd missed in his old eyes. "I don't wish to bring harm to you or your people."

"*Our* people," Grayswa corrected. "You are one of us."

She nodded, embraced him, and then did something she had never done as Arc. She cried. Kwana held her brother and sobbed into his shoulder.

THE FIVE EYSENS began to rotate as the Odeon chips levitated between them. At first, the spheres moved slowly, like a basketball being spun on the tip of a player's finger. However, soon they were going so fast, each appeared as a blur.

"There have been five spheres inserted thus far," Trynn told them. "We are inserting another right now, and there are indications we will need three more after that."

"Nine," Rip said, confirming the number.

The Eysens spinning in unison produced a sound similar to that of a jet engine, except as a musical score, a thunderous classical composition. Loud and beautiful, but dangerous. *Beautifully dangerous.*

"Each insertion gives us more opportunities to make changes," Trynn said, sounding calm and surrounded by silence, when the opposite was actually occurring. The Room of a Million Futures was rocking with exploding images and excruciating sounds. *This must be a taste of what it is like to travel through the Spectrum Belt.* He thought of Shanoah. "And each one makes it exponentially difficult to control the prior Eysens. In some part of the Far Future, there are ten spheres creating absolute chaos."

"You said only nine."

"There is another," Trynn said, his tone foreboding.

"Markol, the man who killed Huang, is working with our opponents. He inserted one."

"Where is it?"

"Kalor Locke."

A chill traced up Rip's spine. "What can we do?"

"We know everything that's happening in our time, the Cosegan time," Trynn said. "We also know all about your time, the Far Future. What we *don't* know, and therefore where the answer must lie, is what is transpiring in the Missing-Time."

"What does that mean?"

"The answer is *in* the Missing-Time," he repeated.

The space became unrecognizable. The five Eysens vanished. Booker, Gale, and Cira all aged in some forced videographer's trick and died in front of him. Rip's anguished cries cut through the noise as a silent crack across a frozen lake. It ended in a painful silence, and in that eerie quiet, he realized he, too, was gone.

"What's happened!?" he screamed. His pleas did nothing except restart the deafening sounds.

Visions enveloped him. Magnificent and horrible places he could never describe. He felt split into a million little pieces, his imagination blown apart, senses lost to an agony of emptiness, filled to overflowing with bits of forever.

RIP WOKE ON THE FLOOR, screaming. It felt like he was sinking in sounds, buried underground, lost in a dream, drowning.

Cira's voice broke through it all. She was screaming, too. And Gale. They were alive. He heard Booker's agonized voice. They'd all made it. Clarity returned a few moments later.

"You won't believe what I saw," Rip said.

"It was awesome!" Cira said.

"I don't know how to . . . " Gale began.

"I saw it, too." Booker struggled to his feet. "Almost an hour went by," he said, checking his phone. "No more planes have crashed. The destruction has stopped. It seems we did . . . something . . . "

"I don't know what," Rip said. "We had minutes an hour ago. How are we still here?" He wondered if they really *were* still "here." After all, he had watched them all die.

Trynn appeared again. Behind him, the Terminus Clock ran backwards, adding minutes, then hours.

"Did we fix it?" Rip shouted. "Do we go on?"

"We just bought more time," Trynn said, staring into the Million Futures. A muted calmness had returned to the Room.

"How much time?" Gale asked.

Trynn shook his head. "I don't know."

"Now what?" Rip asked.

"Get the tenth sphere."

"What will that do?"

"Lead us into the Missing-Time."

"Didn't we just go into the Missing-Time?" Booker asked, feeling exhausted.

"No," Trynn said. "You didn't make it in."

"Then what was *that*?" Booker asked, astonished.

"That was you just approaching the entrance to the Missing-Time."

"How do you know the tenth sphere will get us in?"

"Because Kalor Locke has the tenth sphere," Trynn said simply.

"So?"

"Kalor Locke has seen inside the Missing-Time. He knows what it holds."

"Surely he'll try to stop the Doom," Rip said.

"He'll use it to bend the Far Future and our time into something else, something he can control," Trynn said. "Kalor Locke is no normal man. He has seen eternity, breathed its secrets, tasted the unbridled force of it. Don't you understand? It's *everything,* and he knows how to take it."

"Can we really stop him?" Rip asked.

"We must." Trynn looked again into the million futures and caught a glimpse of Shanoah. "It is our last chance."

END

of book six

To be notified of future Cosega releases
Sign up here or follow me on Amazon here
The next installment

coming next

Cosega Shock

Book Seven of the Cosega Sequence

GLOSSARY

Airsliders – Jet-propelled scooters equipped with laser munitions.
Annjee – Government scientist, old friend of Trynn.
Avery – Caretaker at Old North Church in Boston.
Blaxers – Booker Lipton's private army of operatives.
Blox – Ability to stop myree, an ancient form of telepathy practiced by Etherens and some others.
Booker Lipton — World's wealthiest man. Rip's sponsor. Searching for Eysens and related artifacts.
Brite lite birds – Type of bird that glowed like fireflies, with colored feathers that instantly burned flesh on contact. Staring at too many at once could lead to temporary blindness.
Camsoen – Etheren settlement.
Cardd – Trynn's assistant.
Change-point – Moment in time when an unknown event changed the trajectory of Cosegan civilization from advancing to even higher enlightenment and technological wonders to

that of a primitive reset that became humanity eleven million years later.

Chief – Head of guardians

Cira – Rip and Gale's daughter.

Clastier – An early recipient of an Eysen.

Cloud sweeper – Bird with gray and white coloring and thirty-foot wingspan.

Cosegans – Rip and Gale's name for the people and society that existed on earth eleven million years ago.

Crying Man – Rip and Gale's name for Trynn.

Draycam – Cosegan wanted for a horrible crime, he had been entertaining the thought of killing the Arc and over throwing the entire Circle.

Dream Senders – Etherens who had deepened their meditative and myree talents to the point where they could send thoughts into the dreams and, in certain cases, meditative minds of people in the far future.

Dreemelle – Provider of Revon.

Earliests – Cosegans term for their ancestors.

Enders – Highly classified subgroup of the predictive league. They studied all aspects of alternate insertions.

Enfii energy – Major Havlos energy and mining company.

Epic-seam – Space-time tear located inside the spectrum belt that allows the Imazes to travel to the far-future and back.

Eternal Falls – Three thousand foot waterfall, one of the natural wonders of the Cosegan world.

Etherens – Part of the Cosegan population who practiced deep meditation, lived with nature and mined globotite and other natural minerals and herbs.

Eysen – A basket-ball sized sphere which contained a complete record of all existence. Named for an ancient word meaning, "to hold all the stars in your hand."

Eysenist – Another name for Eysen makers, scientists who create and study Eysens.
Far Future – Cosegan term for period of time when modern humans such as the Egyptians, Leonardo da Vinci and Rip and Gale live.
Finebeale trees – Type of tree in Cosegan time.
Flores – Bush that produced lemon-sized wild berry that tasted like chocolate and custard.
Flyers – Guardians wearing jet packs
FlyWatcher – Self-propelled flying camera with 360 degree view.
Fray – Imaze member on mission flight with Shanoah.
Globotite – Rare air mineral required in Eysen making and insertions.
Glotons – Photon glow light sticks used by Imazes.
Goeze – Triangular vehicles of light that enlarge depending on the number of passengers and payload can fly or drive. Sometimes called "light energy vehicle," or LEV.
Grayswa – Etheren elder, the oldest living shaman.
Guardians – Cosegan security force.
Guin – Trynn's late wife, mother of Mairis.
Havloses – People on the other side of Earth during Cosegan time.
Health-lounges – Cosegan social gathering spot where natural juices and infused mineral waters are served.
HI MEMS – Hybrid Insect Micro-Electro-Mechanical System. Weapons created by implanting into insects during the larva stage - possessed by Both Havloses and Varangians.
High-peak – Trynn's secret lab.
Historics - Holographic pop ups which display the history or facts of a subject, person, or place.

HITE – Hidden Information and Technology Exchange, the covert technology handler for the US government.
Huang – Colleague of Rip's and brilliant Eysen researcher.
Imazes – Part of Cosegan population who live and work in space. They attempt flights to the far future.
Infer-gun – Laser weapon capable of inflicting death or merely stunning depending on the setting.
Insertion – Act of placing Eysens into the far future.
ISS – Imaze Space Summit on a high and massive plateau.
Jenso – Woman who helped design the Cosegan light cities, and Circle member, sometimes called "the moon mystic."
Joefyeser – Etheren globerunner.
Julae – Etheren globerunner.
Kalor Locke — A deadly rival of Booker's and the Foundation for Eysens. He used to run a secret government agency.
Kavid – Etheren, Prayta's friend.
Kaynor system — Section of the universe near the spectrum belt.
Killtrons – Havlos killer robots. Killtronics, or Killtrons, for short, were lethal, highly-acrobatic killing machines with AI-assisted operating systems which can be controlled from a faraway base, and also have the capability to act autonomously.
Light woman – Dreemelle, provider of Revon.
LightShaping – Cosegan method of manipulating various forms of light for manufacturing and construction.
Lumen Tower – Location of Markol's lab in Solas.
MAHEM – Laser-sighted Magneto Hydrodynamic Explosive Munition possessed by both Havloses and Varangians.
Mairis – Trynn's daughter.
Malachy – Saint Malachy an early recipient of an Eysen.
Mind-crystals – Cosegan computers (a million times more advanced than PCs and Macs.

Missing-Time – Period between the end of Cosegan time and beginning of modern human history.
Mistwave Forest – Coastal forest around High-peak.
Myree – Ability to read thoughts and in some cases communicate through minds.
Naperton – Small Cosegan coastal town.
Nashunite – Mineral required in Eysen making.
Nogoff trees – Type of tree in Cosegan time.
Nostradamus – Sixteenth century seer.
NSA – The US National Security Agency.
Nystals – Havlos naval base.
Oordan-field – Area of space, sometimes considered part of the spectrum belt.
Ovan – Old scientist who does equations to help decide who gets Eysens in the far future.
Prayta – Etheren woman who supplies Trynn minerals.
Predictive League – Affiliation of thousands of Cosegan scientists researching the Far future and Eysen effects.
Pulsers – Colored asteroid-like energy masses that can threaten ships in or near the spectrum belt.
Quatrains – Prophecies written by Nostradamus.
Qwaterrun – Havlos port city where Trynn had set up the new Eysen facilities.
Revon – Cosegan herb that, at the risk of serious side effects, substantially increases cognitive performance.
Roemers – Giant butterflies with three foot wingspan.
Room of a Million Futures –Vast space as part of an Eysen research facility that displays countless holographic projections showing ever-changing views into the Far Future.
Salvator Mundi – Painting by Leonardo da Vinci, depicting Jesus Christ.
Savina – Colleague of Rip's and brilliant Eysen researcher.

Screamer gun – Lethal laser rifle, named for the loud sound it made when fired.
Scopes – Goggles that deciphers light.
Seismic-seven – Imaze desperate technique to "reboot" ship during spectrum bombardment.
Sennogleyne – Mineral required in Eysen making.
Seven Sections – The division of lands among Havlos populations.
Shank – Powerful Circle member.
Shanoah – Imaze commander – Trynn's girlfriend.
Sinwind – An outlying Cosegan settlement. Where Trynn was to meet Dreemelle.
Skyways – Moving, floating and ever changing sidewalks, also skyway energy project Trynn had been leading.
Slights – Places in Cosega cities where light and surveillance does not reach.
Sodew – Herbal infused mineral water.
Solas – Largest Cosegan city and also the Capitol.
Spartan – Varangians laser rifle
Spectrum belt – Section of space that must be crossed to reach the Epic-seam.
Spressen – Warm herbal drink favored by Cosegans.
StarToucher trees – A type of tree in Cosegan time that grow to five hundred feet tall.
Stave – Imaze and Shanoah's late husband.
Strandband – Cosegan command center worn on wrist that can access and project continuous stream of data.
Suicide protocol – Imaze oath and final directive - in case an Image is stuck in the Far Future, immediate suicide is required.
Teakki trees – Type of tree in Cosegan time.

Teason – Etheren settlement where Grayswa, Julae, Prayta, Kavid and Mairis reside.

Tekfabrik – Multipurpose nano-fabric capable of changing color, size, and texture. Self-cleaning.

Terminus clock – Linked algorithm displaying the time remaining until the Terminus Doom destroys humanity.

Terminus Doom – Mysterious prophesied end of humanity.

The Arc – Leader of Cosegans, one of the oldest women.

The blind – Cousin of a black hole, a place in space where communications and electronics fail.

The Bullington – Image ship piloted by Maicks.

The Circle – Cosegan council of elders. The leaders of the Cosegan society.

The Conners – Image ship piloted by Sweed.

The Enders – Subgroup of the predictive league. Enders studied all aspects of alternate insertions, and sought to establish other avenues to utilize the Eysens in anti-Doom efforts, and defeat the end times.

The Foundation – The Aylantik Foundation is a secretive organization with seemingly unlimited funding, employing futurists, scientists, engineers, economists, as well as former members of the military and intelligence communities.

The Reach – A 3000 foot building of light and sound. Tallest occupied building in Solas.

The Stave – Image ship piloted by Shanoah, named for her late husband.

Time-breathing – Issue of coping with changes in quality of air between eras affected by the weight of human existence, their triumphs and tragedies, their love and war, truth and lies.

Tracer – Field unit leader of the guardians. Second in command under the Chief.

Trynn — Also known as "Crying Man." He is the most important Eysen Maker. Shanoah's boyfriend.

Tunssee – Cosegan city.

Twistle trees – Type of tree in Cosegan time.

Varangians – Kalor Locke's army of elite special ops. They took their name from "The Varangian Guard," a band of Viking mercenaries.

Varvara Port – Regional trade port of the Havloses.

Visuals – Marble-sized floating cameras that could be deployed by the thousands.

Weals – Personal spy for the Arc. Former guardian.

Welhey – Circle Member and friend of Trynn.

Wild Wandering River – A 2900 mile river that ended at the Eternal Falls.

ACKNOWLEDGMENTS

Cosega Strike was a challenge. I'm not sure about other authors, but for me, all books are a bit of a challenge for a variety of reasons. This one, maybe more so, because of what the world has become.

Many of you have contacted me to comment on how my books, especially *The Last Librarian* (Justar Journal series) and The Capstone Conspiracy, predicted (five to seven years ago) so much of what is happening today. That's what authors, particularly ones who write technothrillers, attempt to do. We look into the future and see what might happen, and then tell the story. Hundreds have written to say it feels like we are now living in a dystopian novel. I agree. It is scary at times, but like the heroes in those tales, we can win, we can create the future we want, the happy ending we so desperately need.

Book six of the Cosega Sequence would not be in your hands if not for all the readers of the original trilogy who bombarded me with (mostly) nice requests for more. When I finally agreed with your demands (I mean requests) and wrote book four, I saw the story had much further to go. By introducing the Cosegan's side of things, it meant there would have to be nine books in the Sequence, which means three more are coming (in fact, *Cosega Shock* is well under way). So thanks for pushing. I love the Cosega books, and hope you continue to enjoy where the saga goes.

To the amazingly wonderful Ro and Teakki. The two

reasons why I do everything and why I survive everything. They help so much with the plots and characters. Teakki especially has had a major impact on recent aspects of the story. And Ro, who in the midst of waging her own battles, somehow manages to keep us going, to keep life beautiful.

And to my mother, Barbara Blair, the person who has never once wavered in her support of me or my work every day of my life. Parenting is no easy job, yet she has made it look that way. She has always been my hero. On top of that, she has read every word I've ever written at least twice, but usually many more times. (She deserves combat pay.)

Joan Osborne thank you for being the final reader - maybe this one will sell enough that I can finally get that Tesla. Gil Forbes is like a character from one of my stories and I'm grateful for his input.

For many years now, Jack Llartin has been my copy editor. I believe he has worked with every book other than the Inner Movement. This one was a bit more challenging, as the gods and gremlins of technology played with the manuscript, and I was in a faraway village in another country without much access to the modern world, and yet he wrestled it under control, and made it better. Thanks to Elena, at L1 Graphics, for creating this cover, one of my favorite in the Chasing series.

And, finally, to Teakki, who patiently waited to show me his latest incredible drawing until I finished writing each day.

Most of all, I can never express enough gratitude to my readers. To all the ones that have read everything I've published, to the ones who have just finished their first Booker thriller or Chasing adventure, it means the world to me that you've decided to spend your money and time on my stories. Please drop me an email anytime. Responding to reader emails is one of my favorite parts of the day!

And to the readers who, with their reading, complete the

book. I'd like to give extra special thanks to the following readers and/or members of the street team for either their support, kindness, reviews (I love reviews), suggestions, and/or encouragement.

(If I left anyone out, I apologize. Please forgive me, and let me know. I can fix it!)

Please don't let the fact that there are so many of you do anything to diminish your importance to me. That this group continues to grow is so amazing to me. It blows my mind and takes my breath away.

In alphabetical order (by first name):

Adam Tanner, Alec Redwine, Amber Hunt, Anne Kaplan, Bill Borchert, Billie Harkey, Blake Dowling, Bob Browder, Bob Dumas, Brian C. Coffey, Brian Schnizlein, Cara Johnson, Carl Howard, Carol M, Cathie Harrison, Cheryl Olson, Chet Keough, Chis Bond, Chris Tomlinson, Christine Moritz, Christopher Bowling, Chuck Gonzalez, Cid Chase, Consuelo Ashworth, Debra Harper, Dennis Lowe, Derek Redmond, Diane Smith, Diane Whitehead, Douglas Dersch, Douglas Meek, Elaine Dill, Ernest Manpino, Ernest Pino, Frank Fusco, Frank Murphy, Gary Human, Gene Leach, Gene Legg, Gil Forbes, Gillian Charlton, Glenda Dykstra, Glenn Legge, Ingo Michehl, Irene Witoski, Jacky Dallaire, Jan Dallas, Janice Gildea, Jean Sink, Joan Osborne, John McDonald, John Nicholson, John Nunley John Wood, Judith Anderson, Judy Hammer, Julie Price, Justin Lear, Karen Mack, Karen Markovitz, Kat Heyer, Kathleen Robbins, Kathy Creecy, Kathy Troc, Ken Clute, Ken Friedman, Kevin Burton, Kyle Dahlem, LA Dumas, Leslie Royce, Linda Loparco, Liz Miller, Marcel Roy. Gerry Adler, Mark Perlmutter, Martha Heckel, Martin Gunnell, Melanie C. Hansen, Michael Ferrel, Michael Picco, Mick Flanigan, Mike Brannick, Mike Lauland, Nancy Lamanna, Nigel Revill, Normand Girard, Pam Gilbert,

Patricia Ruby, Paul Gyorke, Peggy Gulli, Randy Howerter, Rick Ferris, Rick Woodring, Rob Weaver, Rob Zorger, Robert Smith, Robyn Shanti, Ron Babcock, Sam J. Rhoades III, Sam Rhoades, Samantha Jackson, Sandie Parrish, Sandra Zuiderhoek, Satish Bhatti, Sharon Moffatt, Stephane Peltier, Sue Steel, Susan McGuyer, Susan Norlund, Susan Powell, Terry Myers, Tom Strauss, Tony Sommer, Tricia Turner, Vicki Gordon, Vivienne Du Bourdieu.

There are so many wonderful authors I've gotten the chance to meet as well. One of them, Judith Lucci, a fellow thriller author, suddenly passed away a few weeks ago. She published her first book a year or so after me, and around that time we met online and often chatted about the craft, marketing, or Virginia, since we were both from there. She was one of those rare people who was loved by all those who knew her, and in the tightknit community of indie authors, she seemed to know us all. She will be greatly missed. If you haven't read her, you might want to give one of her books a try.

This is a small group of others authors who've made a difference to me: Robert Gatewood, Mike Sager, Craig Martelle, Michael Anderle, Mark Dawson, Nick Thacker, Ernest Dempsey, John Grisham, A. Kelly Pruitt, Eric J. Gates, Dale DeVino, Phil M. Williams, Jennifer Theriot, Haris Orkin, Brian Meeks, Jennifer Theriot, Michelle McCarty, Mollie Gregory, and Zoe Saadia.

There are so many friends of mine who are creatives as well, many from Toas, where parts of this story are set. Their work inspires my work (and my life): Tony Schueller, David Manzanares, Geraint Smith, Michael Hearne, Don Richmond, Lenny Foster, Jared Rowe, Jimmy Stadler, Scott Thomas, Carol Morgan-Eagle, Deonne Kahler, Bart Anderson, Ernest James, Jenny Bird, Angelika Maria Koch, Brad Hockmeyer, Verne

Verona, Brooke Tatum, Markus Kolber, Terrie Bennett, and many others!

Speaking of reviewers, the prolific readers and top Amazon reviewers who have been a great support of my work deserve extra recognition. Thank you so much, and special gratitude to, the remarkable Grady Harp, and to whoever the reviewer "Serenity" is!

There is a goal among some authors to turn readers into fans, fans into super fans, and super fans into friends. I am fortunate to have been able to achieve that goal on numerous occasions.

Thank you.

Thanks for sharing the adventure!

Please help spread the word

If you enjoyed this book, I'd really appreciate it if you would consider posting a review wherever you purchased it (even a few words).

Reviews are the greatest way to help an author.

And, please tell your friends.

I'd love to hear from you

Questions, comments, whatever.

Email me through my website, BrandtLegg.com and I'll definitely respond
(usually within a few days).

Join my Inner Circle

If you want to be the first to hear about my new releases, advance reads, occasional news and more, join my Inner Circle at:

BrandtLegg.com

ABOUT THE AUTHOR

USA TODAY Bestselling Author Brandt Legg uses his unusual real life experiences to create page-turning novels. He's traveled with CIA agents, dined with senators and congressmen, mingled with astronauts, chatted with governors and presidential candidates, had a private conversation with a Secretary of Defense he still doesn't like to talk about, hung out with Oscar and Grammy winners, had drinks at the State Department, been pursued by tabloid reporters, and spent a birthday at the White House by invitation from the President of the United States.

At age eight, Legg's father died suddenly, plunging his family into poverty. Two years later, while suffering from crippling migraines, he started in business, and turned a hobby into a multi-million-dollar empire. National media dubbed him the "Teen Tycoon," and by the mid-eighties, Legg was one of the top young entrepreneurs in America, appearing as high as number twenty-four on the list (when Steve Jobs was #1, Bill Gates #4, and Michael Dell #6). Legg still jokes that he should have gone into computers.

By his twenties, after years of buying and selling businesses, leveraging, and risk-taking, the high-flying Legg became ensnarled in the financial whirlwind of the junk bond eighties.

The stock market crashed and a firestorm of trouble came down. The Teen Tycoon racked up more than a million dollars in legal fees, was betrayed by those closest to him, lost his entire fortune, and ended up serving time for financial improprieties.

After a year, Legg emerged from federal prison, chastened and wiser, and began anew. More than twenty-five years later, he's now using all that hard-earned firsthand knowledge of conspiracies, corruption and high finance to weave his tales. Legg's books pulse with authenticity.

His series have excited nearly a million readers around the world. Although he refused an offer to make a television movie about his life as a teenage millionaire, his autobiography is in the works. There has also been interest from Hollywood to turn his thrillers into films. With any luck, one day you'll see your favorite characters on screen.

He lives in the Pacific Northwest, with his wife and son, writing full time, in several genres, containing the common themes of adventure, conspiracy, and thrillers. Of all his pursuits, being an author and crafting plots for novels is his favorite.

For more information, please visit his website, or to contact Brandt directly, email him: Brandt@BrandtLegg.com, he loves to hear from readers and always responds!

BrandtLegg.com

BOOKS BY BRANDT LEGG

Chasing Rain

Chasing Fire

Chasing Wind

Chasing Dirt

Chasing Life

Chasing Kill

Chasing Risk

Chasing Mind

Chasing Time

Chasing Lies

Cosega Search (Cosega Sequence #1)

Cosega Storm (Cosega Sequence #2)

Cosega Shift (Cosega Sequence #3)

Cosega Sphere (Cosega Sequence #4)

Cosega Source (Cosega Sequence #5)

Cosega Strike (Cosega Sequence #6)

Cosega Shock (Cosega Sequence #7)

CapWar ELECTION (CapStone Conspiracy #1)

CapWar EXPERIENCE (CapStone Conspiracy #2)

CapWar EMPIRE (CapStone Conspiracy #3)

The Last Librarian (Justar Journal #1)

The Lost TreeRunner (Justar Journal #2)

The List Keepers (Justar Journal #3)

Outview (Inner Movement #1)

Outin (Inner Movement #2)

Outmove (Inner Movement #3)